I0533811

MOCKERY

second edition

MOCKERY

SECOND EDITION

A NOVEL OF
POLITICS &
TRUTH BY

Philip
Kraske

encompass
EDITIONS

© 2012 by Philip Kraske All rights reserved.

Published by Encompass Edition, Kingston, Ontario,
Canada. No part of this books may be reproduced, copied
or used in any form or manner whatsoever without written
permission, except for the purposes of brief quotations in
reviews and critical articles. For reader comments, orders,
press and media inquiries:

FIRST EDITION 2010

SECOND EDITION 2012

www.encompasseditions.com
or
www.philipkraske.com

ISBN 978-0-9880428-8-9

Cataloguing in Publication
Program (CIP) information available from Library and
Archives Canada
at www.collectionscanada.gc.ca

To Esther and Mara

El pasado es indestructible; tarde o temprano vuelven todas las cosas, y una de las cosas que vuelven es el proyecto de abolir el pasado.

The past is indestructible; sooner or later everything comes back around, and one of the things that come back around is the project to abolish the past.

—Jorge Luís Borges,
On Nathaniel Hawthorne

And a word travels far—very far—deals destruction through time as the bullets go flying through space.

—Joseph Conrad,
Lord Jim

1 The crucial clue that got me off the dime took place on a gray, flat March day in Saint Paul, back when Rolf Obermeyer was still bravely introducing himself as "a former Gotchell-campaign official." He and his ever-shrinking crew were still wrestling with—or paying off, or burying—the odds and ends, the IOUs and ASAPs, of their losing campaign. As you remember, Senator Alan Gotchell—and Governor Worthington Frakes, his opponent—had seen victory snatched from their dropped jaws by Independent candidate Mitchell Taylor, both campaigns derailed by scandals just weeks before the general election. The interview with Obermeyer was my first foothold up the cliff to my bestselling exposé. And the rest, as we historians love to say when we actually publish a book that someone buys not at fifty percent off, was history.

What we don't love to say is that the book was all wrong. What happened, how it happened, who, why—all wrong.

That's my story.

I found Rolf's fluid, roving bulk slouched behind his ancient desk as he worked the phone, his white business shirt a choppy sea of wrinkles, sleeves rolled past the elbows, one doughy arm flung up behind his bald head in order to flaunt the yellowish, perfectly oval wet spot at his armpit. His stink of sweat and Marlboros wrapped me in its gauze and ushered me in along with his wagging hand. With resignation, I looked at the shut window—Rolf hated a draught—through which I could see the hopeful, white dome of the Minnesota state capitol building.

I sat down in front of his desk, a lovely oak piece that had nothing to do with the rest of the functional office. Way back when his candidate was ahead eight points in the race for the presidency, he had planned to take it to the White House: "My grandma's, Sam—full of curlicue carving and old as the hills. Brought it up the Mississippi with her, all the way from Czechoslovakia. And now—just think—it's going to the White House. The old gal would just cry!" Back then he had been head of logistics for the Gotchell campaign; now he was head of its sand-and-shovel brigade.

"Yeah, well, that's sorta the problem, Sol," he was saying. "We've sorta got our *available* funds, ah, pretty much slotted for right this minute. Which is why I was thinking that, ah, going forward, a little ongoing patience would really constitute the most, ah, proactive stance on this count. And the senator—who still has plenty of say in the Senate, remember—he won't forget someone who, ah, had the courage and see-it-throughness to move together with us to a sort of, of *long-term ongoing closure* on this thing, if you see where I'm drifting here…

"No, Sol, no! Where do people get that stuff? Strum and Dirge, pure Strum and Dirge.…Oh, eighteen months, twenty-four on a good day, Sol—just till we get some traction under our belts, from a financial point of view.…Yeah, absolutely…Oh, you betcha…and believe you me, Sol, I feel that deep—way down here in my Czech soul—really I do."

Spoken like a true ex-director of the Minnesota Department of Natural Resources.

Obermeyer drummed patient fingers on his blubber, shivers rippling through half his torso. Finally: "*Really?* Hey, Sol, hey. And I mean that from the bottom, huh? That'd be great. No kidding: the kind of thing that makes my job a real aspiration to human nature.… Right. Right. Hey, you listen to your Uncle Rolf here, Sol, we're gonna keep you posted straight through till payback. We're all of us here a really far cry from the sort of attitude that says…

"Absolutely, Sol, absolutely. The senator's a player, Sol, always will be. He's gonna be writing a book, he's got an article coming out next week in *Newsweek*, he's, ah, he's gonna be making grand-a-plate speeches—gots one coming up just next month, in point of fact. So don't you worry. Anybody who gets behind us going forward, hell, we're gonna get right behind them back, and I say that without the kind of qualification you're always hearing nowadays from everybody and his brother....Okay, Sol....Hey, and I appreciate it, that'd be great....Okay, okay....Hey, I'm gonna be on your phone so often you're going to think of me as your mother-in-law!...Right. Right. Bye."

Rolf hung up, huffed, and unstapled the smile from his open, bread-loaf face. "So if two of your millions go AWOL for a while, Sol, just relax and enjoy the other ninety, okay? Greedy son-of-a-bitch." Beneath the blubber, Obermeyer had steel, too.

He looked at me, making his lardy neck squish a new way over his too-tight collar. "Know what the problem with money is, Sam?"

"Let's see....You can never find a shirt that goes with it?"

"No: it won't give you an orgasm."

"Ah. Well, I meant *besides* that."

"I mean, hell, you'd think that when a guy made twenty or thirty mill, he'd just die with pleasure at all the stuff he could buy. Head for Miami and burn ten grand a day. But does he? Does he my Czech grandma! Guy gets his first twenty and the only thing he can think about is his *next* twenty."

"Ah, the greed of man," I lamented. I took my leap into the dark. "So: were *you* there when Terry Letizzle brought in the Frakes video?" I was referring to the outtakes of Governor Frakes cursing senior citizens, a major political base. Gotchell's people—a.k.a. Rolf's people—had slipped it to CBS News, and sunk Frakes.

Obermeyer took this question on the chin, and his eyes glazed over. After a long moment, he decided that a new cigarette was the better part of valor. He tapped one out of the pack, visibly apologizing to a picture duct-taped to the wall beside the window. It showed a crayoned house, flower garden, three dogs, three kids, and a sky filled with admonition: "Daddy, don't smoke!" The ashtray was full. He lit up.

After two puffs: "Ah, that, that is a very information-rich subject, ah, Sam, that, ah, I'm not really all that permitted to go out and comment on at this point in time. Why don't you, ah, take it up with Michael or Jan or Milt? Or heck, go to the senator himself? He was there. I mean, given the outcome of the election and the, ah, sudden flip-flop reversal of fortune that we've all suffered, I just can't go around, ah, taking liberties—at least not on any kind of, of, you know, just-like-that basis." Words were buckshot to Obermeyer; he sprayed them into the air till they hit his idea.

"So it *was* Terry who brought it in?" Terry Letizzle had been the candidate's bodyman during the campaign.

Obermeyer waved the fleshy palps of his fingers, defending himself as if I were an onrushing bull. "Now I didn't say that, Sam. That's, ah, that would constitute a total twisting out of my words. I mean, c'mon: that's pretty high-octane stuff—what you're asking there is. I'd just be going straight out of my league, y'know, going out and making comments on it." He puffed his cigarette more and, I thought, guiltily.

"C'mon, Rolf—the election's long over," I said. "Off the record. My publisher said that anything I could dig up about the two scandals would sell my book."

Obermeyer shook his head in broad, gusting swings, the fat sloshing back and forth over his collar. "Zip, Sam. That's zipped lips from the word go."

I performed an amiable shrug and took Obermeyer into organization for the party convention. There was a lot of talk about bad blood between Gotchell's people and the party—seating of delegates, platform planks, keynote speakers. Could he give me any background for that chapter of my book?

This for twenty minutes.

Then, with a glum scowl, I said: "But just on this video thing: it *was* Terry Letizzle who brought it in, wasn't it? Off the record? Please? I had to track down the three-quarters of the Baton Rouge Palace night staff till I got a lead on him."

One of Obermeyer's charms was his childish sense of wonder. His eyes bugged out, and he launched himself forward across the desk, blubber catching up with him later. *"You tracked down three-quarters of the night staff of the Baton Rouge Palace Hotel?"* he gasped.

"Damn right. It finally hit me late last month: whoever brought it to *you guys* surely looked at it first. But let's say that he received it *just before* bringing it to you. Like from someone inside the Frakes campaign. Like after meeting this person at the Frakes–Gotchell debate—say, backstage or something. Always a possibility. And further suppose that he's one of your campaign staff—not unlikely. Now, since the Gotchell campaign was bunked at the Palace, and the

Palace's only mobile TV-VCR stand was already in Milt's room recording the last debate, where else could the guy get hold of a VCR? I checked around and found one: in the conference room down in the hotel sub-level. The big TV down there has a built-in VCR. So I tracked down the staff working there on the night of the debate."

"Jesus—three-quarters," Rolf murmured in admiration. "That must fifty people minimum."

"Sixty-two, 'cause management wouldn't name names for me. I had to stand out in the employee parking lot at the end of each shift and nab people coming out. Anyway, I finally got hold of this nice old cleaning lady from Cape Verde. She was the one: she let him in and stayed at the door while he checked out what was on the vid. She said he was tall and skinny, under thirty, and had bright red hair."

Rolf rolled his eyes dismally. "Yeah, that's Terry, all right."

"And here we are. See, Rolf? I have a description *and* a name. I just need someone's nod on it."

A careful drag on the weed. A squeamish scowl.

"A-a-ah, all right, Sam. I'll give you, ah, yeah, I'll give you that little morsel. Now it's off the record, it's total mum, it's something you picked up as per the wall of the men's john, got it? Milt was pretty damn heads-will-rolly about talking vids and stuff. But I mean, if it's just *confirming,* okay."

"There in the hotel after the last debate, right?"

"Ah, after, yes, just after the third debate that would be. Now, really, Sam, I've really gone the distance for you here—young guy on your way up—let you have pretty much carte-blanche run around here for your book, but there are just some things in this old world that have to go top level for anyone to go delving around in. Every campaign generates a little caca, you know. We're not perfect here or anywhere else for that matter."

I nodded with sage reassurance, though I was nearly jumping out of my seat with joy. *Finally: a name, a solid lead!* "Great, Rolf, I sure appreciate the help. Maybe when I have more of it, you can give me a thumbs-up on..."

I stopped because Obermeyer wasn't listening. He had twisted his head low and to the side, a kid looking at his ice cream that had fallen off the cone. I could see the fringe of sweat on his too-tight collar. A sigh.

"Oh, hell, you've got it. Now you're gonna go around thinking we're the White House Plumbers running smash-and-grab on the opposition, aren't you?"

Actually, I would have suspected that more of the Frakes campaign and its posh director, Phyllis Kirk, than of Rolf's gang; but I said nothing.

Silence crowded into the little office along with the cigarette smoke. "We're still off-record," Rolf groused.

"We sure are."

"Okay. Look, it...fuck." Obermeyer regarded his cigarette and sighed. "Look, it just fell into our hands, Sam," he blurted unhappily. "Okay? Straight stuff now. Nobody paid for it, nobody stole it. All right, after Jover's antics in Frakes HQ you might not believe that, but I swear on my Czech grandma's grave it's true." More tobacco. "After the third debate, we're all sitting around trying to make happy to the senator, and Terry—God knows where he came from—is suddenly over by the VCR coughing and waving and trying to get attention, and finally we look up and there's Frakes on the screen cussing out his constituency and flushing his presidency down the toilet. It was our last chance, last hurrah, seventh-inning charge up the hill, all that. We *had* to go with it."

Not taking my eyes off him, I jotted a few notes on my notepad in my lap. "He didn't mention where it came from?"

"Nope. Nothing. Got all mysterious and said he'd bargained for it, but not even his mother would've believed him and neither did we." A huff. "Not that anybody pressed him all that hard," he added sarcastically.

"We. As in..."

He scowled at the table. "Jan, Milt, the usual band of mariachis. I never touch the hardball stuff, Sam—you know that. I'm nuts and bolts. Give me the parts, I'll build your Cadillac. Besides, we were pretty worried that Frakes' people were going to release something on the senator—especially now that he'd beaten the hell out of Frakes in that last debate. We wanted to strike the first blow."

"You were worried about Frakes' people releasing what, exactly?" I asked.

As I said, deep down Obermeyer had steel. Now it came out. His finger leapt and stabbed. "Don't play the fucking Virgin Mary with me, Mr. Walker. You know *what* just as well as I do. Frakes' people had footage of the senator pulling some sweetie-pie into his dressing room after a speech. Every reporter covering the campaign knew it. You did, too."

"Yeah," I admitted.

Obermeyer stoked himself with more tobacco. "In that way, I'm *glad* Mitch Taylor won. At least *he* did it fair and square." A righteous drag. "Fool, though. See that fresh-water bill he sent to Congress last week? Could've been a draft for one of his stand-up routines."

"You're saying, then, the dressing-room tape might have been true. I mean, despite denials and religion and all the rest of it, Gotchell was still grabbing asses?"

"Of course he was!" Another drag. "Tell ya one, Sam. Got a cousin out in Minnetonka. His kid's studying advertising, leaned on me to get her on the campaign. Smart girl, speaks Spanish 'cause her mom's—what is it?—Nicaraguan or something south-of-the-bordery. Just the kid you want to send down to Chicago, ball the Latino vote, right? But I couldn't put her on, I just couldn't take the chance. She's twenty-two—gots an ass you'd light up Broadway for. If that bastard'd caught her alone, he'd've bent her over the nearest armchair, no questions asked."

"I see what you mean."

"Motherfucker. Know what his pick-up line was?" He imitated Gotchell's nasal tenor: "'Oh, I'm just a poor, tired presidential candidate and my wife's so far from home. Every day it's people, people, people. I need intimacy. I need release from all this tension. Please, just a few minutes, honey. I know it's above and beyond the call of duty, but this is a presidential campaign. People *make* sacrifices in a campaign.' That was the bullshit he gave his girls—and don't ask who told me very much in the first-hand vernacular, sitting right where you are. Just after we'd won Texas and I'm seriously starting to think about public or private for my kids. Fuck. And then I get a lesson in the good senator's 'religion.' Too nice a kid to ask for damages, thank God. Stuffed twenty grandful of slush in her hand and cashed a favor to get her a job on The Hill. And don't think it was hush money, Sam; it was an *apology.*" Another puff. "Fucker. Try breaking your back on a campaign knowing that your opponent has a vid that can torpedo you any time he wants."

This, too, I would attribute to a "senior Gotchell campaign official" in my future book *The Saddest Election,* but the story summed up the dark side of the Gotchell campaign that I did my best to bring out: everyone knew that Gotchell's hands were as hot as ever and that Frakes' people had a video to prove it.

We listened to the smoke for a while, Obermeyer with his big head propped on the heel of one hand, elbow on the desk.

I said, "Still, funny thing is that even in the wake of the Frakes out-takes, *his* people—"

"Never released their tape of Gotchell and the babe. Yeah. Yeah. Go figure." Obermeyer shook his head. "Sudden remorse? Forget it—that was *Phyllis Kirk* in charge of the Frakes campaign; remorse is for the little people. That leaves a gesture of fair play. But that's out too, see: 'cause then they would've dropped the charges against Jover instead of banging the drum with them till they sank us. Nope. I've thought about it up, down, over and out, Sam. No answer. Maybe they figured it was no use, anyway. Hell, what was Mitch Taylor's jump first week post-OutFrakes—twenty points?"

"Twenty-eight."

Obermeyer puffed more. "Nope—I draw a complete blank on it. But I'll tell you something: if I ever come across Phyllis Kirk in a dark Motel Six, I swear to Christ I'll hang her up by her thong-straps till she spills it—just to have it all straight in my head." He stubbed out his cigarette with one, vindictive thump. "If you want to do us all a favor in your book, Sam, get to the bottom line of *that* one."

2 Four years have passed since the Miracle Election, so before I go on, it's probably a good idea to refresh your memory.

It was the weirdest finish since Warren Harding's electoral tie was broken in a smoke-filled room. Briefly:

The general election was close, if not boring, into the first ten days of October. Taylor, like past Independent candidates, was making a showing strong enough to win federal election funds, but little else. His voter base consisted of defections from the major parties in roughly equal amounts. His Democrats disliked their candidate's reluctance to improve the social safety net, and his plastic personality.

His Republicans disliked their candidate's idea of subsidizing "essential American industries," and his flat personality. Mitchell Taylor had ambiguous policies ("We need strong cities!") but expressed them with wit and warmth.

Electoral Dullsville. As one *Boston Globe* columnist wrote, "Here we are, less than two months from a presidential election, and the weather report is the most exciting part of the news."

And then the scandals broke, and nobody gave a damn about the weather.

Five weeks before the election, the chief of security for Senator Alan Gotchell's campaign was caught trying to enter Frakes campaign headquarters with a false security pass. It was a perfect forgery, with the exception of its fat, red stripe: it should have been fat and blue.

The rest you surely saw on the famous security-camera footage. The duty guard stopped Arnold Jover as he walked through the metal detector, and Jover got huffy. The guard, a five-foot-two-inch bodybuilder who soon parlayed his fame into a role on a beach-police TV series, took offense at Jover's brush-off, seized him in an arm lock with one brick-like hand and radioed his partner with the other. The partner came, the police came, and the next night all America watched the video of Gotchell security chief Arnold Jover being led away in handcuffs.

Senator Gotchell's fustian denials only made matters worse: if he couldn't control his organization, what did that say about his future White House? Nobody wanted another Watergate; the senator's candidacy was finished.

Not to be outdone, the Frakes campaign was rocked three weeks later by embarrassing outtakes – that is, unused footage from the filming of a TV spot -- leaked to CBS News. That's the tape, brought in by Terry Letizzle, that Rolf Obermeyer was referring to. Wasn't that a shocker? Frakes, the Ohio apple farmer with his toothache pallor, stands holding a red-white-and-blue candle (symbolic of the "melting down of the American economy"). He flubs a line and breaks into a rictal scowl:

FRAKES: "Why the hell do I have to mention this junk about Medicare? It's pure bullshit, y'know, besides bein'—"

MALE VOICE OFF CAMERA (dryly): "Because we need Florida,

Governor. Gotta have it."

FRAKES: "Yeah, well..." A pause. "Blood-suckin' leeches—every one of those toothless farts! The country can go to hell, can't it?—long as they get their orange juice and bran for breakfast!"

An indecorous thing to say about one's most important constituency, which showed its appreciation by dropping his polls off a cliff.

An early post-campaign writer located the CBS producer who had received the Frakes outtakes (fate's prescient rhyme; the scandal soon became "OutFrakes"). He admitted only that the tape had come from the Gotchell campaign. "Don't ask me who or how. All I know is that I took one look at it, recognized the spot that *was* eventually made from it, and knew I had the hit of the campaign."

A hit it was. Frakes' polls plummeted to Gotchell's level, and in a throw-the-rascals-out surge, the nation turned to Mitch Taylor, the suave late-night-talk-show-host-turned-mayor—mayor of Albuquerque, that is. He surged ahead in the last weeks of the campaign on the strength of his agile sense of humor, passable Spanish, and legendary twenty-five-year marriage to actress Mary Ann Stall. He slid across the finish line with just the required number of electoral votes and 40.5 percent of the vote. To his and the planet's amazement, he had won the White House.

The Miracle Election thus centered on two mysteries.

First, how had the Frakes outtakes got into the hands of the Gotchell campaign? (As you've just seen, I now knew: Terry Letizzle. But how had *he* got them?) And second, why had Arnold Jover, ex-Navy Seal, ex-FBI, ex-spotless citizen, tried to enter Frakes campaign headquarters? What on earth had been worth the risk? The tape of his boss, Senator Gotchell, was a possibility, but hardly a sure one; for, assuming that Jover wasn't going to rifle the campaign's huge video files amidst a dozen staffers burning the midnight oil, how would he have known where to find it? Had someone in Frakes' campaign told him? A good soldier, he has never said. Investigators could not pry a word from his set Seal lips. Jover did six months in minimum-security, walked out past three hundred screaming journalists, and disappeared into a private Arizona military academy, where he personally instructs ten-year-olds in the proper making of beds, and bounces an Eisenhower dollar the regulation eighteen inches off each one every morning.

And as long as we're on the subject of a video of Senator Gotchell's philandering technique, let's hover for a paragraph to remember just why such a sequence was deadly to his candidacy.

Alan Gotchell was a handsome and twice- (now thrice-) married man, then fifty, who had plied the halls of Congress for eleven years. Only women had he plied even more. With zeal and industry, he had become one of the greatest of congressional womanizers, earning the nickname "Gotcha" Gotchell. He managed to dampen this tag in the year prior to the campaign, however, invoking a religious conversion. He joined a church and started a congressional Bible-study group. He even trotted out his "personal spiritual advisor," a fire-breathing evangelist of unimpeachably dark skin who proclaimed Gotchell's new godliness. It was a moral Brooklyn Bridge, but the public bought it.

And Gotchell's organization intended to protect it. Any video of sexual shenanigans was a fake, they told pining reporters. And none of Gotchell's people broke ranks. Three young female aides on the campaign flatly denied any improper advances. Zero. The Secret Service people, with their bureaucrat's feel for the side of the bread that holds the butter, stiff-armed all inquiries.

On Governor Frakes' side, though, things were less clear. Did they have such a tape? What was on it? The answers I got ran from just-about-pretty-categorical denial (Phyllis Kirk, Frakes' cagey campaign director) to "Yes, I saw it or something like it," from Laura Prestini, an advance woman for Frakes. I had interviewed her a few weeks before my talk with Rolf. Her version was this:

"The 'Gotcha' vid? Yeah, I saw it," she told me with her now-famous little-girl giggle. "About five of us did—though don't ask me to tell you much. I was pretty ripped. In this humungous L.A. hotel suite the night the convention closed. Whole hotel was like one big party. We were just *so* totaled out by the primaries and *then* the late campaigning for superdelegates. It was the first breathing space we'd had since New Hampshire. We were in there partying and putting on vids—some of them these disgusting porn things. Somebody—I think Phyllis Kirk, yeah—put on something, 'from headquarters files,' she said. And she had this cheesy look on her face.

"Anyway, suddenly there I am at like four in the morning watching Alan Gotchell holding open a dressing-room door—he's got his suit jacket and his tie off, and you can make her out in the back of the room; shot's taken from way down a hallway, looking in. And he's laughing with a Secret Service guy and sort of, like, escorting him out, you know? And they both have these juicy, good-old-boy grins on their faces, and then he goes back in—Gotchell does—and you can kind of see her there in the back. And the Secret Service guy—I think he was Afro—closes the door and kind of grins to the other guy who comes into the picture. They're standing in front of the door with their hands folded. You know—one of these sleazy grins that guys always have when stuff is going on? I mean, you don't *see* anything, but it's perfectly obvious what's going on."

That was the best description that I found, though it was no scoop. Laura had told other people, too, during and after the campaign; that was one reason I interviewed her. Another Frakes campaigner at the same party told me he might have seen it, but wasn't sure. Another mentioned watching films and hearing Gotchell's name mentioned, but again, nothing concrete. The media people at Frakes campaign headquarters swore they had no record or recollection of such footage in their archives. "There's nothing to it. Total ghost," one guy there told me. Mentioned by every post-election book, the "Gotcha" Gotchell video lodged ultimately in the stratosphere of Hints and Allegation. There it stayed.

Stayed, that is, until well into the first year of the Taylor Administration, when yours quite truly, Sam Walker, then thirty-one, a penniless and widely unknown writer of history books, pushed into doing a how-it-was-won election book by his lubricious editors, took a good lead and an anonymous tip—see Chapter Four—and turned them into the biggest political scandal since Watergate.

And how I regret it. For my book, *The Saddest Election*, eight million copies sold in nineteen languages, was flat wrong. Which is why I'm writing this addendum to my book, and publishing it on the Internet, free of copyright, complete with video clips: to be sure the truth finally gets out. I also wish to thwart any accusation that I'm going to make (more) money out of the story.

Not that it matters; the lawsuit resulting from this addendum will likely shred the fortune I've earned from *The Saddest Election*.

Anyway: up with the curtain. The Taylor presidency is now

history, Rolf Obermeyer and a few others have agreed to let me use their names, and the air is clear for me to publish the full story. I'll take you through how I wrote *The Saddest Election* and how I later discovered that it was a sham with my name on the jacket. And if this account shatters a few pretty truths and sugary icons, so much the better.

3 As I said, before *The Saddest Election,* I wrote history books. My pine bookshelves proudly displayed my two published works, one on French-American relations between the two world wars, the other on American foreign relations with Latin America during the Eisenhower and Kennedy Administrations. To supplement royalties, I also did French-English translation by Internet. Then out of the blue, my editors, Walt and Janine, suggested over a New York Ritz lunch that I might boost my career by doing a "contemporary history" project—namely, the next presidential campaign. From the quality of the grub, as opposed to the insignificance of the writer, I should have known that a scam was on.

I later discovered why: the Bigfoot writer they had engaged for the job had withdrawn after a disagreement with Walt, who was refusing to finance Bigfoot's lavish research expenses. (Bigfoot, shitfaced, related this to me on the floor of the Republican convention.) But at the time, touched by the sweet, avuncular concern of my editors, I said yes, and spent nine foodless months dodging between the two campaigns and sleeping in fleabags, bus stations or, for a treat, the back seats of rental cars. Five months post-election, when I talked to Rolf Obermeyer, my June deadline was pressing, my savings flagging, and my desperation rising for some—any—unique insight into the Miracle Election.

Londoner Walt was beginning to drop ominous hints about "the dreadful toll all this must be taking on you, Sam. Look—hell—here's one to mull over: why not scrap the bloody book project? Just scrap the whole damn thing. Give us five thousand words—'Taylor Rises and Others Fall,' say—and I'll twist an arm or two over there at *Vanity Fair* for you."

So you understand why I was willing to camp out in the drizzly employee parking lot of the Baton Rouge Palace Hotel and why

Rolf's confirmation of Terry Letizzle was so important.

And why I jumped on it right away. Who the hell was Terry Letizzle? That was the next step: to vet him before I stuck my tape recorder in his face and extracted the story of how he'd gotten hold of the OutFrakes tape. I walked from Obermeyer's office straight into the general office, where the skeleton staff was at work, and where, with a few reasonable exceptions, I had the exclusive run of the files to research my book. Calling oneself an historian, I had found, lulled people into trust. Campaign officials were grateful that at least someone was focusing his book on the campaign machines for the longer understanding of history, if only to scrub their own reps. I had much the same deal at Frakes HQ in Ohio, where, as you'll see, the rep scrubbing would be far more vigorous.

Five months post-election, the Gotchell campaign had shrunk and shrunk till it now occupied just half of the fourth floor of the building, which had started life in 1903 as a warehouse for a horse-feed company. Like most structures of downtown Saint Paul, it has a façade of fancy brickwork that our more prosperous age can no longer afford. Cast-off equipment, awaiting the sharks from second-hand-office-supply firms, stood piled up at the dark end of the floor, reaching nearly to the wooden rafters, these fat as water mains and held together with bolts as big as your fist. On the wall hung a giant floor-to-ceiling poster of Gotchell. It had consisted of four parts, but now only the lower two remained, exhibiting the over-studied choice of his tie and the crenellation of his lower teeth. Tied to a coat rack, a deflated balloon hung swaying in the draughts, shriveled and moribund like the campaign. The country had moved on.

The skeleton crew had diminished even more since my last visit three weeks earlier. The eight survivors, mainly accountants and legal people, all men, had crowded their desks together as if for warmth at the lit end of the floor, and amidst a sagebrush of cables worked in flannel shirts and Vikings jerseys, a coffee pot perking to one side, coats hung on the backs of chairs.

"Hey, if it ain't the post-mortem guy," called one of the flannel shirts, Todd Stohl. He was a broad, bearded lumberjack of a man; it was almost laughable to see him wiggling his fingers over computer keys. It was Todd, incidentally, who had first connected the cleaning lady's description with a name for me, this during a phone call the day before. Four or five of the others stirred and rumbled a hello my way. Todd served me coffee and one for himself—just to make sure that this extra coffee break looked like courtesy.

"So whatcha lookin' fer now?" he asked, slapping his heavy hair away from his temples. Todd eternally needed a haircut.

"Odds and ends on itineraries," I answered vaguely. "Entourage lists and résumés. I need to see who was along on a couple of campaign trips. Oh, and maybe some video."

Todd nodded. "Well, most everything you can find in the PC if you know what yer lookin' for."

"I know pretty much."

Todd sat me at an unused computer, jammed a few cables into place, and got it going. I spent the rest of the day there.

Terry Letizzle had graduated from Ohio State University in Columbus with a Master's in political science. His résumé, however, went downhill from there. He had stormed out into the world and landed a job heading the sports and gardening sections of a Columbus department store. There he stayed, with the years rising to the level of "whole department buyer" for the sports section. Before and during this job, he worked on the election campaigns of two state-congress races and one for the U.S. Senate. Terry was some kind of jinx: all three lost. His résumé listed two addresses in Columbus—his parents' house and his own—and what was clearly a temporary one in Minneapolis while he worked on the Gotchell campaign.

He listed his marital status as "single but working hard at it."

I knew that the losing senatorial candidate—previously a congressman in Washington—was a friend of Senator Gotchell's. A phone call confirmed that Terry's entry into the Gotchell campaign had been through that connection. He had left his sports-department job, moved up to the Twin Cities, and, according to Social Security records, was a full employee of the Gotchell campaign two months before New Hampshire. His desultory job title was "Assistant 4," the campaign equivalent of water boy.

He was, however, *Gotchell's* water boy—his valet, from the looks of it. Travel records showed that Terry traveled with Senator Gotchell from the first primary straight through to election day. They were on the same buses, the same whistle-stop train tours, the same campaign jet. Everywhere that Gotchell went, Terry was sure to go. He was away only one day, in June, to attend his father's funeral, according to a note I found.

I had surely seen him during the campaign, but I drew a complete blank on the pale, undefined face with red hair on his ID sheet.

Then I slogged through some accounting records till I found Terry's weekly expense sheets. If you want to know what Napoleon or Einstein were really like, look at their expense sheets. The laundry bills will tell you more about your subject's opinion on hygiene than a dozen interviews. Taxi tips will shine a light on their generosity, bar tabs their need for liquor, and restaurant bills their idea of their importance. Was their rental car a four-speed tin can or a Chrysler? Expense sheets bare the soul.

Terry's expense sheets were interesting not only for their humble content but their honesty. Scanned into the computer files, they spoke of shaving cream and blades, computer disks, a variety of expensive silk ties (this just before the first presidential debate), convenience store items like mineral water and pretzels, notebooks and pens, bi-monthly twelve-unit boxes of condoms (did Terry really get around that much?), taxis, eight umbrellas from a Portland supermarket, and scores and scores and scores of meals for between one and five persons, these always carefully, religiously in the economy-class range—far below Gotchell's presidential standard.

He hadn't even charged the campaign with the flight to his father's funeral in Columbus. There were no charges for clothes, either, though nearly a year on the campaign trail would certainly justify a sweater here and a summer shirt there. Nor was there anything like a massage, a double whisky, a bottle of aspirin, extra socks, or a new cell phone. No clothes, no room service, no cable movies, only many Burger King dinners; Terry liked a good Whopper. I scrolled through all forty-odd weekly expense sheets twice; nothing even close to luxury appeared among them. Terry was a true believer. It seemed to be his pride to live in Spartan conditions for the cause.

With the exception of the condoms. Why on earth had he put that most personal of items on his expense sheet? Boxes of them— a dozen at a crack every two weeks or so—top-quality brands that cost a bundle. Yet no celebratory steak dinners after winning Super Tuesday, no new suitcases, not even a tube of toothpaste.

Just condoms.

I looked up at the guys at their screens and asked, "Hey, did Terry Letizzle have a girlfriend on the road?"

Laughter.

"Just his hand," answered one guy.

"Wasn't for lack o' tryin'," said another. "With girls, I mean, not his hand."

More laughter.

Todd Stohl smiled and said, "Terry was not Don Juan, Sam. He asked a lot of girls for dates, but you know how that stuff goes. He was too desperate, too eager."

"In everything," someone added.

That answered that: the condoms were for Gotchell.

As Rolf had said, "Gotcha" was alive and well, whatever his "personal spiritual advisor" said. Gotchell's wife Cindy, Miss Idaho from ten years earlier, knew nothing: she rarely campaigned with him. The campaign's standard line was that Cindy tired easily and had to be ready to support her man at key times: "Cindy is Cindy, y'know, Sam. Cindy picks her spots," was Rolf Obermeyer's delicate offering. From the less abashed, I'd heard that nobody wanted her opening that perfect mouth without an hour of coaching beforehand.

Terry's purchases were a neat solution to Gotchell's sexual obsession: nobody paid attention to Assistant 4's expenses, and Terry could step up to bat for Gotchell if anyone like me raised the issue.

But more to the point: two dozen condoms a month! Other post-campaign books had hinted broadly that Gotchell was up to his old shenanigans, but the proof was slight. It seemed clear now that Gotchell had women waiting in every whistle-stop. I wondered: had Terry been in the video Laura Prestini had described—say, shuffling with the Secret Service out of Gotchell's dressing room? Had he arranged the liaisons himself?

All of this searching and wondering took a lot longer than it reads here. It was late in the afternoon by the time I had noted my discoveries and printed out a few screens. Most of Todd Stohl's co-workers had gone home for the day. The last thing to do was take a good look at this Terry. Who the hell was he? Why didn't I know his face?

I went over to Stohl. "Todd, can I see some video footage? I'm going to interview Terry Letizzle—looks like he might have some interesting takes on the campaign—and I need to jog my memory, remember what he looks like."

"Uh, right, Sam," said Todd, his face and beard swinging involuntarily to the clock. It was five-twenty-five, and Todd's quitting time was five-thirty. "We'll have to get out the VCR," he muttered. "Tell ya what. I'll set 'er up quick for you and get out one of the boxes of videos, and you can just look through whatever your heart's content is here."

We traveled down the room to the pile of campaign dross. Todd waded in, his big feet knocking over computer screens, and jerked a television free—it had a VCR built-in. He passed it to me easily, as if were an XL pack of toilet paper, and I nearly staggered and dropped it. "Careful now. Just take it over a ways and plug in somewhere. Now let's see: some vid of Mr. Right-Hand Man." He rolled his eyes; Obermeyer had done the same thing with regard to Terry.

"What's the matter?"

"Oh, you know, Terry was just kind of..." Todd scowled. "Look, Sam, don't get the wrong idea, okay? The guy was energetic as hell, always up and enthusiastic. He did a lot of the grunt-work here nobody else would do—especially pre-primary. But once things got hot and heavy..." He patted the pockets of Tact for the right words. "Look, alls I know is, once the campaign got cranked and he was doing errands for Gotchell, he was a total pain-in-the-asshole. When Gotchell wanted something, Terry was on the phone screamin' fer it and he didn't stop till he had it in his clutchy little hands. You'd think he was workin' fer God—more clearanced than thou, like. Okay, now you gotta have guys like that on a campaign doin' the gofer work; I'm not sayin' that. But I mean, hell, he coulda, you know, finessed it a little better..."

"Fervent."

"Yeah. 'Fervent' like '*over*fervent.' And you're going to talk to *him?*"

"Yeah, he was with Gotchell a lot. I thought he might have a few good stories."

"Yeah, he'll have a few," Todd murmured thickly. "And you can make up your own mind about which are worth writing down."

I wrote that down in a notebook later on, just to remember. I was starting to wonder about this Terry.

Todd looked blankly at the mountain of campaign material. "Okay. Now. *Terry.* Footage of *Terry.* Terryy-y-y-y. Where would?... No, wait a minute, this'll be easy." Todd went back into the pile and puffed about and brought back a box full of video cassettes. "Here—this one has the three presidential debates. He comes on at the end."

Lightning shot through my stomach. "Like at the end of the third debate?" I blurted. "When everybody comes on stage to congratulate the candidate? That could actually be really interesting."

Todd didn't understand my enthusiasm. "Um, not exactly with everyone, Sam. At the end of each debate, y'see, Terry's job was to go onstage first and take off Gotchell's mike pack out of his suit jacket." A grin split his beard. "I don't think Terry quite kisses his ass in these, but I didn't really look that close."

*N*obody had ever looked at Terry close. Even now, watching the frozen frame, I felt only the vaguest stirring, barely rising to a memory: a red-haired guy near the candidate's limo, hand proprietarily on its hood; him handing Gotchell a cell phone during a parade; him signing papers at a hotel as the rest of the campaign dragged their gray faces off to the elevators. It was a plain, round face, slightly pale, slightly lost. You forgot his face because something inside told you to, as with street people who scream at lampposts.

I ran the third debate footage to the end and picked out his red hair instantly. I was at that debate, by the way: Baton Rouge on a raging, rainy mid-October night. Like everyone else, I arrived dripping, and the auditorium stank of damp business-suit shoulder padding. Gotchell came to the debate boiling with rhetoric. Though the Jover scandal had bitten deeply into his polls, he had come back somewhat, and this debate was his last chance to get back into the race. Frakes had not yet suffered his scandal, remember, and was still fourteen points up on Gotchell nationwide.

A fiery, almost cruel, debater, on every question and response, Senator Gotchell pounded Frakes into the floor that night. The electricity in the auditorium changed from funny to grave to operatic. His open path to the White House clouding, Frakes floundered;

Gotchell found a way to twist whatever he said into a new axe to throw at him. Frakes looked pathetic, kept fiddling with his watch, with the knot in his tie—eventually pulling it out of center—kept huffing and looking offstage. He finally whined to the debate moderator, "Hey, now let's just wait a doggoned minute here. First this guy just ups and misstates my position, then he gets to go on and on all night about it. I'm not gettin' my fair share here!" Calm as an undertaker, the moderator assured him that each reply was rigorously timed. Gotchell fought down a grin.

Due to his decent showing in the polls, Mitchell Taylor was allowed seven minutes at the end of the debate to air his views. "Wow!" he chuckled. "I feel like a stand-up coming on after *Death of a Salesman.*" His funny, warm, off-the-cuff talk—the perfect coda to the debate—gained him a critical shove in the polls. His numbers surged into the low teens the next day, so that the Frakes scandal, seventy-two hours later, shot him to the White House.

Anyway. Terry. His third-debate cameo. I released the pause button.

Hardly has the moderator said good night when Mrs. Gotchell rushes onstage, in her emotion breaking away from escort-Terry's arm. Her perfect ex-Miss hair billowing, she throws herself upon the victorious gladiator, showing all America that no maggot like Arnold Jover is going to destroy her faith in her man and he shouldn't yours, either. The two kiss like long-separated lovers as Frakes watches with lumpy envy.

Eileen Frakes, no Miss Idaho, trudges onstage. In her tight face, you see the trashing of all her plans for new White House china.

Meanwhile, Terry has stopped at the far right, almost out-of-frame. Keeping a religious distance, he waits for the Gotchells to finish their smooch. Terry is thin, hair too curly to do much with; his shoulders stooped from too much slouching when he was a kid, thus the neck cocked forward as if bent. The ID card dangles crooked from his jacket lapel, and the collar of his shirt is too loose, which only emphasizes the thin neck and weights the round face. He holds his arms soldier-straight, tapping an electric Morse on his thighs.

And then, if you took a good look at him, which no living soul had ever done before, you notice an odd angle to his right arm, and then its cause: a bulge under his right armpit, on the side away from the camera, which makes his arm hang out. Well, for the moment, the bulge could be anything: a box of well-wisher chocolates delivered to Mrs. Gotchell backstage, a book, a thick notepad of Things To Do, a box of tissues just in case emotions run too high and threaten the tender brushwork of the makeup lass.

Or even what it was—a black video cassette box of the old VCR type; this was the last election in which that format was still used.

At long last, the lovers quench their desire, and Terry moves forward to them. And what impresses you now are his eyes, alight with purpose and worship. His hero has slain the beast. He has risen from the dead. The polls will sing arias tomorrow morning. Campaign people and dignitaries are now rushing onstage like fans after a prize fight, but Terry scarcely notices them.

Five steps bring him to the side of his master. On the last one, he bows smoothly in Japanese reverence and lifts the right flap of Gotchell's suit jacket, the senator barely flinching. To use his right hand, Terry needs to have this arm free. He takes the package out—it *is* a video-cassette box, after all—and slips it under his left arm. Terry unclips the transmitter from Gotchell's belt, the microphone cable slithers out, and Terry coils it up. He sets everything on the podium, and, moving away a few steps, conscientiously tucks the video box back under his other arm, on the off-camera side.

Highly Eminent Personages stream past him now; Rolf Obermeyer's lard blocks him for a moment. And until the scene cuts to the post-election analysis, Terry remains there, straight as an honor guard, watching his hero being fussed over, warming his scarecrow frame in the embers of power.

Remains—once more with feeling—with a video cassette box under his arm, just hours before presenting it to his own—that is, Gotchell's—campaign organization, which passed it on to CBS so that the whole nation could enjoy Frakes' tantrum.

"I got you, I got you, I got you," I muttered over and over. "I got you!"

You'll have to indulge my triumph, but after all, it *was* only on a hunch that I had recently spent four rainy days in the employees' parking lot of the Baton Rouge Palace, and my hunch was proving right. With smugness rising to somewhere near euphoria, I watched that crowd of campaign big shots swarming around the candidates and knew that one of them on the Frakes side had slipped Terry the video. No, I wasn't quite certain, but I had been plodding the dusty trail of the Miracle Election for half a year at that point, and even not-quite-certain tasted like a cool piña colada in the middle of the Sahara. I was on my way to *The Saddest Election.*

4 Two days later, I received an anonymous note. I had spent these days mainly at Gotchell HQ in Saint Paul completing my background research on Terry, and preparing to go to Columbus, Ohio, to interview him; and making copies of the three debate tapes and looking for more footage of Terry, mainly with the goal of having a few photos of Terry for the eventual book. For I had—unwisely—called my editors in New York and told them I was onto something, something worth pushing my June deadline back for.

"Forget it," was the answer, in addition to Walt's amused skepticism that a young pup like me could find important leads where veteran reporters had come up empty; editors are such snobs. Janine pointedly reminded me that if I was going to finger someone in particular, she wanted plenty of "visual" to work with when she "put together" the book. By the way she talked, you would have thought I was going to hand her a scrapbook of notes rather than a finished manuscript.

The note I found flapping on my car's windshield in the soggy March breeze. I lifted it off, hearing my fragile finances shatter around me, and cursing the Saint Paul parking police: only my rear bumper was gouging the sanctity of the crosswalk. My spirits lifted wonderfully, though, when I opened the envelope and saw that it was a note with an explosive tip on the election.

> *Dear Sam Walker:*
> *This is to inform you that Laura Prestini, head of advance to the Frakes campaign, used to be good friends with Terry Letizzle (Gotchell campaign org.). This is no coincidence. They were in contact before the election.*

Standard white envelope, standard office paper, laser printer, no indentation, no closing. The paper had been folded in perfect thirds that make you confuse the top and the bottom of the letter, and left to the clammy care of the windshield wiper. I can still see the marks of its grip as I write this, four years later. It had been placed on the windshield just minutes earlier: the time it had taken me to zip into Mama Lisa's Pizzeria, fill a softball-sized bowl of salad, cover it with olive oil and vinegar, and eat it while reading Mama's copy of the *Saint Paul Pioneer Press*. Not more than fifteen minutes.

And Laura Prestini? I mentioned her some pages ago; let me fill out the picture here.

She was not quite "head of advance to the Frakes campaign," as the letter said, but head of advance work *in the Midwest.* Laura's job was to go ahead of the campaign to arrange hotels and photo ops, rent sound equipment, start the hype, bone up on local issues, pretty-please the local police into cooperation, and generally straighten the paths of righteousness for the coming of Our Candidate. Like Terry, she held a master's in political science from Ohio State University and, starting as a teenager, had worked on four straight winning campaigns. A sharp, swift operator. In fact, the reason I had interviewed Laura was that she had been in charge when the good governor made a five-star fool of himself:

Frakes had spent the campaign treating the press in either a business-like or contemptuous manner, depending on whom you talked to. Matters came to a head one afternoon in an Indianapolis park when, during a press conference, he refused to answer a follow-up question. Steve Sharpe of the *Dayton Journal Herald* questioned a contradiction between Frakes' speech of the previous day and his campaign platform—on unemployment compensation limits, just for the record. Frakes gave a half-baked answer. Politely, Sharpe began a follow-up question: "Excuse me, Governor, but wouldn't that mean that—" Frakes turned away and took a question from another reporter.

Which was not the first time that had happened.

Nor the second, nor the tenth.

Sharpe roared at the top of his lungs, "Goddammit! That's enough of this. Governor, you can't just answer what you want and blow off the rest! Who's coming with me?" He turned and stalked off across the grass, most of the press corps following him; and in thirty seconds, Frakes was standing on the amphitheater stage before a patch of trampled grass and some two hundred citizens, embarrassed as if they had witnessed a lovers' tiff.

"Go ahead—walk out," Frakes bellowed, when he had lifted his flaccid farmer's jaw off the boards. "It just goes to show you that stuff about hobgoblins having little minds full of inconsistency." (The actual quote from Emerson, often invoked by politicians to get themselves out of a jam, is as follows: "A foolish consistency is the hobgoblin of little minds, adored by little statesmen and philosophers and divines.")

"So the governor jumped down from the stage and started to press the flesh with people—which he doesn't like to do, really. And I gave the media ten minutes to smoke their cigarettes and calm down," Laura said into my tape recorder. "And I walk across the park to where they're all griping and polishing their lenses and I try to reason with them. But no go—they're all full of piss and vinegar, like, 'You can't do that to us.' So I just look at them and say, 'Well, maybe I don't like it, either, but that's the answer he wants to give. Write it any way you want.' And I walk off."

Laura, however, wasn't the only Frakes campaign official on the spot. One of the media specialists had sent along an assistant that day.

"The dumbass panicked," Laura said, almost spitting the words. "First time on a campaign, national or otherwise, and he thought the sky was falling. *Without telling me,* he called his boss in L.A., and L.A. called the campaign brass—you know, Michael, Phyllis, Don, the consultants. Suddenly everybody's flying in, all very serious and worried like real, grown-up campaign officials, and we sit down in a Holiday Inn suite and order in the chop suey. Took us six smoke-filled hours to pound out a half-ass answer: a milky apology, a solemn promise to be more forthcoming on answers, a few lines on how a vigorous, informed press is the cement of modern democracy, blah, blah, blah—stroke everybody's ego a bit. And back on the road."

I had interviewed her some months before receiving the windshield note, in January, at the small public-relations firm she ran in Columbus. She was twenty-six then, had dark, shoulder-length hair that framed tiny silver dots in her earlobes, smarty-pants blue eyes flecked with ice, and an unfortunate Italian nose. Her body was slim—maybe "petite" is the word—though with full breasts, almost too full for such thin shoulders. A crucifix hung in the shadowy valley between them; now and then, in a single movement, she scooped it out with her thumb and gave it a top-to-bottom stroke with her forefinger. She sat tipped back in her executive's chair, legs crossed, palms flat on the armrests like the reigning queen. The Perrier bottle stood at the ready before Her Highness. Cashmere caressed the royal neck.

Only that nose nagged, like a guy with his pants zipper down. Before her operation, it curved south into an Italian hook. Look at girlhood pictures of her, and you'll see it fairly shrieked from her skinny, adolescent face. It must have been the bane of her youth. Was it the prod that—like shortness for men—drove her into politics? For politics attracts the unattractive, and where love won't find a way, power and an executive salary will do nicely.

I noticed a Barbie doll in an evening gown on the window ledge beside a fax machine. She—it?—was smiling into a mirror on a Barbie-sized dressing table, running a comb through her hair, preparing for a max-cool-fun evening; clearly the set was decades old. I looked around for her boyfriend Ken, but all I saw was a trophy— "Balance Beam, First Place"—in high-school gymnastics. No, Ken seemed not to have arrived yet, or maybe had never been invited.

*T*his is no coincidence. Keys in hand, I probably stood by the car for five minutes re-reading the note; call me a slow reader. *What* wasn't a coincidence? Their friendship despite political differences? The fact that they used to be friends and now were not? Or that they had talked during the campaign? As anonymous notes go, it didn't have a lot of substance.

But it was an interesting tip, a second name—a second point that created a line of investigation. Speculation on a connection between the two campaigns, of someone in the Taylor organization arranging the double scandals, was so strong that heavy-hitters like the *Times* and *Post* and *Journal* had quietly dispatched teams of journalists to investigate, to no avail. Advance people scoping out the same speech site for Frakes and Gotchell might gripe about their salaries; opposing PR staffers might haggle over airtime before the same station managers. But no—beyond this occasional rubbing of shoulders, the two campaigns shared little more than a thriving mutual suspicion. At the end, the reporters tiptoed back to their newsrooms and said that they had found no connection between the campaigns, that the Miracle Election of the first Independent candidate in American history had been just that: a miracle.

I had the inside track.

For ambiguous though it was, the message had eminent authority. Only the circumstances indicated this. Someone—someone who knew me and knew what I was doing—had taken great trouble to plant it and get away without being seen. They (I prefer "they" to the bulky "he or she") had monitored my movements, found out where I was, and followed me all that morning. Todd Stohl being nervous about letting the original tapes out of the office overnight, I had first picked up the videos of Terry that I needed to copy, gone to a video place that could copy the half-dozen bits for me, then gone to a pharmacy to buy eye drops for my fiancée, then to Mama's for a bite. It was just down the street from Gotchell HQ, where I would go to give back the original videos.

In short, I'd given my follower quite a morning before they could be sure to catch me away from the car for fifteen minutes or more.

And lest you think I am exaggerating their caution, get this: after the first read-through, my historian's instincts jumped to the fore, and I handled the letter and envelope only by their edges, with my palms. I would later have them dusted for fingerprints by an expert: they would turn out to hold none but my own.

"Laura Prestini, head of advance to the Frakes campaign, used to be good friends with Terry Letizzle."

Two minutes and about seventy steps returned me to Gotchell HQ, where after returning the borrowed videos, I put my third-debate copy into their VCR and gave it a good, hard, Sherlock Holmes-type stare.

Sure enough, towards the middle of the Frakes campaign crowd—Phyllis Kirk leads everyone out, of course, hair perfect, lavender-silk suit pulling hard on the over-fifty-white-female-professional vote—Laura Prestini comes onstage. More to the point, Laura has a black purse slung on her shoulder, and yes, it is easily big enough to hold a video cassette. She stands in the pack around Frakes, makes a comment and smiles to the guy beside her, who now forgets Frakes and chats her up, figuring that a largish nose really can be overlooked in view of the fine chest that goes with it.

The crowd shifts and jostles, and I noticed how skillfully—how fully, yet how casually—Laura keeps her back to Terry, across the stage. And Terry's soldier-straightness struck me now as less military, less reverent than simply rigid. Rigid with fear. You can see the footage here on my website—you decide.

This is no coincidence. They were in contact before the election.

After watching this a half-dozen times, my face by the end just inches from the screen, I took out the cassette and straightened up, tingling all over. Across the floor, the computers of Todd Stohl and his buddies beeped and burped, and I was struck by the thought that every keystroke they had ever made in this room might have been useless. Was Laura a plant in the Frakes organization, working to her old classmate Terry? Had they also sunk Gotchell? Had Taylor's people hired them to swing the election his way? Or were they working together on behalf of a foreign power trying—though with greater imagination than bin Laden's boys are likely to muster—to discredit American democracy? You could have listed conspiracies all night, and I still remember Frakes staffers doing just that over double whiskies as Taylor surfed the ever-rising wave to the White House.

My ruminations were cut short by an arresting text message from my fiancée: "555." This was the code she used to tell me that she had seen someone following her and would go to the pre-arranged hiding place. I yelped a good-bye to Todd and the guys, grabbed my stuff, and dashed for the car, reflecting as I ran that the life of a history-book writer isn't usually this exciting.

5 I dislike books in which the narrator talks about himself. Unless readers have been warned that an autobiography awaits them, I believe a writer is best read and not seen. For glory, he ought to be content with a dashing jacket photo or a DVD segment of him sipping whiskies with Clooney or Crowe, who will star in the movie version—something for Mom to brag about over bridge. Otherwise, the writer should write, and leave the limelight to the glib and photogenic.

A few facts about myself are necessary, though, to continue the story of how I wrote *The Saddest Election.* At least these facts are not dull. Being spied on is worrisome and creepy and enervating. Dull it is not.

I met my Moroccan wife Naima (that's na-EE-ma) when I was in New York just after the election. At the time, I was talking with a couple of New York Taylor-for-Prez officials, trying like every other campaign writer to get *something, anything* on Taylor. A kindly cousin of mine in Queens had donated sleeping space on his La-Z-Boy to my cause. One night I was hustling home from an interview, alert for any incarnation of Jack the Ripper, when Naima walked past and, in a whisper, asked if I spoke French. My answer was yes: I had lived in Nantes, France, from the age of seven to eighteen. My late father had run a junior-year-abroad program for Americans in that city's university.

With a cry of anguished relief, Naima threw herself into my arms and knocked us both to the pavement. I mistook this for anguished dementia, shoved her off with an elbow-jab in the neck, scrambled to my feet and snatched away my satchel. I was several thrusting strides away when she screamed at me not to leave her, she was in trouble, she needed help, she was starving.

Thus do great romances begin.

Naima was Moroccan, illegal, and homeless. She had been thrown out of her house in Tangiers because she had gotten pregnant. It didn't matter that she was the pride of the family, having taken a degree in virology in Rabat, and supported her four worthless brothers and oppressed mother with her research on crop viruses for the Agriculture Ministry. Pregnancy is a sure sign that *you know what* took place, and Naima's shit-for-brains siblings were scandalized that she had actually gone and done what they try day and night to get women to do. Out she went into the street, though they told her with brotherly frankness to stay in town because, after all, she did still belong to the family and they did still need her salary. She said a teary good-bye to her mother and told the outraged guys she would write from abroad.

She got an amazingly proper abortion from a college-friend's brother who was a doctor. Then she sized up the well-developed mafia racket that runs motorboatfuls of dupes over to southern Spain for the Spanish Guardia Civil to round up and send back. She sought a surer and cheaper method. She hung around the port for a week until she found and seduced a middle-aged Panamanian ship captain who, amidst winks to his crew, stowed her in his cabin on a freighter bound for Newark. She put up with his bad breath in return for the transportation, and Captain Alfonso, to give him his due, always used a condom and was *"gentil."* He sneaked her out amidst boxes of dates into Port Newark, gave her a hundred bucks and the address of a Panamanian friend—who turned out not to be there.

She jumped into my arms two sleepless days later; no hotel would take her without ID or passport. Naima had wisely tossed both into the Atlantic. It's the old immigrant game: it's harder for U.S. Immigration to send you home if they can't prove where home is.

Naima enters our story, now five months illegal and very leery of immigration authorities, on the day I discovered the windshield note. To observe the requisites of falling in love in more tranquil surroundings, she had come back to Minneapolis to live with me. Here the risk of being tripped up by Immigration was smaller than in a big port city, and my mother was nearby with her pick-and-shovel French, which she used mainly to talk Naima into having children with me.

I had told Naima many times that the police could not stop anyone on the street without a good reason, but like most people from the Third World, Naima never quite believed this. Don't be surprised: there I'm hassled by Tangier's Finest just for parading my shabby infidel mug alongside her Islamicness. Your private business is their public business, and pity the fool who thinks otherwise. So Naima grew up with a smarting respect for the authorities. In Minneapolis that first year, she always had one eye peeled for the pant-cuffs of officialdom.

Which turned out to be a good thing. At almost the same moment I was mulling over the windshield note, she did spot someone watching her.

Equipped with her new, if virological, English, Naima audited classes in her subject at the U of Minnesota, preparing to resume her future career. Foreigners breathe a quarter of the university air and most of it in the science courses, so her accent presented no problem. On that day, she made her usual checks of strange faces in the classrooms, glanced in the mirror of a sports-clothing shop, and peered from behind the magazine and greeting-card racks. Before entering a bathroom, she checked to see who was around in the hallway, then checked again to see if any of those people were waiting for her when she came out. This was her daily routine, regular as a diabetic checking blood sugar.

And I'd always smiled at it.

The watcher was stout and powdered, with a fading, red perm and thick hips and a round tummy that had lodged babies now of roughly high-school age. Naima spotted her on the bus and later in one of the dark theater classrooms in the medical-studies complex—spotted her across the theater because the woman, no virologist, had taken out a magazine to read and was turning pages during the lecture.

And was still turning them across the cafeteria while Naima drank her morning root beer, that culinary Mount Rushmore which Naima considers "the greatest thing since the slice of bread."

Then, at noon, the woman's cell phone rang. She pulled it out, spoke briefly with someone, hung up, sighed with lid-closed relief, and walked out. Naima called me, very frightened, sure the police were about to pounce. I hardly knew what to think—that she had been detected by Immigration was nearly impossible. She does not look Arabic. Her features are mostly African; she traces her roots to Senegal and is darker than most African-Americans, tall and slender. Dressed in jeans and a sweater—she had held no truck with veils and the like since her very secular university years in Rabat—she could easily pass for American.

I picked her up in a university parking garage, third floor, as arranged. She scrunched down in the back seat till we were a block away.

"Sam, I think we should not go home. Probably they are waiting for us."

"I don't think so. They would have arrested you this morning. Why should they wait?"

"That's nonsense! It must be the CIA! They are looking for Middle Eastern terrorists!"

I assured Naima that the CIA had more interesting suspects to tail—privately, I was less sure about the FBI—all of this in French, of course. I drove to our down-at-heel apartment on the university's

West Bank (of the Mississippi, that is). We drove up and down Cedar Avenue twice before parking and saw nothing suspicious. We went in, and just to calm her, I told her to wait in the neighbors' apartment while I checked out our own.

Which brings me to the espionage part of our story.

Our neighbors across the hall were Paul Skoglund and Bob Klein, both of whom worked in the music business. Bob was a sound engineer who occasionally rented time in Prince's high-tech palace. Paul played trumpet and piano in the studios for whomever paid. They were good guys—always there with the needed tomato or cup of sugar, reliable with the care of plants. We also kept an eye on each other's apartments, lest the penniless come to filch from the dimeless.

Paul had news.

Just after noon, he heard the bulky locks clank in my apartment door. He glanced through the spy hole in his own door and saw a man dressed in janitor's garb locking the door of my apartment. His back was to Paul's spy hole, but Paul saw to his surprise that he needed both hands to turn the lock, which meant that he wasn't using a key to do it, but probably a combination of lock picks. Then he picked up a tool kit and thumped down the stairs and out the street door. Half a block down Cedar Avenue, he jumped into a BMW—a vehicle that rarely caresses a janitor's backside.

I left Naima and Paul together and crossed the hallway to our apartment. More to ease my own foolish fears than anything else, I checked through all the rooms—all three of them, that is: the kitchen, the bathroom and the living room that doubled as bedroom and tripled as a study. All was quiet: no bear traps, no hit men.

So: what?

My campaign-election notepads—about thirty. They were not as I had placed them. Receipts that I kept to deduct on my expenses had been moved around. But not much. Had I not known that someone had been in the apartment, I would not have noticed anything, assuming that Naima had shifted them. And my desktop computer. I turned it on and checked a few things, and quickly discovered that about ten files in my word processor had been saved to a flash disk that morning, the last one just after noon, which was about the time that Naima's shadow-lady, talking on the phone, had sighed with relief and disappeared. Obviously, she had been keeping an eye on

Naima; the thief alerted her when his work was finished. Her hours being irregular, they had needed to keep her under watch. Me, I spent nearly every day—and certainly every morning—out of the apartment, a fact that a few phone calls could have established.

Had they been watching me, too, in order to put the note on my windshield? I wondered.

At least our problems had nothing to do with Naima's illegal status; that was a relief. The whos and whys were less clear, however, unless you figured that my election-book competitors were trying to get hold of the few soggy trial chapters for my book; those were the contents of the copied files. I considered this seriously for a couple of reasons. First, I was one of the few writers still working on how-it-was-won books; only one came out later than mine. And all the books that had already landed in the stores, holding no interesting revelations, had fallen straight into the remainder bins.

Second, the operation had clearly been carried out by amateurs. Naima would never have spotted a professional tail, like a private detective. And the man who had entered our apartment might have had plain bad luck in being spotted—that could happen to anyone—but a pro would have rifled my computer and notes without leaving traces. And he would have used a vehicle less suited to the escorting of a supermodel.

On the other hand, he was serious about the job: he knew enough about lock picks to pick the sophisticated lock of our apartment door and the easy one downstairs that opened on the street; this indicated careful preparation.

We didn't call the police—they might have asked questions about Naima—but from then on, we assumed the intruders were checking our e-mail, and maybe the phone, too. Paul and Bob started keeping an eagle eye on our door.

Thus began my six-week lambada with Big Brother.

Naima was still pretty upset, so I bit my financial lip and took her out for a steak washed down with enough red wine to stun an elephant; she had discovered the illicit joys of Christian drink, even if she still observed Ramadan, the annual Muslim month of fasting. But once she had fallen tipsy into bed, I wandered around the apartment, thinking and thinking, for it had occurred to me over the last glass of Rioja that maybe someone else was on to the Terry–Laura story. A pile of royalties awaited anyone who could throw light on the Miracle Election—enough to be worth hiring a team to see how I'm doing and make sure I'm lagging sufficiently. That meant I had to move my fanny, and quick. The next step was to go to Columbus and grill Terry Letizzle.

And Laura.

6 Four years later, it still pains me to write about Terry Letizzle. When I think About him now, he reminds me of an ecstatic kid yelling to his parents to watch him, he can ride his bike no-hands—then sails right out into a busy street. My memory of him is colored by his shrill loneliness and awful fate, and the guilt that the years seem to have knitted into these. For this reason, I merely sketched his story in *The Saddest Election.* Now that four years have passed, I fill out the picture here. Once an historian, always an historian.

His house was a tiny, frightened, white wood box, vassal to the spacious brick structure next door from which it was separated by a scrubby little no-man's land with a compost heap in the middle. The lawn beside the house—it was on a corner—held four cherry trees in a square formation. In the middle of them, planted with weird prominence, two iron, T-shaped clothes poles vibrated in the wind, relentless like the moan of freeway traffic down the block. The hedge had been trimmed too enthusiastically and showed only sticks. There was no garage, and the mailbox displayed a tilted five.

Parked down the block, I watched Terry arrive from work under a faceless spring sky, his red head sharp against the white of the house. He wore a dumpy parka and dark dress pants with brown leather shoes. I knew nothing of his work since the election, but I was pretty sure the dress pants led up to a white shirt and a company suit jacket with a name-tag that served to distinguish him for consternated shoppers looking for an adjustable basketball hoop or the correct size of undershirt. God had penciled in Terry for a life of waiting on others.

After twenty minutes, I figured Terry had shifted gears and changed his clothes, so I drove up and parked and walked up the cracked walk to the front porch, calculating that the entire building would almost fit in my apartment; surely it had but one large room for both sleeping and living. I remembered his résumé and wondered if Terry had "worked hard" enough at finding a wife; for an answer—to me and the doorbell—I had the hurried footsteps of a friendless man. I hoped Senator Gotchell had been magnanimous with condoms and lovers, but I doubted it.

"Hi! How are ya? You're Sam, I'm Terry," he established, grabbing my hand. His was strong, though the freckled flesh was perishable and spongy.

"Hi, Terry. Thanks for making some time available on such short—"

"Sure, no problemo. You said you're doing a book on the election?"

"Right. It's a—"

"That's great, that's fantastic. Well, what did you want to talk to me about? I mean, I'm really flattered by the attention and all, but I can't *imagine* what I could tell you." All of this in bursts of syllables and stale breath that made me want to duck. His thin frame still barred the entrance, and I wondered if we were going to have the whole interview there at the front door.

"Well, just a little of the day-to-day running of the campaign—the details. According to people I've talked to, you traveled almost constantly with Senator Gotchell—"

"Nothing 'almost' about it. I was his right-hand man. Got him up in the morning, fed him, set him on the campaign trail and gave him a push. I wasn't his right-hand, man, I was his backbone!"

Which was still in the middle of the doorway.

"Right. Well, that's basically what I'm looking for: background color. What did Gotchell eat for breakfast? How did he like his collars pressed? Did he say a prayer before giving a speech? The moods of the campaign, the ups and downs of the primaries, interesting little—"

"Oh! Oh, okay. Yeah, that's fine, no problemo," he said, and I wondered what might be a problemo. He pulled me into the house by the arm. "C'mon in and sit down. You can stay for dinner, can't you? I'll make us some pizza—it's really good. I'm a great cook. Just watch."

Thus headlong was he entering the pages of American history.

Only a tiny percentage of what Terry told me that evening gave me material for *The Saddest Election*, though our conversation filled two sixty-minute cassettes and part of a third. Almost all of it was exaggerated and, because of the personal nature of his stories, little could be verified.

On and on he talked, well past the beer and the ham-and-mushroom-pizza—excellent, as advertised—which we ate in the kitchen under a fluorescent light that fluttered schizophrenically. For once in his life, someone was interested in him, and Terry had no intention of letting him go. He spattered words from an oceanic supply, hands darting, Adam's apple pumping, eyebrows twitching, nerves so loose that I wondered if he weren't a reformed junkie. (So strong was the impression that I later asked his old college friends from Ohio State if he had taken drugs; the answer was no.) He just could not sit still. He must have run to his bedroom-study, the only other complete room in the house, fifteen times for news clippings and photos.

"Got it right here—no kidding, I really do," he pleaded from some closet. In between serving me and getting clippings, he was drumming his fingers on his thighs, on the kitchen table, on the beer bottle—I asked him to stop, and he obeyed—except for the silent Morse code with his right ring finger on his left palm. He was a man who needed a dog, something to occupy his feverish hands and absorb his loneliness.

"You heard it right, man," he told me, pointing at his ear lest I try to listen through my mouth. "Nine o'clock in the evening, practically past my bed time, and there's yours truly still going through the bills on the computer with this Mexicano babe with tits like two basketballs—no kidding, man, just like *that.*" He cradled the air to show me. "And I'm trying to find out where the hell Gotchell's four suits got sent, and the campaign plane's taking off for Sacramento in like ten seconds, and all the woman really wants to do is get my phone number or better yet, just go down on me right there without asking name, rank or serial number. I mean, can you dig that?" A pianist's flick of the hand to the beer bottle, which he upended weightlessly into his mouth.

"All of the friggin' sudden, the receipt pops up on the screen, and by the grace of God the suits are still in the shop—which means *another* search while this babe is like trying to fondle me through the hanging clothes and plastic and stuff. Finally, I spot the suits back in the corner, grab them off a rack, and she's asking me what hotel I'm staying in and won't take no for an answer, so I blurt out, 'The Hilton, Room 205,' hoping to God on high there really is a Hilton in Phoenix, and off I run to the taxi that still has the meter running. Duty being duty, ya know. But that's campaigns for ya, man, politics being the ultimate aphrodisiac, just like Kissinger said."

(The story was false, in case you have any doubts. The manager of the dry-cleaning shop, a Gotchell supporter, personally did the work on the suits and took care of Terry when he came in for them. There was indeed a mix-up, but she called Terry on his mobile phone before he was five minutes away in his car with the wrong suits. She *was* Mexican, by the way, but her age was fifty-three, well beyond babehood.)

Such were Terry's campaign stories. He was everywhere doing everything. His sure hand guided the campaign, and all womanhood cursed his dedication to it. Every Gotchell memo needed Terry's pen, every platform plank his hammer, every opportunity's window his prizing fingers. He was the linchpin of the organization, the brain behind the brawn, and to hear it from Terry, the hapless senator never made a move—never scribbled a change in his speech—without consulting him: "Ter'—how does this sound? Awful, right? Give me something better. C'mon, anything—I'm on in two minutes." Relations with China, solar-power policy, media statements, political ripostes—all had made their marks on Terry's weathered brow.

He had a beautiful voice; that was the best you could say for him. It dashed up and down a baritone scale like the low notes of an organ, marvelously clear and sonorous, reminiscent of Obama's. And he was a great carpenter. He had rebuilt the interior of the house—formerly a stables—right down to the wainscoting in the bedroom-study, even the ceiling. He listened to my praise of all this, but to my surprise shrugged it off. His deceased father, a retired automobile factory worker, had done similar work for extra income. And he seemed to have passed on to Terry a disdain for manual labor. So to Terry, the carpentry was little more than drudgery, and no more artful than cutting the grass.

"The counter?" he chuckled at my compliment. "Hell, you just measure and cut, put in a few supports. Anybody could do it."

"*I* couldn't do it."

"Yeah, but you don't need to. You're a writer—a *political* writer. You have a voice."

"You have a voice, too."

"Oh, come on, man. Like people listen to Terry Letizzle whenever they get a chance."

I got down to business while I still had tape in my recorder. "Terry, before I forget, just let me get down some detail here. First, your middle name."

"Martin."

"Martin. And you're from Columbus here?"

"Akron, actually. I came to Columbus when I started at OSU, and I've just stayed on. Still go over to State for poli-sci happy hour on Fridays." He grinned.

"Great place to pick up chicks, man. I don't know what it is about politics that—"

"You studied political science?"

"Yeah, picked up a Master's," he said carelessly; it might have been part of a two-for-one sale.

Terry mentioned the year, and I snapped my head up with a respectable imitation of surprise. "I was just talking to someone last month who said they graduated from OSU. Poli-sci., the same year, I think. You know who?"

Terry said he didn't, though the alarm in his liquid-black eyes rose like the squeal in a teapot. I told him who, and the rest of his fingers joined the ring finger in typing on his palm. "Oh, yeah—Laura." She might have been the girl who had dumped him last weekend. "She used to come to the poli-sci happy hour, too. At Rutherford's. That's a campus bar. She's in PR now, I think, or at least she used to be. I haven't talked to her now in—hell, like, ages."

"Run into her during the campaign?"

"Sure—here and there." At this point, he tried to launch a lecture entitled "Campaigns are small worlds, really," but I was waving him back into the pits before it picked up speed.

"So you had time to chat."

"We talked about what hotels to avoid, mainly. You know the worst hotel in America, man? It's not some rent-by-the-hour joint, but actually—"

"Speaking of Laura, I need your comment on something. She told me that her campaign had a video of your man Gotchell going into his dressing room after a speech with a pretty aide and, well, pushing out the Secret Service detail. Any truth to that?"

Terry jumped up and rushed the dirty dishes to the sink, where they toppled in with a clatter. "Senator Gotchell has always been faithful to his lovely wife. Of course, he *looks*—everybody looks, man, that's okay, that's in the rules. But that's it, and you can put that in your book." The defensiveness in his tone was new to me.

"What's your take on Jover trying to get into Frakes headquarters? Laura told me that in her organization, they figured he was trying to get hold of this videotape."

Terry started washing plates and glasses, forearms moving like piston rods. "Lemme tell ya something, man, I knew everything that happened in our organization. Arnold Jover's illegal entry was his own work. He was a cowboy. We don't know why he did it, and we don't *wanna* know. If there's one thing a campaign organization can't use, man, it is a *cowboy.*" He snatched a metal pad and gave the pizza pan a cruel scrubbing as if to expunge Jover from it.

"Campaigns and people," I said with melancholy. "The more I research I do, the more I discover a campaign all depends on the personalities involved."

"Damn right, man, absolutely. This senator said it best: 'I can't be responsible for people who go off on their own and try to short-circuit this democratic process.' He must have repeated that a hundred times, but did the American people listen? Like hell. Goddamn Jover ruined it for everybody. If I had him here, I'd wring his goddamn neck, you know."

I wondered. I ate some grapes he had in a bowl on the table and tried to imagine Terry working up that kind of rage. Maybe.

"What if I told you Laura told me about the videotape she passed you at the third debate?"

He stopped—he was rinsing the pizza pan, and now the water just ran and ran over it. His stillness was as striking as his flurry. Finally the pan slipped a little in his loosening grip and slid through this fingers and made a witless clunk in the bottom of the sink.

I realized then how small the kitchen was, lit by the single, aguish tube. The mangy refrigerator jutted into the floor space like a peninsula. A small TV hovered high on an ugly wall bracket.

He swatted the water tap shut and stood hanging his head, wet hands gripping the counter's edge as soap suds ran down the garbage cupboard.

"Ah, the great *democrat,*" he sneered. "So *just.* So *responsible.* So *concerned* about free and fair elections. She didn't happen to tell you just how incompetent she was—or is, rather, did she? Like: not just the outtakes video but with Jover and the goddamn security pass?" He swung around. "That's right, Sam—it was *her* idea, *her* information, *her* pass she photocopied, though knowing Laura, she probably *forgot* to mention that part of it. And long as we're on the subject, Sam, let's get something real straight for your book, okay?"

"Okay, but don't—"

He took a step forward, and I reached for my beer bottle to make something of my flinch.

"She told me that security stripe on the ID was *red,* not blue. Blue was the *right* color. She should have said *blue.* Got that on your tape here?" He slapped his hands dry on his pants, then snatched the recorder off the table and spoke into it. "Laura Prestini told me, Terry Letizzle, that the stripe was *red.*" He banged the recorder on the table and looked at me as if daring me to object.

"So you –"

"That bitch. It was *her* fault, not mine. So if I got back at her, it's what she deserved. Of course, nobody'll believe me. I'm just fucking little Terry Letizzle who tries to help everybody out and does it with a smile on his face because life is hard enough. But it's true."

I weighed this and added empathy to my voice. "All right. Let's take this step by step," I said.

But Terry was listening to the future now. "And now look what's going to happen: *you've* got hold of the story! This is going to go all over the country! I knew this would happen! *I knew it!*" He broke down crying. He staggered back against the sink, wiping his eyes on the heels of his wet hands. "They're gonna come down right on top of *me!*"

I searched for something consoling to say. "Terry, it's not like it was all your fault. It was *Jover's* decision to try for the tape. Or whoever it was that knew about—"

He shook his head. "Arnold's the only one I told. He seemed

reliable. Really he was just a fuck-up. He ruined everything."

"Well, okay, then! You were just—"

But the conversation was over.

"All the good background I gave you doesn't count for much, does it? I try to be your friend, and you throw it back in my face. Don't worry—people do that to me all the time. Even women. Especially women, especially classy babes like Laura. So go ahead. Drag my image up and down the street till it's just a carcass."

"Wait minute, Terry. Remember it was *your bosses'* decision to turn the tape over to CBS. You were just—"

"Oh, now you're trying to humor me. People humor me all the time, too—customers, Laura. I hate that. I turned my back on her, know that? Right in her face I dissed her. You can take a hike, too. C'mon, get the hell out."

"Terry, hold on. I'm not—"

"I'm not holding on to anything. This is my house and nobody tells me what to do in my house. Now get out! Get out, get out, get out!" He was screaming. "Try to give you a hand, help you out for the good of history, and I end up eating shit for it. Always. Just get out. Get the fuck out of my house. This is the one place where people can't shit on me." He was still crying, and he grabbed my coat off the back of an unused chair, slashing the tears off his face. "This is all going to come down on *me!* I knew it! I knew it would come out!"

"But there's no—"

Terry opened the back door and threw my coat outside. "Just get out, and tell that bitch when you see her that she's not getting half what she deserved. And she can take her bygones and shove them up her tight little ass!"

A few seconds later, I was out in the dark side yard brushing off my coat. I turned off the cassette and patted my pockets to make sure I had all the tapes. I could still hear Terry inside, crying. My first idea was to let him calm down and then knock on the door and try to reason with him. I put on my coat and practiced different lines of contrition: *Gosh, Terry, you were right. I apologize. I was getting a little ahead of myself there* Or: *Look, Terry, this is going to come out, one way or another, and this is your best chance to spin it your way.*

I disliked the falseness, but I certainly wasn't going to let the story get away from me. I had a thread of the Miracle Election mystery in my grasp. Jover's entry had been *Laura's* idea? His security pass had been a copy of *hers?* She had even told him the color of the stripe? Well, if the photocopy she had sent Terry was in black and white, that would have been necessary.

After five minutes, Terry was still sobbing on the kitchen table, not into his arms, but bent over like a rag doll sitting in the chair I'd used. I watched him from the lawn until I realized that a nearby streetlight made me slightly visible. So I retreated beyond the bare hedge and set up watch in the shadow of a van parked at the curb. As luck would have it, my movement started the neighbor's dog barking. Terry jumped up from the table and a moment later slammed open the back door.

He had a gun in his hand.

I couldn't move, which was the right thing to do, anyway.

He squinted into the dark, panting—a sob stole out—and I had a bad moment when he came down two of the three steps to the lawn. But there he stopped. His body jerked and his mouth opened as if he were going to shout a threat. Then some caution—legal? moral? physical?—prevented him. He peered around, the gun held upright near his shoulder as if it weighed a lot, and maybe it did—it was a bulky chunk of steel that made his wrist keel over; the butt pointed drunkenly at an angle. He looked like an actor who had never handled a gun before. Still, watching his shoulders heave up and down, I had the distinct impression that the gun was loaded and that he was mad enough to use it. A leaf from last autumn fell across his face, and he slapped it angrily away.

He wasn't there long—not thirty seconds, probably not even ten; time doubles when an armed man is looking for you. Finally, he turned and placed a foot on the upper step and, after a last look, went back inside. He crossed the kitchen and put a hand—without a gun—up to the wall, as if leaning against it after a long run. He turned off the light. No others came on, and when I drove past the little house an hour later, it was still dark.

I have always resented Senator Gotchell's absence at Terry's funeral. He was in Washington at the time, and Columbus is just an hour away by plane. Instead, he sent a message written by some harried staff member, praising Terry's "drive and tireless work for our democracy," lamenting that he "could not have been a guide to Terry in his hour of need, and thus pay back, if only one iota, some of the valuable emotional support he gave me during the campaign." Voice quaking, Terry's pink-haired mother read it as if from an Olympic medal, and the reporter quoted from it twice; her report on a dead-slow news day played up the former-campaign-aide angle.

The TV crew was tasteful about the mourners, briefly filming the friends and family on the sidewalk as the hearse arrived. The cameraman even managed to create the sensation that a multitude had come to pay Terry their last respects. In reality they numbered about a dozen: his remaining family, some cousins, the regional manager of the golf-supplies branch that Terry ran, who sat with a cell-phone ear jack in his ear; his mother's sniffling sisters and neighbors. No girlfriends, either past or present.

Laura Prestini, however, did come—ten minutes late, alone, ensconced in dark glasses like a movie star, sitting alone near the back of the church, head down. She spoke to no one and departed during the final hymn. Yet in her hunched shoulders and limp neck, I saw genuine horror at Terry's passing. She hurried out along the wall, eyes down, hand covering her face as if she had just discovered the body herself, and I found myself grappling with the incredible notion that they had been lovers.

I sat at the back, up in the choir loft, having told the organist that I couldn't handle being with others at a time like that. Actually, I was concerned that they might have heard my name in connection with the death, as I had given a statement to the police. (While I was at the police station, the chief stepped in briefly and introduced himself. He had known Terry. The chief had been a candidate for state congress years earlier, and Terry had worked on his losing campaign. "Always kind of wondered how that guy'd end up," the chief muttered, implying that suicide figured on his list. He told the woman taking my statement to "just keep it to generalities." Even in death, no fuss was to be made over Terry.) When I gave my condolences to the family, however, his bewildered mother and two brothers had no reaction to my name. Just as well.

The day after our interview, Terry spent the morning tidying his affairs and then shot himself. He must have been damn frightened at the threshold of death: the first bullet nipped his forehead and burrowed into the refrigerator. For the second try—some minutes later, blood pouring down his face and an elderly neighbor banging frantically on the side door—he marshaled his nerves: a perfect shot through the temple. He had written a suicide note of sorts. The blood had to be wiped off, as Terry, with more transcendent matters on his mind, had fired in its direction. It was found to read, "God bless America."

America would never return the favor. Once my book came out, she threw him in the historical dungeon with Benedict Arnold.

7 I spent six days after the funeral going through campaign records on Laura Prestini at the Frakes campaign offices—six days, including the Sunday, because there was a lot more material to cover than with Terry.

In contrast with Gotchell's homey place in downtown Saint Paul, Frakes headquarters was divided in two, the executive and financial offices in downtown Columbus, and the main part at an airplane hangar at Columbus Airport. The latter was a rat nest of dividers and computers and copiers and posters rippling in the ruthless draughts. Every work desk had an electric space heater under it, for the cold air spread everywhere at ankle level, like army ants sweeping over their prey. The heat gave each worker a quick caress and rose quickly to the white steel beams and aluminum roofing high above. I saw workers tapping at keyboards wearing driving gloves. Such are the unique sacrifices of political campaigns.

The headquarters was still busy. Citing personal reasons (a frail euphemism for the outtakes scandal), Governor Frakes had suddenly resigned his office. His lieutenant governor having declined to step up to the job because of renewed heart problems, a special gubernatorial election had been set for June. What few computers had not been commandeered for the campaign were relegated to a back corner of the hangar, which was good for me because the questing tentacles of cold rarely stretched that far. All of the space heaters having been snatched up, I could research in relative comfort by wrapping a *Columbus Dispatch* around my thighs.

The item I probably spent the most time on was Laura Prestini's expense sheets. Unlike Terry, she was liberal with her expenses, at least during the primaries. Her meals ranged from good to down-right sumptuous. To the campaign she had charged massages, running shoes, tampons, an electronic agenda, rounds of golf, and a day at Disneyland. (These were small potatoes compared to her boss, Phyllis Kirk, who considered her lavish hairdos and extravagant suits the least that the Committee to Elect could do for her.) She also purchased a "Squeel-EE" burglar alarm for her suitcase, though it was the smallest of three available models. I imagined that with the constant travel, much of it on commercial airlines, some of her things had been swiped.

By mid-September, however, as the national campaign revved into overdrive, Laura's expenses had dropped off. Suddenly, she was eating for half the money and buying next to nothing. A receipt of twenty-two items bought in a department store actually made me laugh: the purchases were no sexier than a pack of gum, Post-its, a cheap shower cap, four black Bic pens, and six key copies. Three were for $1.89 apiece and three for $1.79—mysteries of marketing. All the same, I made a note to ask Phyllis if she had jerked Laura's chain on expenses. And I printed out all Laura's primary-campaign and general-campaign expenses sheets *and* receipts, just to be sure I had proof of the differences.

Then I moved to the other question: What were her movements just before the third debate? Had she picked up the outtakes video somewhere, or a copy of it? I checked her travel records and hit pay dirt.

On the day of the third debate, October seventeenth, she had taken a commercial flight from Kansas City to Columbus. She arrived at three-thirty-five. Eighty-two minutes later, at four-fifty-seven, she was on a flight to Baton Rouge, site of the third debate. The campaign log, however, showed that Frakes had three campaign stops that afternoon—Lawrence, Kansas, then both Kansas Cities—before a flight to Austin, Texas, and later Baton Rouge. The next four days Frakes would be on the east and west coasts.

These Kansas-area stops were all Laura's shows. Of course, her presence might not have been necessary, but what was she doing back at headquarters? That was suspicious. With eighty-two minutes between flights, she could not possibly have left the airport. Was she picking up Frakes' suit for the debate? And if not, wouldn't it have made more sense to pop over to Columbus in the next few days, when Frakes would be out of her area? Travel records showed that she was often in and out of Columbus—usually only for hours, clearly no farther than headquarters at the airport; and she could go for weeks without spending more than a day here, presumably sleeping in her own bed just for the joy of it. Hence the big question: might she have come in that day to pick up the outtakes video that sank her candidate?

I sat mulling, looking up at the ceiling, till my eye fell on a black security camera tucked into the skirmishing beams and ducts of the hangar. The camera was part of the same security system that had filmed Arnold Jover's attempted entry here months earlier. I wondered if it might also tell me something about Laura's quick swing through Columbus Airport on October seventeenth.

Ten minutes later, I was on the opposite side of the hangar, rummaging through boxes of security video with Zack Stram, the daytime security chief, a lanky, bored Georgian whose labors on this earth consisted of watching black-and-white monitors and filling out forms. He enjoyed having company.

"Sure, she's in here. Gots to be—'nless I used her already. Like I said, after that attempt by that Jover guy, s'curity got tightened up a notch. Wasn't that bad before, mind, but now we started checkin' folks comin' and goin', scatter-checkin' bags an' briefcases, checkin' ev'thing that moved and some of it that didn't. And we had to start savin' every reel of s'curity video—you know, just in case something turned up missin' later on? 'Cept Campaign Central never did get 'round to tellin' us to get rid of it. I'm reusin' it little by little on the new gov'nor race here. But your reel should be here somewhere."

And it was. After moving around several rows of cases, Stram's long hands closed over a film can labeled "October 12-24." I asked if he had time to show it to me, and he laughed. "Time? Lordy, man, I got nothin' but. S'curity, that's a prison sentence, that is."

Her plane from Kansas City had arrived ten minutes late that day, and Laura was in and out of Frakes HQ in one minute and forty-three seconds, according to the security tape's digital clock. The hurry was understandable. She would have less than an hour to dash across the tarmac, check in for the flight to Baton Rouge, fight her way through security, and get to the gate. Maybe the lateness was due to the weather; it was windy that day, and her hair was a blown-over mess that she was fastidiously pushing into shape with one hand as with the other she pulled her suitcase up to the security desk.

You've seen the black-and-white video again and again, but just for the record: tight slacks, a white, high-waist sports jacket stained on the right sleeve; no doubt the campaign had been hard on her clothes. It was unzipped to show the dark, clingy sweater with deep V- neck that offered a lovely sample to the bored guard (not to be confused with Alex Jill, the one who had caught Jover, who by now was in Hollywood flexing his muscles before a casting director). The high angle of the security camera augmented this view and by good luck reduced the effect of Laura's nose, then still a hook.

Four-ten P.M.: Still smoothing her hair, Laura Prestini approaches the security counter and shows her security pass to the guard. She signs in—right-handed—at the security counter.

"Signin' in, that was a new r'quirement, too, after the Jover thing," Stram added beside me, munching honey-coated sunflower seeds.

Laura smiles flirtily at the guard and points to the big suitcase and her black purse with the cell-phone pocket on the strap that she's dumped on top of the counter: *Can I just leave these here a moment?* The guard nods and says something that makes her laugh. She steps up to the metal-detector booth and from her jacket pockets takes out a sparsely populated key ring and a few other things. She places these on the counter, steps through, collects them again, and walks quickly away as the guard boosts his torso atop the counter and leans over it to get a good look at her backside. Laura sways away off camera.

"That's Baronowsky, dumb Poh-lock," Stram said around another mouthful of sunflower seeds. "Majorin' in finance and *I-talian,* if you can believe it. Says you meet all these sugar-butts tryin' t' be opera singers. They gotta study I-talian, y'know. But hang on: he says it's just him and one other guy in the class, and the other guy's a faggot. Gots the whole field t' hisself!"

"Smart man. But you need long arms to reach around a soprano," I said as we watched Baronowsky: he checks his watch, makes a note, and jots his initials beside Laura's name. I was grateful that the camera was not the usual grainy quality; it was well focused, the image sharp enough to see writing on the registry; the top quarter of the page was filled.

"Hey! That's jus' what I said!" Stram cried. "But no, no, no, he says that's the best part. Says you catch 'em when their still undergrads, they just slide and glide in your hands. Real high-strung, he says, want it two-three times in a row!"

"Is that right? Gonna go a long way, this Baronowsky." (Not so, I'm afraid. I talked to him not long before writing this addendum to my book. One of his singers had gotten pregnant, and poor Baronowsky had dropped out of school to support his new family.)

Laura returns. With a video cassette box in her hand.

A black video cassette box of just the kind that Terry Letizzle, may he rest in peace, would hold under his arm on the evening of that same day in Baton Rouge.

Yes, you've seen the footage a hundred times, but indulge me for a paragraph and let me relive the tingling in my back as I leaned forward on the rheumatic folding chair in Zack Stram's cozy cinder-brick office where the cold could not penetrate, where the paperwork spilled off the desk and the laughing angel of a *Playboy* calendar watched over us, in my nostrils the odor of his honeyed sunflower seeds that I will forever associate with that moment. Here was my book shooting to the moon. My writing career. Financial security, which till then had been only a dream. The resources to marry and have children with the perfect wife who had literally fallen into my arms. Here was the key to the Miracle Election.

Four-twelve P.M.: Laura is back, carrying a black video-cassette case. She puts the video on the counter, laboriously empties her jacket pockets again, steps through the metal detector, twists at the waist and collects her things. She steps to the registry book and signs, Baronowsky now on tip-toe peering down her sweater.

To my surprise, she does not put the cassette in her purse. No. Laura crouches to her suitcase, lays it down on the floor and puts the video on top of it—Baronowsky now leaning across the counter to watch, though all he sees is her behind because Laura has her back square to him and her left profile to us. She takes a something from her off-camera-side pocket, but luckily passes it to her left hand, so we see it: it seems to be a tiny pocket flashlight. She aims it—either at the suitcase or the video on top—and presses the button with her thumb. Laura starts; so does Baronowsky.

"What's that thing?" I asked Stram, who stopped the video.

"Ah, that's for one o' them damn 'Squeel-EE' alarms. Gots one in her suitcase. Comes with one o' them beamers: infra-red or nuclear or somethin'. It turns the alarm on and off. That's why she jumped. Even the damn all-clear beep'll clean your ears out, it's so loud."

Laura pockets the device, unlocks the latches of the suitcase, and takes the video cassette. She raises the suitcase top to vertical, regaling all America with an exhibition of her undergarments which clearly run to the lacy, and works the video-cassette in amidst an assortment of frilly panties and thongs.

"Look at that! Look at that!" Stram shouted. "Wears them little skinny things up her ass, don't she? Bet you anything you want she's wearin' one right there!"

I didn't bet, too busy taking note that in the upper left corner, nestled atop a half-cup white brassiere, is *another* black video box.

Laura closes the suitcase, snaps down the latches. Takes out the little device, aims it, presses the button, jumps slightly less with the beep of the activating signal.

Up goes the suitcase handle. Purse over the shoulder like a city slicker. And then the big finale: smiling warmly, she reaches out and caresses Baronowsky's cheek—then pinches it so sharply that he jumps back, grabbing it with both hands. She grins, turns on heel, grabs her suitcase, and walks off camera, Baronowsky staring open-mouthed after her.

"Christ alive! I love those tough, flirty ones!" Stram laughed, as all America soon would. "Won't let you outta bed till they've taken every last ounce! Hey, let's take another look!"

"Spirit she has," I said, croaking a laugh just to be polite. My heart was beating too hard for anything else. "Hey, just what is this 'Squeel-EE' alarm?"

"That's right—didn't see 'er in her baggage." Zack had grabbed the video remote control and pushed the rewind button. "Bad little moth'fuckers, them Squeel'EEs. Ain't you hear 'bout those?"

"Guess not."

"It's like this big, aluminum clothespin—kind with the spring in the middle, y'know? 'Bout as big as your hand. *In theory,* you stick it in your suitcase on top o' your stuff and close it so's the teeth open.

Y'activate it with that button once your bag goes through s'curity at the check-in. You can do it a good fifty feet away. People been buyin' 'em 'cause with all the extra s'curity and terr'rism, them wiseasses in Baggage Handlin' been havin' a damn field day."

I said I had read about this somewhere.

"Wiseass opens a bag with a Squeel-EE in 'er, the mo'fucker lets fly a screech that'll cure constipation. Prob'm is, folks don't always pack their belongin's tight around 'em, so they end up slippin' sideways and fallin' over in the bag and *whoop!* You can hear those son'bitches goin' off a hundred yards 'cross a busy runway. FAA's gonna ban 'em."

The alarm was probably a good idea, I was thinking, considering that she'd just snatched the Frakes outtakes to pass to Terry at the debate. But my god, what a traitor! What on earth had driven her to bushwhack her own candidate?

8 There were a few last matters to clear up while I was at the airport, among them Laura's expenses, which had dropped off in late September. A coincidence, or had she taken flak from the campaign brass? I pulled my coat around me and crossed the blustery tarmacs to the offices of Phyllis Kirk's airline.

SwanJet Air at that time serviced only the center of the country between Denver and Nashville. In the four years since, it has expanded to Winnipeg, which allowed the company to sweeten its title: SwanJet International Air. Phyllis had lent the Frakes campaign a hangar for its headquarters and a comfy 757 for its travels—these in exchange for the post of campaign director and, in case of a victory, that of (First Woman) Chief of Staff.

Phyllis Kirk was of that aridly joyful type of woman who has everything except youth and tries to buy this back from the surgeon. The result was facial skin so tight that you could play a drum roll on it, and a spidery throat with many vertical creases, as if she were squeezed too tightly by her belt at her waist. Her coiffeur had tried to make her hair look full and abundant and light, and succeeded only in imitating a cascade of feathers. On the day I talked to her, her hair was cinched together near the scalp at the very top of her head. The long, pluming, tumbling pony tail—for lack of a better term—swooned sideways over one shoulder or the other, not so much permed as choreographed.

As you can tell, I don't like Phyllis—though I liked her back then. From the very beginning of the campaign, she had helped me generously, allowing me wide access to the campaign records and guiding me into aspects of the Frakes campaign that hadn't occurred to me. Most importantly, she arranged with her own airline and that of an associate to give me employee rates. I later acknowledged her help in *The Saddest Election* and in it treated her deferentially. This time around I am not so charitable. Phyllis, you see, told me a little fib— threw me a little curveball—that windy March day. If she hadn't, if she'd been straight with me, *The Saddest Election* might—*might*— have been a proper accounting of the facts.

So much for that.

Her Majesty's office consisted, on three sides, of wood paneling and, on the fourth, of an Andersen window-wall overlooking the Columbus Airport runways. The paneling held the usual gallery of pictures with presidents and senators and CEOs, adduced to fine-tune the visitor's understanding of her greatness. What else? The desk, a vast chrome affair, lay across the Persian rug as a pet lion might, gold pens waiting at a tense angle for her oiled hand. On two corners, cut flowers arranged professionally stood in magnificent vases. These came from some unpronounceable Tibetan village, never visited before or since by Westerners, to which her money had wafted her.

Beside all of this, like a separate set on a TV stage, was a sort of living room—sofas, coffee table graced by a model Dreamliner, armchairs—all immaculate as if never touched by human buttocks.

"Sam! How lovely to see you," she said that professional warmth that informed you she *was* happy to see you as long as you didn't waste her goddamn time. She guided me over to the lounge area and, sitting on the sofa, suggestively laid one suggestive leg over the other as if to suggest something more vigorous than another droll chin-wag about the campaign.

I anchored myself in an armchair at a right angle to her sofa, but within caressing distance of her shoe. With Phyllis it always seemed polite to imply that the sylvan pounce was not far from my mind, either. Her long-stemmed cigarette holder gave her the air of a villainess. She wore a billowy, white jumpsuit that might have been made from parachutes, all bundled together at the waist by a palm-wide belt of lime-green elastic. The material was easily transparent enough for me to see the matching lime-green thong and brassiere. Well, fashion is fashion, and like kids' tantrums must be tolerated.

She smoothed the underside of my calf with her shoe and asked, "So, how goes the contemporary history of this country's stupidest election ever?"

"Going just great, actually, Phyllis," I said, invoking the stringer-reporter cheer that appealed to her. "I'm going to start writing soon. There are just a few more things I needed—background color, you know." I flipped a few pages of my notepad.

"Yes, I would imagine that in an election like that, you'd need all the color you can get."

I never like to make it obvious what I'm looking for, so first I took her through her post-election problems with the FBI, which had investigated whether the use of her company jet and hangar had constituted campaign-finance violations. (They hadn't.) From there I moved to the Frakes organization in the southern states to allow her to grouse once again about how slow they were in putting things together for Frakes' appearances.

"Pain in the ass," I agreed, shaking my head. I flipped more pages. "What about your Midwest area? Laura Prestini? Ever have a problem with her?"

Phyllis Kirk blew a cloud of smoke up to the ceiling, where it thickened like a mist. "No, Laura was divine. A little hard to handle sometimes—well, just once, really—but she was right on the ball. You could ask Laura to put together a twenty-stop bus campaign for tomorrow, and she'd have it ready with a coffee pot perking at five A.M." Another puff. "She did it, too—in Illinois, just after the damn OutFrakes tape came out."

I frowned at my notebook. "Why do I have 'ask Phyllis about L. Prestini, September' down here? Something about her expenses, I think—her charging too much to the campaign. Or maybe early September, give or take."

"Oh, the expenses problem. Laura was getting a little too lavish for just an advance woman. So were a few others. Don't remember what it was: clothes, maybe, or expensive food that should have gone to a more deserving—i.e., wealthy—mouth. Like mine." A smile and another playful tap at my leg. "You know me, Sam: daughter of diplomats. No fun like that till you hit the thirty-two-percent tax bracket. I'm so sorry."

I chuckled. "So you did give her a warning about the expenses?"

"All part of campaign management, Sam. A general meeting with the six advance chiefs. Had to knock two or three of them back into line expenses-wise before the general campaign started. Laura was one of them."

I was going to ask something else, but a sudden, tender recollection dawned on her. "You know, it's funny you should ask about that. It was really a bit of a scene. Laura took the dressing-down hard—much harder than she was supposed to. Turned beet-red, apologized right then and there—to everyone, tears in her eyes. Gave a speech on what an honor it was to work on the campaign, how proud she was to work with capable people. Offered to pay back whatever I felt was right, with interest. I thought, 'My god, how did you ever get into national politics with a guilty conscience like that?' Thought she had more moxie. The others just took it with a poker face and said they'd be more careful."

"Did you ask her to pay back the money?"

"No, of course not. I just said that it wouldn't happen again if she wanted her West Wing pass. Poor woman had to go outside and get a drink of water in the hall. I had no idea she had such a thin façade." She sucked deeply on her cigarette and blew a pensive cloud at the ceiling out the side of her mouth.

I took note and moved to my second important question: the reporters crisis in Indianapolis. I wanted Phyllis' take on it.

"Yes, but first…" She stood up. "What do you think looks better, Sam? Like this?" She pulled her elastic belt up towards her chest, which outlined her breasts more. Then she pushed it down to better outline the curve of her thin waist and good hips. "Or like this?" She swung around and let me see how utterly the lime-colored thong disappeared between the cheeks of her butt.

"That looks just great."

"I guess it depends, doesn't it? On whether you're a tit man or an ass man."

"I guess it does. Me, I go about halfway. Depends on the lady."

"What about on *this* lady?" she said over her shoulder.

Through the parachute silk I judged her backside had far more muscle than mine. "Right there is perfect," I answered.

Phyllis sat down, satisfied, and puffed her cigarette. "The reporters thing was just a few days after the expenses thing, I think—and it *was* her fault and she had no business managing it. That's what *I'm* here for."

"And—what?—Laura ran after the pissed-off reporters and talked to them, but nothing doing, right?"

Phyllis threw the onto the table with a bang. "You're damn right there was nothing doing! Essentially, she told them to shove it! How would *you* take that? You can't do that with the media. You've got to hold their hand, kiss whatever part of their anatomy is necessary, indulge their sense of power. I mean, what's the difference between *our* campaign and, and a bunch of polyester-clads that put up a climate-change fly-by-night party? *We* get airtime, that's what. That's why Mitch Taylor won, isn't it? Suddenly he was getting six minutes a night on the evening news—three of *our* minutes and three of Gotchell's."

"And suddenly we had a three-party system," I said.

"All thanks to the media. No, they are the goose that lays the golden egg, Sam, and Laura simply told it to stop beefing and get on with the laying. First thing we knew we had an ultimatum on our hands: either the governor apologized and agreed to follow-up questions or they would deal him dirt."

"That's what I wanted to ask about: the fall-out from that. Did you chew her out? What was Laura's part?"

Phyllis shrugged. "Actually, I flew in from Tallahassee figuring that a light reprimand would do. Really, Sam, I put some serious thought into it. I remembered how badly she'd taken the one on campaign expenses, and I planned to keep the reprimand just as low-key as possible. Hell, she was a terrific advance person, one of my best. It was a strange situation, the reporters walk-out; never happened before. I didn't blame her for making the wrong snap call; I still don't."

"Right. So…"

"I told her—nicely—what her mistake was and told her not to make it again."

"To treat the press with kid gloves."

"To grovel, to be more exact." She fiddled with a new cigarette, leaning forward to the coffee table to give me a less-encumbered view of what she had to offer down her blouse. "And I thought that all went well. Laura was a little stiff in the face—okay, no offense taken. But no sooner did I get down to crisis management with the three other campaign heads than she tried to crash the party."

"You mean she hadn't been invited?"

"No. She barged into our meeting room bursting with political-science ideas and tried to take over what I can assure you was a very tense, three-Valium meeting. She wanted to make up for her mistake, and that's understandable, Sam, but this was no time for twenty-five-year-olds to run the show, no matter how perfect their tits are. I finally had to tell her to get the hell out. I finally had to have security *escort* her out."

"You're kidding!"

"Not a bit." Phyllis re-crossed her legs significantly. "She was livid."

"Laura? Livid? How livid?"

Phyllis grimaced and blew out some smoke. "Sam, I *don't* like telling tales out of school," she said. And this was true: Phyllis was no gossip. "People lose their cool—their *cools*—now and then, even me. And when that happens, barring shots fired or punches thrown, I consign it all to the forgive-and-forget file: case closed, move on."

"C'mon, Phyllis. Just the headlines. Just give me a feel for it."

"Headlines." A shrug. "She told me—screamed at me—that we'd be ten points ahead in the polls if we'd get our heads out of the sand. How's that?"

"Wow. What did you—"

"Threw it right back at her: I told her that amateurs who lose their heads don't get hired on at the White House."

"That must have stunned her."

"Hit her like a two-by-four. Stopped her in mid-sentence, figuratively speaking, of course. She turned around and stomped out." Another puff. "Okay, I was sorry, I *am* sorry, but Jesus, Mary and Joseph! The sky was falling! This was no time to test out if Marshall McLuhan was really right or not. Ansel on the conference phone, Winston outsmoking me across the table, Harry Fine from the ad agency crying and gnashing teeth. I mean, my god!"

I jotted a note on my pad—memory aids that would allow me to fill in complete quotes later on.

Phyllis tapped my knee with a sharp fingernail. "Now, let's also get something straight for your records here, Sam, and don't you forget this part: the next day, first thing in the morning, Laura Prestini called on me *personally* and apologized for the scene—I accepted this—and needlessly sent me a bouquet of roses, not even at campaign expense; I checked."

So did I, later; it was true. When I looked up from my flying pen, Phyllis was talking about the scandals.

"Jover was caught, and we all started looking at curtain designs—the stuff of dreams, Sam, dreams! Next stop Washington! 'Chief of Staff Phyllis Kirk'—doesn't that sound just lovely? Secret Service men like Stallone at my beck and call. 'Just set my intelligence briefing by the poached eggs, dear. Now come over here and let's play bodyguard for twenty minutes before we go up to the Oval.' Not all of them would be as tight as you are, *surely.*"

I laughed.

"Yes, those lovely, delicious, marvelous three weeks—the best. And then those spiteful shits at Gotchell's campaign slipped CBS a worthless outtakes video from *months* earlier, and it was all over."

"CBS always did hate you."

"I should have seduced someone over there, that would've done the trick." A mirthless smile. "Just kidding. Whom is an ancient post-menopausal like me going to seduce?"

It was an obvious invitation to tell her she could seduce any red-blooded guy, and normally I would have stepped up to it, but I feared Phyllis might take it too seriously, and said nothing. I regretted it; my silence hurt her.

She jolted up from the sofa and stood, brittle, at the floor-to-ceiling window, one arm cocked under her elbow to hold up her cigarette. She watched one of her planes take off and slide into the gray lid of sky. "It really was too bad. You know I had a whole plan ready to revamp the airline industry? Low fares, decent staff compensation, *and* the safety standards." She paused, listening to be sure I was writing this down. So I did, and now you've read it—twice, if you read *The Saddest Election.*

I could tell the interview was ending, and skipped down my list of questions to the most important one: "Phyllis, was Senator Gotchell's man Arnold Jover looking for a videotape that your people had? Everyone's heard about a secret video taken of Gotchell pulling a young female aide into his dressing room after a speech, and pushing out a couple of Secret Service agents. Primary season, would've been, from the sound of it. Anything to that?"

No answer. I went on.

"I can't find any confirmation, though. Just that some of your people saw it at the post-convention wing-ding in the hotel suite. But the recollection of it is pretty hazy—one person even mentioned *you* being the one who put it on. I can't get any detail at all, though. And Secret Service sends me packing."

Phyllis had not moved before, but there was now something frozen about her posture. Cigarette smoke rippled upward past her prune neck and coiffure. Finally, the ash drooping from her cigarette made her turn and tap it into an ashtray. She returned to the window and watched a flimsy single-prop struggle into the air.

"Yes, I saw it, and it was pretty damning, I'll tell you. The poor girl even resisted a bit before Gotchell more-or-less pulled her in— you could tell they were lovers before, though; at least a woman can. Just that the poor thing was embarrassed about doing it *right there* in front of everyone. Not that Gotchell cared. To him it was all in a day's work. There were three or four people around: aides, Secret Service—the usual Sears-and-Roebuck lot. Everyone sort of smiled and turned away to their cell phones. She kind of laughed—well, really just grinned—and in she went with Gotchell, who was holding the door open for her. Then he pulls the door closed behind him. But just before it's fully shut, a last Secret Service man—or a woman? Yes, a woman, it seems to me—hustles out, making a joke of it: Don't want to keep Mother Nature waiting! And they take up their places on either side of the door, and the others drift away down the hall."

I wrote this down, word-for-word, in my self-styled shorthand. "Do you remember the young woman? Any description at all?"

Phyllis took a puff and pursed her lips. "No—sorry, all gone. Shortish hair and slacks seem to ring a bell, but that's about it. The camera was some ways away down the hall."

"Looking into the room or sideways?"

"Sideways, it would be. You weren't looking into the room, that's for sure."

"And the hall was like, like a school building, with lots of doors, or…"

"Non-descript. A long cement corridor, the ugly kind you find under a stadium."

"With the hinges on your side, so the door opened—"

"Other side. The door opened to the camera."

"And the door? It must have opened into the hall. Wooden, metal, with a knob or—"

Phyllis turned sharply, making her hair rear and settle again. "Sam, let's not get too deeply into this, all right?"

I stared.

"I'd just rather not go into it, that's all. The film was brought to me in summer—late June, early July. One of my aides had received it anonymously from somebody who hated Gotchell. I didn't ask for details."

"All right." I treaded lightly. "The thing is, Phyllis, it could have been from *years* ago—before Gotchell's supposed religious conversion."

She looked at me as if I were a fool. "Senators don't usually walk around with a full detail of Secret Service, Sam. Besides, the face, the high hair line were the same. It was clearly recent."

"Ah. Right," I said with becoming stupidity. "Anybody else see it?"

"My aide said he hadn't looked at it; it was for my eyes only. I saw it at home and stored it away to show the kids when the moment was right. I waited for the convention party and ran it on the VCR— once. Exactly once. We all had a good laugh and then I got rid of it."

My head jerked up; I couldn't help it. "You…just…*got rid of it?*"

"Uh-huh," Phyllis said casually. "Threw it in a Dumpster behind the hotel. Sneaked down the next morning before breakfast, made sure nobody was around, in it went. Good-bye, thanks for the memories, but I don't win elections that way."

Slowly, I bent over my notepad again and wrote that down.

"Now, Sam." Still standing, Phyllis gripped her lime belt with many rake-like fingers and pointed one at me. "Now. You are going to put something in your book for me, got it? And don't forget that you owe me a bit. *More* than a bit. Ready? You will put in this:

"'For nearly a month that summer, Phyllis Kirk held in her hands the power to destroy Senator Alan "Gotcha" Gotchell—long before his Jover scandal. Gotchell had successfully built an image of re-formed womanizer, his support among women in the forty-to-sixty-five bracket especially was beating the hell out of us. Phyllis recalled an evening reading the polls in some God-forsaken Marriott and sucking on her martini olive, in the throes of temptation. The White House was hers for the taking: one phone call, one quiet meet with someone from the *Journal,* and this election was history."'

Her hand swept away to the window. *"'And she threw that video away!'* Got it? 'She pulled it out once for the convention-night bash, enjoyed a nice, beery har-dee-har with the mid-level staff, and, in the interest of goodness and American democracy, *she threw it into a Dumpster.* And she made up her mind that if any copies turned up in the future, she would confiscate them and destroy them. Because that is not how Phyllis Kirk plays this game, Sam. Twenty years in national affairs under my belt, all fine and well. But that is *not* how Phyllis Kirk plays this game. Which is a lot more than you can say for our opponents—our compatriots, too, remember—in the other party.'" She straightened up. "Okay, end of quote. I'll run through that again if you didn't get it all down."

I scribbled fast. "No-o-o-o-o, that will do," I said. "That will sure do it."

And it did. Check page seventy-four of *The Saddest Election,* hardback edition, and you'll find the whole story.

Her side of it, that is. I still had Laura's to go.

9 That evening, I talked briefly with Naima from my Columbus fleabag. She was calling from the street in front of the house—beyond the earshot of listening devices—and she wasn't happy. Naima had checked the normal mail and the e-mail, as every after-noon about six P.M., and called me if anything important came in.

She now told me that the computer was doing strange things: the hard disk was buzzing like mad for the first two minutes whenever she turned the set on. Suspicious, she had called Randy Nuttle, a U of Minnesota history professor and friend of ours, who came right over with his son Stewart—one of these teenagers who could fix a computer with a hairpin. Stewart skulked through the hard drive and found that the intruder had installed some kind of program that allowed him to snoop.

"It's sending out information about what's on your hard disk, Sam," he told me when Naima had passed Randy the phone. "Stew says he might be able to find out where, but it's possible he'll alert the program that he's on to the game."

"No, forget it," I said. "I don't want them to know. There's nothing important on the hard disk, anyway, just campaign notes."

I told Naima not to worry; if the incident proved one thing unequivocally, it was that they were interested in me, not her. This calmed her down somewhat. But I also told her it was more important than ever to act naturally, to keep them on the line. Because once I got the Terry-Laura business straightened out, I was going to take a crack at the spies. For one thing, I wanted to see who these blissful amateurs were; for another, the wild idea occurred to me that one of them might have left the Laura-Terry tip on my windshield, and might have something interesting to tell me in exchange for my dropping charges.

I also began, very discreetly, to watch my backside as well, using a few of Naima's tricks. Not to keep you gratuitously in suspense, however, I have to say that my effort gained me nothing. I never saw anybody.

I had my usual on-the-road dinner of canned ravioli and canned spinach, both heated in the hot water of the fleabag-room's sink for thirty-five minutes. I would have slept in the car—my finances were at their very end—but the weather had turned cold; better poor than pneumonic, I always say.

Over my meal, I watched a TV special about President Mitchell Taylor's first hundred days in office. It ended with a short interview with Taylor himself. Never, the reporter noted, had a new president so taken the country by storm. "From forty-one percent of the vote to a sixty-three percent approval rating!" she gushed. "How do you do it?"

And President Taylor had his answer ready: "Well, Jenny, a good suit never hurts."

Aaaah, those were the days.

He was funny, decent, passionate if not always well-informed. There were doubts about him because of his inexperience in national and international politics, but he dispelled these by putting together a White House staff of equally warm, avuncular personalities from think-tanks, universities and major corporations. Many of Taylor's top staff were holdovers from the vilified previous administration—in the name of "continuity," buzzword of the Taylor White House. That 63-percent approval rating must have felt pretty sweet after the 36 their labors had rated just a hundred days earlier. The more realistic among them surely wondered how many points were due to the good suit.

In retrospect, it seems, about half.

The first eighteen months of Taylor's reign were great fun. His gorgeous, daffy, twenty-year-old daughter, Brenda, seeing her chance to do something more sensual than study accounting at a leafy East Coast college, pranced through a garden of million- dollar offers from modeling agencies, Hollywood moguls and perfume makers, plucking here and there. She dated movie stars, made love in a couple of action flicks, and generally sold her father to lots of drippy twenty-somethings.

Remember her appearance on the red carpet at the Oscars? The swimsuit photo in *Sports Illustrated*? (*The Washington Post* revealed that it was only White House pleading that kept her off the cover.) Remember her one-season contract with designer Irving Matiz and very public break with him? "Oh, I just got tired of hanging with a guy with arms skinnier than mine," she told *Vogue*. Six months later, Matiz and his chain of chichi boutiques were cowering in the grip of Chapter Eleven. She was—let's use that great cholesterol-blob of a word—"cool." And if she was, America's youth howled, so was her dad—seriously.

"What gives me nightmares," said Taylor, and this quote made *Bartlett's Familiar Quotations*, "is to think of someone coming up to Brenda and I [sic] and asking *her* for an autograph!"

Every president earns his superlative; Mitch Taylor's was "the funniest."

Until the tide turned, anyway: terrorists, tired of vexing airport security, started to blow off car bombs on city streets, one every six weeks or so. After the fourth or fifth one, Taylor performed a speech worthy of Hollywood, but the fervor was hard to maintain as the economy soured even more. And then there was the report leaked to the *Times* that the FBI believed that the terrorists were more familiar with Wheaties than camel meat.

After the mid-term elections, Brenda checked into a chemical-dependency farm for a long, long stay, and Taylor found himself fielding questions about his own drug use from many years ago, and maybe not so many, during his talk-show days. Catholics took poorly his offhand crack about the Pope's headgear: "a beanie." Then came his dangerous call for Taiwanese independence of China, which he prefaced in the worst possible way: "This is just one man's opinion, but…"

Prices rose, interest rates rose, market queasiness rose; doing business became an art form. Sensing the public's boredom with him and his vivid ties, the media pounced. The Republicans and Democrats, who had chafed at his "Teflonality" for two years, were right behind.

"C'mon, you guys. I thought you didn't *do* this kind of thing with me!" he said at one battering press conference, stretching for a laugh that never came. This quote as well should have made *Bartlett's*, for his reelection bid ended right there. After that, he looked like, well, what he was: a clever talker. After many months of drying out, Brenda graduated from the farm with ten more years on her face; she would be of no help on the campaign trail. Polls falling, aides resigning, Taylor hocked up a "great pride in being a steward of the presidency at a time of crisis in our nation's politics," and withdrew from the upcoming election. The country accepted this with relief, and the Taylor family soon after bought a retirement ranch in the middle of New Mexico, far from the madding crowd and its high-powered lenses.

Remember all that? Then remember this:

"Well, all I can say, folks," said the newswoman, smiling into the camera at the close of *100 Days—FaceTime with President Mitchell Taylor*, "is hang on to your hats. Here is a president who has the best staff in a generation—and the best tailor in Washington."

I snapped off the television and said, "Here is a president who never in his wildest dreams expected to win the American presidency."

It was true. Taylor had run for the White House on a lark. He was a great campaigner, but it turned out he knew even less of politics than the luscious Brenda did of acting. It was inconceivable that he had paid off someone like Laura to sabotage the two major-party campaigns.

Wasn't it?

Another idea: had Phyllis Kirk, through one of her "aides," put the note on my windshield? Maybe she had heard something about Laura and Terry. Maybe she—or some spy—had seen them together backstage during the third debate, when Laura surely passed Terry the video. Maybe she'd investigated them—money was no object for her—with the idea of extenuating her failed campaign for the sake of posterity, which was certainly on her mind: *You are going to put something in your book for me, got it?* Hence people searching my computer: she wanted to see how I was progressing. Still, she certainly would have hired better people than TweedleMom and TweedleDad.

Well. At ten o'clock that night, I called Laura and made an appointment with her for the following evening, "just to clear up a few odds and ends."

"Sure, love to. It'll have to be too late for dinner, but I can give you a drink," she said in her political-pro's voice.

I hung up, relieved. She sounded happy to talk to me. I took one of my notebooks and, on a fresh page, planned my line of attack; she would not be as easy to ambush as Terry.

10 It should be easy for you to imagine Laura Prestini on the historic evening I spent with her—before she was "Laura." For she was just as you would expect: crisp and neat and ironed, sporting a white cotton shirt with Indian embroidery on the sleeves, open down to the third button, as the fashion gods were dictating that year. She wore a corduroy vest open over it and a pair of custom blue jeans that did what they could for her narrow hips. Two chaste, blue dabs at the earlobes, the crucifix on the gold chain, no rings.

In fact, Laura always looks brand new, as if just issued from a mail-order catalog, here peering challengingly at the distant mountains as she wears our rugged, U.S. Army-tested spring/fall hiking pants with reinforced knees; there flipping a perfect burger on the barbecue while we view her softly feminine stone-washed denim shirt with superb drape, available in three colors: "winterwheat," "maplewood" and "coaldust."

You can imagine her, that is, except for the nose.

She opened the door, and the first thing I saw was a clump of surgical bandages around it, the extremes reaching to her ears. The center of her face was a blotchy purple.

"That's right—I got a nose job! Just got out of the hospital yesterday!" she laughed in that burbling, girlish giggle of hers. "Hi, come on in. Great to see you again, Sam. How's the book going?"

I entered and took off my coat and set up my tape recorder and made small talk all the while. Though I said nothing, the nose operation astonished me: I hadn't noticed any surgical bandages on her at Terry's funeral the day before. Of course, I'd only seen her walk out quickly and from up high, but even still….

"When did you have the operation?" I asked.

"Friday."

The day after the funeral. That answered that.

"I'll be paying it off like *forever*," she was saying. "But, like, I had a little money? Like enough for the down payment? So I said, 'What the hell? I'll treat myself!'"

She went to the kitchen for drinks and snacks, and I had a chance to look around. The apartment was also straight out of the catalog: the reds and oranges and browns of the sofa, the light-green pillows with matching red-and-orange-and-brown trim, the light-green blanket with red-and-orange-and-brown trim hung with precise casualness off one arm rest; all of which matched the red, orange, brown and green floral pattern of the curtains and lampshades.

The two minimalist armchairs were blocks of polished maple with obese cushions inside; they reminded me of those barrels in which people used to hurl themselves over Niagara Falls. Beyond them, at the arched entrance to the dining room, a lit cabinet of crystalware stood like a geyser of ice. A calm dining table awaited the next dinner party. I wondered if a decorator had done the place for her; it was just that perfect. (The answer, just for the record, is no. In a later interview, not with me, Laura said she had done it all herself.) Laura had not eaten ravioli out of the can the night before, that was for sure.

I moved to the bookcase, behind the sofa, for clues to the furnishing of her mind, and found a vaguely disappointing mixture: hardcover books at the top and foot-high stacks of women's magazines ("Ten reasons not to SAY YES TO SEX") at the bottom. Sitting on top of them, I found a brunette friend of Barbie's dressed in a miniskirt. Still no Ken. Among the hard covers were Bob Woodward's million-a-crack investigations, Ogilvy on advertising and others on PR, Stephanopoulos proffering grave-but-cool takes on everything; it stood beside three mint copies of *The Bridges of Madison County*. Three or four books were by people with M.D.s.

One of these was a curious school-bus-yellow volume called *Creative Penance: An Unofficial Guide for On-the-go Catholics*. I took it out, much intrigued; I found the pages were much thumbed and underlined. Chapter Three: "Was It a Sin? Eight Basic Questions." Chapter Five: "'Fessing the Hell up." Chapter Six: "Picking a Penance Worthy of the Crime." Chapter Ten: Modern Penance: The Difference Between Self-Flagellation and an Hour for Your Favorite Charity." I put it back on the shelf beside a furry, pink dog with dewy eyes. The sign around its neck asked, "Are'nt you gona hug me?" I picked it up and, sure enough, it had been made in China, where spelling just ain't what it used to be.

But it was the ferocious wooden crucifix hung in the middle of the bookcase that dominated the room; it practically attacked you. It must have been three feet high, with a blood-streaked porcelain Christ glaring down and to the right to see the latest Judas that had strolled by. It gave me the creeps. Half the face was covered in blood, and the flesh of the sword wound was torn with a realism that Hollywood would approve of. Before Laura returned, I staked my claim on the sofa in order to put it behind me. But I wondered: How on earth did the Tasteful-Living Single Woman jibe with a monstrosity like that?

Laura ran in with two gin-charged Cokes, talking on a cell phone tucked between her ear and shoulder. She put potato chips on the coffee table (also minimalist oak) and pressed her hands together to beg me for forgiveness, then zipped back to the kitchen. My tape recorder on the coffee table picked up her voice, slightly nasal from the surgical bandages:

"Yes, I know, we *did* have to jerk out our order at the last minute last year, but we *did* make it up to you by giving you the BrightPens work, and now we consider our relationship finished....Oh? Quality? Oh, really? And what about the BrightPens thing, just for one example?...Yes, well, we don't pay for the excuses, dearie, we pay for the work, done right, on time…"

Cool as marble.

The conversation lasted a good five minutes. Then she dashed in from the kitchen on a good-little-girl skip-run, her arms straight at her sides, hands stiff. "Sorry 'bout that, Sam. Business. I'll try to make up for it with a terrific interview. Go ahead, ask me who Phyllis was sleeping with—anything. *Especially* that."

"Can't. The editors said I had to keep the book to under three hundred pages."

Laura laughed and sat on (or maybe in) one of the maple blocks, crossing her legs under her as if at a picnic. "Hey, did you ever ask Phyllis about the 'Gotcha' video? I really don't remember if it was *her* who put it on, or—"

"Just the other day, actually. It was her, all right."

"Told ya. Whoops—forgot my glass!" She was back in a flash. "Okay, ready. Quality time for Sammy," she said, pressing down the bandages of her nose; the side ones had jiggled loose. "See?" She held up her cell phone and turned it off. She reached for a potato chip, but threw it back. "Whoa—can't."

"You're on a diet?" I said incredulously.

"No—penance." A smile. "I'm Catholic." With that curious flick of her thumb that I recalled from our interview in her office, she slid out the crucifix between her lapels. "See? Like very."

"Catholics have a thing about eating potato chips?"

She laughed. "This morning I had to tell a lie, so no snacks for five days," she said, tucking the cross back into its comfy little place.

I remembered *Creative Penance*, and wondered if it didn't explain the not-at-campaign-expense roses she'd sent Phyllis Kirk. A curious, unfinished creation, Laura was. She had created a persona that she didn't yet fill. The dowager apartment, the inviting cleavage that had nothing to do with the deft PR manager, the legs crossed under her as if this were a bull session in the dorm hallway and not an interview about a presidential campaign. It was a cramped sensation, like trying to see through someone else's glasses. Still, there are people who just don't look like themselves outside their habitats—you would hardly recognize Rolf Obermeyer in a T-shirt cutting his grass on a Sunday morning—and I figured that Laura was one of them.

At any rate, I made a mental note that I wasn't seeing the real Laura, at least not yet.

She was giggling. "Yeah, and those are vinegar-flavored potato chips—my favorite."

I ate one—yummy—opened my notebook and glanced one last time at my attack plan.

Four years on, I listen to that conversation as if it were a crime scene and her answers the sheet-draped furniture in it. We sat, interviewer and interviewee, amidst the loving reds and browns and oranges and light-greens, Christ in his bloody outrage above us, and as the tape goes on, the whole country, even Terry, seems to wait breathless at the dark windows like neighbors of the murder victim, stealing looks from the doorway, squashing their ears against the walls, relaying tidbits back to the others and sifting them for clues. Guilty? Innocent? Did she do it?

Listening to the tape, I blurt out things like "Follow that up!", "Don't ask that, ask this!", "Don't give her so much running room!" and I swing back and forth in my swivel chair and bite my lip and remember that I was young and poor and I was breaking the biggest story in American politics since Watergate.

I followed my plan, taking her through a few personal details, getting her accustomed to answering my questions. Her family particulars might interest you. Her parents lived in Kettering, Ohio, her father a county-government comptroller, her mother a homemaker. Her older brother, who also lived in Columbus, was a systems analyst for a company that made bulletproof windshields, though he was preparing to enter a Catholic seminary.

The PR agency that Laura ran had only ten employees, but the business was profitable; the three investors who owned it were happy with her work. "Our clients run the gamut: a wetlands-preservation group, a smallish women's fashion chain, the OSU football team, a chemical manufacturer, the state dental association, a new company in—"

"A wetlands group and a chemical manufacturer? Isn't that kind of—"

"Contradictory, right?" She smiled. "Everyone asks that. No, the issues involved are completely different—though I don't tell the wetlands group about ChemWell. They're practically *religious* about that kind of stuff." Then: "Is something wrong, Sam?"

I found myself looking around as if a bird had entered and were flapping around the apartment. "No, nothing, I guess. It's just....It's awfully quiet in here, isn't it?"

"Yeah, the walls here are great. When people have parties, it's no problem. You pay for it—tons—but it is like *so* worth it."

"Yeah, I would imagine." I could almost hear Christ glowering at the back of my neck. The stereo played Mozart, but it could not disperse the silence; it trickled like a stream into an ocean. We talked about how Laura had been in political organizing since she was a high school senior, when she'd helped her neighbor run for city council. She had worked on campaigns every two years, right up to Frakes' gubernatorial campaign, and later his run for the White House, her first national campaign.

"Won't be my last, though," she said. "That was my first losing campaign, the first blot on my record. I can't leave it like that."

"People tell me you were terrific in the campaign," I said. "Phyllis Kirk said you ran a very sharp operation."

"She did?" Laura's legs unfolded beneath her and she sat right up, neck stretched like a goose in flight. *"She* did? Are you *sure?* Did Phyllis Kirk herself say that to you directly?"

For a moment I doubted my own memory, she was so shocked. Her ice-blue eyes burned at me.

"Yeah, just the other day, actually," I said. "She never told you?"

"Yeah, at the end of the campaign, but I never took it seriously. I thought she was just, you know, the usual..." She giggled, embarrassed. "Hey, here's one for *you:* did you know she's angling for a position on President Taylor's business-rights commission?"

I did, but I let her tell me about it at length and regain her balance. Why did Phyllis' approval amaze her? The two run-ins must have really shaken her up.

"I mean, at the end of the day, she's nothing but a geisha, you know," Laura laughed, but bitterness pressed in her voice. "I could tell you stories..."

I shook my head. "Kiss-and-tell is for movie stars. But as long as we're on the subject of Phyllis Kirk, there's a follow-up I wanted to ask you about." I ruffled a few notepad pages for the sake of appearances. "That blow-up with the reporters in Indianapolis—we talked about that the last time?"

"Oh, right." *'Right' but she didn't like to talk about it.*

"What was the fall-out in your organization from that? Did anybody take blame?"

Laura took a long pull on her Coke. "Yeah, I did—unfairly, too."

"What—sanctions, make you lick envelopes?"

"No, just like a bawling-out and then on with the show—typical campaign beef. I had a campaign to run, so I left them to wring their hands over it."

She went on, and I remembered Phyllis: *I finally had to tell her to get the hell out. I finally had to have one of the security people escort her out....I told her that amateurs who lose their heads don't get hired at the White House....Turned around and stomped out...*Phyllis' version was certainly more credible.

"Finally, Phyllis and our useless campaign managers agreed on the asinine plan of just giving in," Laura finished. "Not *my* idea at all, let me tell you."

"Which was?"

"Which was why answer them at all?" Laura blurted.

The fluid PR queen was back, the hands flat on the armrests except when they flared up to gesture, the head tilted articulately to the side as she held forth.

"The press needs *us* more than we need them. Surprised? It's true. They need"—her perfect fingernails popped up from the armrests and scratched quotation marks in the air—*"the story.* That's how they pay their mortgages. Actually, I think Governor Frakes always had that about right: give them the essential tidbits and let *them* fill in the picture where they have to. Like I always say: the goal of PR is to put the frame."

"The frame?"

"Just the key word or phrase. PR puts the frame and the reporters paint in it."

I shrugged. "That's a bit condescending, if you ask me."

"Are you kidding? It's a compliment!" She smoothed back the tapes of her nose and smiled patiently. "Sam, dear, don't get me started on reporters—especially print ones, they're the worst; TV ones don't give you so much trouble. To put it in ten words or less: if PR doesn't put the frame, reporters don't know where to *begin*."

"Or maybe they begin in a place you don't want them to."

"Make the frame strong enough and they won't. They can't. If they do, they look stupid."

I frowned. "Now hold on. That's—"

"Look, I did my thesis on this." She drank and put down her glass with a smart *clack* on the agate coaster. "Take the Gore-Bush recount mess in Florida in 2000. Remember? The voting ballots were badly designed, the difference between the two candidates was a few hundred votes, they were in recount after recount because they couldn't decide on a proper standard for half-punched ballots, the judges were trying to set rules based on conflicting electoral laws. Meanwhile, the whole election hung on Florida's electoral votes. Total chaos, right?"

"Right. So?"

"So Bush won because of a *masterpiece* of Republican PR. Why? Because his people immediately—immediately, that's the key, you know—they immediately established the frame: deadlines. That was the framing word. Florida election certification, then the Electoral College on December twelve, then Inauguration Day. Once they'd done that, the media took it from there: stories about the electorate getting impatient, people wanting a winner, James Baker saying again and again that the country needed to move on. See any stories about people willing to be patient? Editorials advocating a solid, unquestionable, well-represented recount even if it took till February? No—not one. Once Republican PR had established deadlines as the frame, all Bush's people had to do was run out the clock in court. Four Supreme Court justices didn't buy the argument, which just shows you how flimsy it was. It was a five–four decision, remember?"

"Yeah." I shrugged again. "Well, aren't those dates important?"

Laura laughed. "See?"

"But that's—" I started angrily.

"Sam, there's nothing sacred about December twelfth—or January twentieth, for that matter. If the sitting president has to stay on for an extra month or two till authorities unquestionably demonstrate a winner, who cares? I mean, *looking back on it,* who cares? It would end up just a funny old anecdote, like, like Mrs. Adams hanging John's wash out to dry in the executive mansion."

"All right. You have a point," I said neutrally. I wondered, however, about the wisdom of changing dates so frivolously. Tradition—the simple respect for form—is one of the few natural strengths a democracy has going for it. "But you've got to admit that's a pretty clear-cut case: deadlines, I mean. I don't know if you could apply that to—"

"Are you kidding? There are loads of historical examples. The Kennedy assassination, for example. Kennedy *slumped* against Jackie. He didn't slump, he *jerked* back—probably from a bullet hitting him, but we'll never know for sure. But *slumped* is the word everyone remembers. You can even find *slumped* in history textbooks. And then there's the classic: 9-11. C'mon, Sam: what's the frame there?"

I was still trying to take all this in. "No...no idea."

"Yes, you do. C'mon: when you think of the Twin Towers and 9-11, what's the first word that comes to mind?"

"I don't know...'Collapse'?"

"Of course! *Collapse.* Which says what? That the buildings couldn't take the impacts or the fires or whatever. Or at least that the basic fault lay with *the buildings.* And that's that: it doesn't matter now if ten thousand scientists sign on to the towers falling as a result of pre-placed demolition explosives. It doesn't matter a bit. Until they make a full-scale attack on the word *collapse,* forget it: they're not going to move public opinion one inch. And believe me, that's going to take a *lot* more work than finding explosives in dust samples from the buildings. Hey, you moved Alf!"

"What?" I said, bewildered.

She got up and went to the bookcase. She picked up the furry dog, dusted it off with a smart whack and set it back on the shelf, but facing the other way. She did not give it the hug that the sign requested. She treated it, in fact, with the brusqueness that I myself would have given it, and it occurred to me that this underlying masculinity was the result of many years of bearing up under the curse of that long nose. She had never been beautiful and had few of the beautiful woman's affectations; perhaps that was why her inviting cleavage did nothing for me: it was a bow to fashion, not sexiness.

"Sorry, I didn't realize…" I murmured.

"Forget it. Just that Alfie always faces west. That's my good side. If Alf faces east, it is like *bad news.*" To the dog: "Doncha, Alf? Superstition, you know." She sat again.

"You're superstitious?"

"Wow! About a few things, like *very.* Like I never wear yellow to an important interview, and—well, a couple other things. Like I never, *never,* buy stocks on a Tuesday." She was returning to her collegiate posture, legs crossed under her. "You mean you don't you have any superstitions?"

"Just one: I never buy anything on a day when I don't have money to pay for it."

Laura giggled and drank. Her hand moved to the potato chips and again dodged away. "You know, the time-frame thing—that was our problem when OutFrakes started. Suddenly, there was the governor on tape saying all those stupid things. We had like no advance warning, no time to wind up a counterpunch to blunt it. Whatever: a tape of him saying—like to a campaign aide or a friend—something like, 'God, Florida is a great state,' or 'Isn't it interesting talking to these elderly people? They're the warehouse of history of this great nation.' Something like that.

"In a big crisis like that, you've got about half a news cycle to come back in—maybe a little longer depending on what day and what time the story breaks. Problem was, we didn't have anything. No time to choose a frame, nothing." She flapped a hand. "Game *so* over."

"That's for sure." I turned to my notes again—it was time to move matters around to Terry.

"Hey, one thing, Sam." Laura seemed to remember something and leaned forward. One bandage came unstuck and she pressed it back into place. "All that stuff about the press I just said—I'd appreciate it if you wouldn't put it in your book. I mean, it's all fine for like background and all, but it makes me sound, you know, kind of like, you know: Machiavelli."

I smiled. "Not a bad man, actually, Machiavelli. A moralist in an immoral world."

"Yeah, he sure could use better PR. But you won't mention it, right?"

I was looking at my notes. "It's not on the main story, anyway. The reporters crisis was just an incident."

"Yeah, but…" A tactical giggle. "You *won't mention it,* right?"

I looked up, startled. "Okay, Laura, I won't mention it."

"Thanks."

"All right, that clears that up. Let's move on to October—the first scandal," I said, flipping back another page. She was comfortable and talkative now; time to pounce. "Arnold Jover, the Gotchell campaign's head of security, is caught trying to get into your campaign's central office because he has a forged i.d. card."

"With a red stripe across it instead of a blue one! Isn't that just like such a laugh?"

"Yes, it was like the Watergate break-in—the tape horizontally across the door bolt, where anyone could see it."

Laura shook her head too many times and too broadly. "And all for what? What could possibly have been worth that kind of risk?"

"Well, that's what I was going to ask you," I said. "Any ideas?"

Laura continued shaking her head.

"Well, I have a theory about it. Remember that tape of Gotchell you told me about? You saw it on the last night of the convention? Him accosting some pretty aide in his dressing room and pushing out the Secret Service agents?"

"Oh, yeah—hey, but don't quote me like too carefully, okay?" She giggled and ran her thumb under her crucifix—just once, then tucked it back into place. "God, what a night."

"Well, my theory is that Jover was trying to get it back before *your* people slipped it to the media."

"Yeah, I've heard that one. Well, at the end—" She stopped because my look stopped her.

"Let's not play hide-and-seek, Laura. Terry Letizzle told me the whole story before he died."

Laura watched me as if I'd pulled out a gun.

"And by the way," I continued, "he insists that *you* told him the stripe was red. What did you do, slip him a black-and-white photocopy of your own i.d. and just tell him the colors in it?"

Laura took a long drink and put down her glass without a sound and watched the condensation on the glass.

"He didn't happen to add on that I literally risked my career to get him that fax, did he? It *was* a fax, by the way. Did he? No." She pressed back her nose bandages again, and this time the skin went white around them from the pressure she exerted. "Or that we had promised to keep the secret?" Her voice had turned high and flinty; she was about to cry. "What else did he say? That I told him red on purpose to get that Jover guy in trouble?"

I nodded heavily. "In different terms, but yeah."

"Yeah, he would. Not that it matters. It's like *so* obviously—"

She stopped. Her shoulders were shaking, and she squeezed her tear ducts as if that would keep them from opening, cleared her throat. It didn't do much good; she spoke in little more than a nasal whisper; and my cheap recorder barely caught it.

"That is so obviously bullshit, though no one will ever believe me. All I ever wanted to do was get the 'Gotcha' video away from Phyllis, and I've ruined myself doing it."

I waited a while. "Why is it so obviously bullshit?"

"Sam, would you wake up! Do you really think those frat-boy security guards looked at passes? One in ten, if that. Campaign workers, hell, they forgot them all the time. As long as nobody walked out with a computer under his arm, the guards just looked at their skin mags and picked up their pay. Finance was the only department that really needed security, and that was all housed downtown with campaign management. Hell, if your aim is to sink the other candidate, you couldn't have picked a worse way than with a stupid security pass."

Zack Stram later gave me a lukewarm confirmation of this, which I'll get into on another page. "So what happened with Terry?" I asked.

"Nothing. I got in touch with him—I don't know, late September—and told him we had the tape of Gotchell and the girl, that Phyllis might well use it towards the end of the race if things got tight."

"It was in the campaign video archives?"

Laura nodded in tight, electric jerks. She reached for the potato chips again, hesitated, and withdrew her hand empty. "I gave him the number on the box and told him where to find it in the vid library."

So the video had not ended up in a Dumpster. It figured: Phyllis was a fair person, but even for her the temptation must have screamed; at least she would have kept it in reserve.

"And the truth about the pass is, even if you don't believe it, I told him not to bother with it. If he simply walked in looking like he belonged there, he could waltz. If they did question him, he could say he had to talk to—whoever—Mark Biffin in Graphics. Jover—I don't know how *he* got into this, that wasn't my idea at all. He shouldn't have even pulled out the pass. It was like a loaded gun."

"All right," I said slowly. I ate a potato chip. "But for the record: are you denying that you told Terry the wrong color?"

An exasperated huff. She was leaning forward off her chair now, talking to the glass, watching the drops fuse and run down to the coaster underneath.

"Okay, okay, it's possible, I admit—which is *not* an admission of guilt, understand?" She looked up, pleading. "For God's sake, Sam, you know how it is! You think something over and over and pretty soon you think you were saying green! *I don't think so, okay?* But, fuck, I'll, I don't know. Look, I told him the pass colors on the phone. I wasn't holding up my pass in front of me when I talked to him—that's true. But this is also true, okay? I also don't think he was writing anything down." She shook her head and wiped her eyes again. "I still say he shouldn't have used it."

I thought all this over. "All right, one wrong band of color on a security badge *is* a pretty chancy way to pull down someone's campaign. So what did Terry do after the Jover scandal? He must have been pissed."

Laura was trying to arrange herself in a collegiate position again, pulling her legs under her again, but this proved uncomfortable. She again sat forward, elbows on knees, one hand feverishly rubbing a forearm as if she'd banged it on something. Was this just the oversensitive woman that Phyllis had told me about? She had sat this way during the funeral—I remembered her thin, hunched shoulders.

"'Pissed' falls about a mile short, if you really want to know. He called me every name in the book and said I'd done it on purpose. So I finally said, 'Look, I'll get the tape for you myself. Happy?'"

"*You?*"

"Of course. I knew Phyllis would use the Gotchell tape if he came back in the post-debate polls. Phyllis wanted Chief of Staff, and she didn't mind getting down in the mud to get there. Hell, why else was it there in the vid library?"

"She could have made copies."

"*Of course* she could, Sam," Laura said leadenly. "But that's what I *told* you: in PR, advance warning is everything. The point was to get a copy to Terry and his people. To have their defense ready."

"Ah. Right."

For a happy moment, she could play the political pro again, and she began pulling back fingers.

"One: you bring out experts who point at the film and say that part looks faked, or it was from years earlier. Or you say, 'Yeah, yeah, we paid the same shyster pedaling it as Frakes did. His name is Herbie Jones, he's a used-car dealer from Xenia. Or say the girl was paid to take off her clothes in the room. She was a whore with a long history of flashing and mental disorder, she did it for fifteen thousand cash, she was later seen buying a necklace at Tiffany's. Whatever. Or—and I told Terry this one myself, Sam—I said to just come out ahead of the curve with the video *themselves* and frame it differently. Put the frame yourself—that's *always* your best bet."

I needed a long drink to digest all of that. She was faster than light. I would have taken a week to dream up all of those.

"The point is that, given a little time to prepare, good PR is invincible. Invincible. An advance on a crisis, even just twelve hours—six hours—makes all the difference."

I was becoming glad of the gin in my Coke. "I guess so," I said, and the words disappeared like mist into the granite silence. Even Mozart had given up trying to penetrate it. "All right. But if you want me to buy your story—that you were just interested in a fair election—fill out the picture for me. You went to Columbus on the morning of the third debate, the one in Baton Rouge. Take it from there—with all the details."

"There's a tape of me in Security, isn't there?" she asked glumly.

I nodded. "I saw it."

She sighed, as if picking up a weight again, and to my rising amazement I realized that the worst was yet to come. As if reading my thoughts, she said, "I knew it was all over—soon as you brought up Terry. God."

She blew out hotly, pressed back a bandage on the side of her face, and trudged back to the topic.

"It was the only chance I had to get away before Baton Rouge. I walked in, grabbed it out of the video library, and ran for my plane.

I never really—" Her voice caught, and she began to cry, hunched over her drink.

"So we're still talking about the *Gotchell* tape, right? Not—"

"I'm still glad I did it," she blurted. More sobbing. "Gotchell was recovering from the scandal with each debate. He's great in debate, even if he's just boilerplating. And after the third one—when Gotchell really hammered the governor?—she would have used it. I know she would've. A chance to sink Gotchell? And on a sex charge? She'd laugh all the way to the Oval."

"Phyllis, you mean."

A nod.

"Give her her due: at the end, she didn't."

"Ha! Bet you anything—*anything*—that I swiped the only copy that existed," she snapped.

"Maybe. I walked in here thinking you'd grabbed the Frakes outtakes that day. To give to Terry and sink your candidate."

"Didn't Terry tell you?" she asked, surprised.

I rubbed my neck. "My interview with him didn't last all that long, actually," I said dryly. "Just when things got interesting, he threw me out."

"And killed himself," she added in a sudden whisper that I didn't recognize, nodding at the floor. Again I wondered if they'd been lovers. "No. It was the Gotchell tape I got that day—that's for sure. That's for really, really—"

Another wave of tears hit her. What the hell was wrong?

"Well, I'm awfully glad to hear you didn't stab your own candidate in the back with the outtakes," I said lamely, just to fill some space. But this only brought on more tears. What was going on?

I took her drink and handed it to her. After a long minute on my tape recorder, she could at least talk again.

"That's just it, Sam. That's just it. I'd carried the outtakes with me for months. I, I, I just couldn't get rid of them. I was there when Frakes made the gaffes. I'd actually set up the shoot, at a little studio in Dayton." She sobbed into her hands. "He was all tired and nervous—just a wreck. So as soon as the techies took the good takes they needed, I slipped the master vid into my bag and then kept it on me. I just couldn't, I just couldn't let it go…Whenever I remembered it, I just—"

She cried freely now, her voice jerking like a little kid's.

"I had…nightmares about someone.…swiping it, Sam. Nightmares. I couldn't…I couldn't even throw it away. I kept looking for…for an in-incinerator. Or a chimney in my hotel room, that was…another one. I thought of sending it to my p-parents for…for safekeeping. I even wrapped it…up and went to the post office, in Rockford…Illinois, I think. Then I got so worried.…I was always so wor-worried that it would get lost in the mail…maybe some postal worker would think it was a p-porno vid and open it up! Oh my god!…So I kept it…kept it on me. I even bought an alarm for my suitcase in case.…This big, loud Squeel-EE…in case, in case anyone tried to, you know, open it." She was crying in torrents now, gripping the little crucifix on her necklace with both fists. "That's…how it happened, Sam. That's…just…it."

I stared at her as I might stare through a fog. I didn't get it; I had no idea what she was trying to say. The recording tape has me saying, with incredible stupidity, "I saw that—the Squeel-EE, I mean—in your expenses."

Her head drooped lower, nearly to her knees. "And I think I saw the OutFrakes vid cassette, too, in your suitcase," I added over her tears. "On that security tape. When you put the Gotchell tape in. The outtakes one was in the left corner."

"Yeah. Yeah, that's it, then: I just threw it in there," she said with black finality through the sobs. One of the surgical bandages came loose and hung out, shaking pathetically like an elderly person's hand.

"And from there you flew to the debate in Baton Rouge," I prompted her. "And before the end of it, you met with Terry backstage, right?"

She nodded. Then, abruptly, her head lifted. Her eyes wandered above and beyond me, to the bookshelves, the furry dog, to Christ. The latter seemed to stiffen her—enough to string sentences together.

"Yeah, I'm, I'm like America's new Dumb Dora, huh? Bigger 'n all of 'em put together. Too bad I'm not blond—that would explain it."

"Explain…what?"

She was panting, not quite crying now but looking away from me across the apartment, though her eyes seemed to be peering across a canyon.

"But imagine the explaining I *will* have to do, Sam. Imagine trying to explain a silly little mistake—like, you know, a waiter giving *you* the normal Coke and your friend the Diet. Whoops! Sorry 'bout that.'" A tattered laugh. "And explaining it on national TV, in front of the whole country—the whole earth. It's only what I deserve, of course, getting Governor Frakes humiliated…"

And she broke off, overwhelmed. She tumbled over to one side in the chair as if she no longer had a bone in her body, and the new, harsher sobs thudded through her like kicks from a mob.

"They'll kill me! They'll tear me to shreds!"

The recording tape has a thirty-second gap at this point. It is broken once, about halfway through, by the crash of my pen falling on the table. At least I think it was my pen. It might have been my jaw or just my naked shock at the stark, vile mundanity of what she was saying: that an American presidential election had been trashed because of a mix-up in videotapes. For, rather than giving Terry the Gotchell tape and keeping his candidate safe, she had given him the Frakes outtakes and bushwhacked her own.

11 Of my last hour with Laura, little need be said. There was a moment while I was in her kitchen heating chicken soup—nervously checking through the doorway to be sure she wasn't cutting her wrists—that I considered not writing at all about her and Terry Letizzle. What was done was done; my book wouldn't change the outcome of the election. We had talked about that, Laura and I, as I stroked her trembling hand and said whatever came to mind: that she had no obligation to talk to anyone, that the matter would eventually blow over, that she was smart and attractive—especially after her nose job—and had a bright future ahead of her. No good: she just kept on crying.

Just once she raised her teary face, the bandages hanging away again like skin on a burn victim, and screamed, "I'll be the shithead of the century! Imagine the jokes they'll make about me! My mother won't be able to go to the store for milk! I'll end up sweeping floors, and they'll *still* laugh at me!" Then: "You couldn't just forget about it, could you, Sam? Or just water it down a little? Or—what the hell?—Terry's dead; tell them he came to my hotel room and raped me and stole it. What's the diff? I'll do a year of penance—I'll live in a convent, I'll treat lepers in Africa, anything! I swear!"

But by the time the soup was ready, I knew what I had to do. In the first place, the truth of America's strangest election needed to come out—just on principle. It was a public matter.

As to the second place—how else can I say it?—I had my bestseller; I had the key to the Miracle Election. Compared to the first point, of course, this was a minor matter; if I mention it at all, it's to put the moment in perspective. I had gotten one good tip and from there wiggled through the crevices of the cave to the truth. All I had to do was write it clearly, and the well-waxed skis of mass marketing would carry me to the Promised Land. I don't mean hundred-thousand-dollar royalty checks; I mean that for the rest of my life I would never lack for an interesting project or a publisher. And that, for a guy who sells syllables by the pound, is everything.

What follows of my interview with Laura is largely from memory; I'd turned off my tape recorder and locked it away in my briefcase just in case she got some funny ideas. It's worth adding, however, that as with my interview with Phyllis Kirk, I jotted quotes on my notepad and immediately filled them out in the car, which for me is a reliable system.

Laura had no specific recollection of taking the wrong tape out of her suitcase that evening; it had but a small sticker with the video-library number. In Baton Rouge, she'd hit the ground running: rental car, hotel, shower, her cleanest evening clothes, a quick review of next-day's activities, a dozen phone calls as she gave orders talking around the ham sandwich and mineral water that she'd ordered from room service.

She snatched the video out of the suitcase, stuffed it in her purse, and ran for the debate hall at Louisiana State University, where she also had responsibilities: seating for Frakes-campaign officials, arranging Frakes' dressing room, and briefly meeting with Secret Service officers to arrange details for the post-debate cocktail with some Louisianan VIPs. As planned with Terry, she met him backstage right at the end of the debate, when both campaign delegations prepared to walk on stage, and slipped the tape to him. She had recommended that he leave it with one of the security people while he was on stage, but he rejected this, afraid of losing the tape.

"I could understand that," she said into her soup bowl, her crucifix wagging over it. With irritation, she pressed the surgical tapes back into place. "I'd lived in terror of losing the outtakes tape for months."

It was not until OutFrakes broke on *The CBS Evening News* that she realized the mix-up; it simply never occurred to her that she had passed on the wrong video. The Frakes organization was completely blind-sided. She called Terry several times that night, but he had either turned off his cell phone or, more likely, thrown it away. After that, with Frakes plummeting in the polls and Laura working eighteen-hour days, she didn't bother. They never spoke again.

"Not that I had anything nice to say to that filthy motherfucker."

I pondered all of this during another storm of tears, and wondered where the "Gotcha" Gotchell dressing-room tape had ended up, as she had never given it to Terry. I asked if she still had it.

"Yeah, it's there," she said, pointing to her bookcase at a half-dozen copied videos beside a tall stack of DVDs. My heart did a somersault of joy. Then: "*The Wizard of Oz* was on the night I got back from the campaign, so I recorded over it—thought that was appropriate. And I checked, just to be sure: it's all gone."

"Kind of a loss for history," I observed, looking amidst the row of videos. It was the one labeled in thick felt-tip marker *WIZ/OZ*.

"Yeah, well, what the hell: it was all over. Not that I'm any fan of Gotchell's. He's a vicious bastard—*and* a congenital liar all throughout his career, not only about sex. But enough reputations have gotten trashed—mine too, now."

I carried the dirty dishes to the kitchen and prepared to leave. I assured Laura that I would be as decent as possible to her, emphasize her hard work on the campaign, make crystal clear that she had only committed a mix-up, and had the country's interests at heart. She took this teary-eyed, but with stoicism, too.

Then, in the doorway of her apartment, came the weirdest exchange of the evening.

She had applied fresh bandages to her nose and recovered a little bounce by then. I didn't worry about leaving her alone. She accompanied me to the front door and stood there leaning tiredly against the door frame. "Well, I guess I'm going to test that old saw about how any publicity, even bad publicity, is good publicity, huh?"

"I'll say." Her key ring hung on a hook beside the door. Like Alf on the bookcase, the key ring was presided over by a stuffed bear with drippy eyes.

"Those aren't the keys I saw in the security video," I said.

Laura looked at it. "What? With good ol' Rufus?" she said with a smile, smoothing his fur with a finger. "No, he stayed here with my neighbor Henry—guy down the hall. He took care of my plants while I was on the campaign." She gave dry giggle. "And a lot better than I do. They never looked so good as when I finally got back here."

"Well, you could have made Rufus famous. That security video is going to get lots of airtime once my book comes out."

"So will I," Laura murmured, and her eyes filled with tears again. "Too bad Terry won't be around to get his fill, too. America hates a traitor."

"That's true, it does."

"Why else did he commit suicide?" Laura said sourly. "Fucking backstabber. I hope it hurt like hell."

"Well, if you feel that strongly, why did you go to his funeral?"

Laura jerked away from the door, not weary at all now. *"Funeral? You went to his funeral?"*

"Yeah."

She stared at me. "Well—I sure didn't. What makes you think I did?"

"I saw you there."

"You mean to Terry Letizzle's funeral—after what he did? Taking advantage of my mistake like that? I'd just as soon spit on his grave!"

I couldn't believe my ears. It *wasn't* her at the funeral?

How could that be? I looked away, trying to remember. Of course, I'd been sitting up high in the back in the choir loft, and Laura had walked away, head sort of down, but...

Laura let fly that famous little-girl giggle. "You still think you saw me, don't you? Wait. What day was the funeral? What time?"

"Thursday morning—ten-forty-five. Well, actually, the hearse arrived late with the casket. Call it almost eleven."

"Thursday morning around eleven. Thursday morning I was with..." She shut an eye as if taking aim. "I was wi-i-i-th...would've been Arlen Barrington. He's operations director for football at OSU."

A patient smile. "Yes, you can call him if you want."

"No, it's no big deal," I said. And at the time, it didn't seem to be one. Besides, Arlen Barrington rang a bell as someone famous—an athlete—and experience had shown me that he was the type of person least willing to talk to a novice journalist. After a warm leave-taking and my assurance that I would send her a pre-publication copy to prepare her for the likely media onslaught, I left.

Still, the question of Laura at the church nagged me. I wondered who on earth the woman had been—so acutely moved by his passing, far more than the rest of Terry's sappy mourners.

12 I spent the following six weeks writing *The Saddest Election*. I had to check out many additional facts in the light of what I'd learned. Courtesy of Phyllis Kirk, I flew to Baton Rouge, for example, and went backstage of the debate hall and, with Laura's hazy recollection as a guide, reconstructed where she'd handed off the wrong video to Terry. I asked Zack Stram about the Frakes staff campaign passes and the attentiveness of the security guards. It was lax, though he wouldn't have gone as far as Laura's flat dismissal of them:

"Sure, some typist swingin' her meatballs past the counter four-five times a day, the boys ain't gonna check her. For the rest, b'fore the Jover thing, call it fifty-fifty. Shoulda been better, yeah, but a strange face in a suit and tie, I'd say that'd draw fire—'less the boys was tryin' to work a phone number outta that Cuban cleanin' lady. Now there was a well-built chassis."

I also checked again with Frakes campaign staffers and asked if they knew about the "Gotcha" Gotchell tape in their video library; they denied it up and down, though one admitted that in the heat of the campaign, the videos were not as well catalogued as they should have been.

Then I talked to—or at least *tried* to talk to—some of President Taylor's campaign people. For one, I wanted to have *something* on the winning campaign. More importantly, I wanted to mention Laura Prestini and see if I got any reaction. Many people would suspect that Laura had sabotaged the major-party campaigns for Taylor, and I wanted to cover that angle as best as I could. It went poorly. Taylor's people were still frantically setting up their administration, never having counted on going to Washington, and I could only get one of their top people on the phone, none for a sit-down interview. He had no reaction to Laura's name, though this was hardly a proper canvassing of the organization. This worried me—only for a short time, however, as you'll soon see.

Meanwhile, as I wrote *The Saddest Election*, my story of The Miracle Election remained secret. No other journalists came knocking at Laura's door. Two more books on the election came out, and as neither one mentioned what I had discovered, both crawled away to the bargain bookshops to commiserate with the previous year's world almanac. I was alone with my scoop. Finally, in mid-May, I e-mailed the manuscript to New York from Randy Nuttle's computer. Then I threw myself into French translation, being flat broke and a thousand in debt to my mother.

But only for ten days or so. My editor, Walt Greene-Halver, saw what he had in his hands and, realizing that perhaps he had better begin treating me as a serious writer, sent me an emergency advance against the real advance, which would instantly make me rich. He dropped everything and, with Jeanine, moved the book into production. I also prepared a condensed version for *The New York Times Book Review* to rev the pre-sales engine.

Then I spent a day with an image specialist—Walt arranged this—a very hard woman who normally worked with Hollywood stars. She taught me how to deal with the upcoming TV interviews: "to look crisp like the guy handing out the sweepstakes money, and not the wrinkled dopes receiving it," was how she put it. I was skeptical at first, but once on the book-tour circuit, I was damn glad of her help.

I kept Laura informed on matters and phoned her for the last time three days before the *Book Review* article hit the newsstands the first week of July.

"So that's how things stand," I told her. "The first pebbles of the avalanche will come tripping down the slope any day now."

"I'm ready, Sam," she told me. "As ready as I'll ever be. I've resigned from the firm; no use dragging them into this. I'm just doing a little consulting on special projects, mostly with ChemWell. Once the article comes out, being me is going to be a full-time job. Thank you for being so kind, okay?"

I had the feeling that she hung up the phone and cried her eyes out again. I prayed that her nose job had turned out well.

Between my interview with Laura and the book landing in the bookstores, I also cleared up the espionage angle of my story, which was a good thing, because this allowed me to establish a crucial point about a connection between Laura and President Taylor's people. Because of a promise I made, I have never mentioned the spying in any interviews or written about it. I can do so now only because President Taylor is out of office.

Besides, a book like this needs a dash of comic relief.

The intruder at our apartment showed up one more time, politely having waited for me to attend a conference at the University of Minnesota on the recent campaign and the consequences of Taylor's election. Naima, of course, was at the university virology department enjoying her microbes. But ever since the first break-in, she had left a tennis ball behind the door—pulling it shut with a piece of string from out in the hall—whenever she left the apartment empty. When she came home that afternoon, she found the ball rolled a few feet into the room.

I determined that my papers had been sifted. They held no reference to either Laura or Terry. The computer also did not concern me, as I had borrowed an ancient and very heavy portable and hauled it around with me, to the detriment of my elbows. To the desktop computer I continued to add a stream of anodyne notes, a time-consuming job when I had ever less to consume, but it was worth it to maintain the façade of normalcy before my Internet-snooping fans.

But with Naima on edge again and my deadline screaming, enough was enough. It was time to unmask these witless wonders of The Great Game.

On a sunny, balmy, shirts-sleeves day in early May, then, some friends and I sprung the trap at the Hennepin County Government Center Building in downtown Minneapolis. It is, in reality, two broad, flat buildings that stand facing each other like boxers at the weigh-in. A web of glass and steel holds the two parts together and creates a high central atrium. It is so high that for local suicides, lacking cliffs and high bridges in the flat Twin Cities area, it is the jumping point of preference, maybe because at the bottom, beside the information desk, a shallow pool of water offers a second lease on life, just in case the Fates are in a charitable mood.

But the advantages of the building for our purpose were that it is broad and airy—you can keep watch across a long distance—and that it has only two exits. These lead down to either side of Sixth Avenue, which the building straddles. And just up Sixth sits a hunched little police station just in case we decided to press charges. It was the ideal spot: it would be easy to spot people following me and easy to threaten arrest afterwards.

And the followers would have good reason to follow, since my e-mails over the past week had been filled with mysterious correspondence about the recent election campaign. The "source," who had dubbed himself "Big Throat," promised me earth-shattering revelations about a foreign plot to subvert the election, and all for the low, low price of five thousand bucks, which was all that my bank account contained after my mother had kindly transferred me the five Gs. No loan, no book, no grandchild, I'd told her, hitting her where it hurt. Up she'd coughed.

I was to meet Randy ("Big Throat") Nuttle at twelve-fifteen at the passports section of the County Government Building; and that was twelve-fifteen sharp, since Big Throat was between his ten o'clock lecture in *Principles of Historical Research 1-001* (which had ended at eleven-thirty) and his one-o'clock *History of Medieval Spain 3-025: El Cid to Fray Luis.* We had chosen the passports section because Big Throat's versatile son Stewart, able with digital cameras as well as computers, could film the proceedings from the second-floor balcony across the atrium. The passports section changes location from time to time, due to the vicissitudes of city administration, but on that day, it was tucked into the pleasant, wood-lined alcove just off the lobby.

All of us carried cell phones, and between these and Stewart's top-of-the-line digital camera, we practically bloated with pride in our e-lint. I sat down amidst the lake of chairs, and within comfortable camera range of Stewart. Five thousand dollars bulged against my heart; I had just drawn them in hundreds from my bank in order to reassure any followers that this was The Real Thing. The money, though, made me damned uneasy. What if the watchers jumped me or Randy ("Big Throat") Nuttle? I thought of how it must be a relief for Mel Gibson or Will Smith to have a script to follow; doing this in real life is a different matter.

My phone rang: Naima. She told me that she was going to watch an experiment in the biology lab and would be home a little late, around eleven-fifteen.

The first part of that message—about the experiment—was the signal that she had seen her middle-aged woman watcher again. The second part—that she would be home late—meant that the woman had disappeared, at around eleven-fifteen.

I told her fine and gave her my love, which besides my love meant I was still waiting for Randy.

But as soon as I hung up, a middle-aged woman in a business suit entered the area. She was stout and had fading red hair—Naima's watcher? Yes indeed: the woman dispelled any doubts by walking up to the waiting-number dispenser near the counter and making a painful show of taking a number and studying it. But she forgot to follow up this gesture by looking at the number on the electronic "Now Serving" sign. She sat down directly in front of me, very erect, tilted a little back, in order to listen to my conversation with Big Throat. This also permitted me a good view of her earphone, whose cable curled up to her ear from inside her collar.

What kind of numbskull hired these bumblers? I wondered.

My phone buzzed again.

"Hi, Sam. This is Stewart—from the library? Listen, I found those two articles you wanted—maybe three. One was right in front of you."

"You don't say?" I said.

"Yup. The other one was behind it in the stacks, maybe fifteen or sixteen shelves. The third one I'm about fifty percent sure on. The last two look like business. Better read 'em real carefully."

"You mean tough."

"Right—tough, mean."

This shook me. "Jesus. You got pictures for me?"

"Not very clear ones. I'll see what I can do."

"What do you know about the Rothstein?"

"On its way. Give it five days."

I hung up—scared. Stewart, who had followed me since my bank withdrawal, had spotted two and maybe three of them. One was the woman in front of me, another fifteen yards behind me in the lobby; he and the third one looked "tough and mean." Stewart had gotten some footage of them, but not very clearly. Randy ("Rothstein") was on his way and would make contact within five minutes.

He did, sitting down in a heap beside me. In a noble stab at verisimilitude, he had put on a long trench coat, this despite the bright day. The woman in front of me stiffened.

"You bring the money?" Randy asked with a loudness that took into account everyone's needs.

"Yeah, I brought it." I took out the envelope. I passed it over to him and looked him right in the eye.

"Have you talked with the guy from the library?" I asked.

"Yeah," he said with a curt nod and passed me a memory stick. And now I realized that he was frightened.

"*Yeah.* In fact, I got a glance at one of the articles, and he's right on the money."

"Jesus. Okay, clear out. Good doing business with you."

But Randy is a perfectionist, and he stayed to get off his lines: "These files should answer all your questions, including a few you never thought of. I'll give you three days for follow-up questions. After that, I disappear. I'm not taking any chances." And he was off, fast, his wrinkled coat wagging.

I counted to fifty and got up. The woman followed me. I walked up to a bulletin board and called Stewart on his cell phone. "Well?" I said.

"Got pictures after all. Looking great. Rothstein left with an African article behind him. The other—Tough and Mean?—is on you."

"Right. Thanks. Now you be careful and get the hell out of there," I said.

The woman had been forced to go ahead of me. She waited to be sure that I was going toward the escalator down to the street level, and went down ahead of me. And walked out of the building ahead of me. She didn't try to make sure I was behind her, probably because the other one—Tough and Mean—was trailing me.

I gave her a good look-over. I was disappointed. Her suit was sternly gray and her shoes sensible, with stout heels. Her feet appeared small as mice under those thick hips, fence-post calves sensibly displayed in white nylons. She walked cautiously as if pregnant, her bag hung on the crook in her elbow, proper as the Queen of England.

Or a bureaucrat.

Of course! A stuffy, martini-lunching, bill-writing, lobbyist-loving, reporter-bashing insider of Washington, for whom the light of the moon is a privacy issue and rock-throwing a First Amendment question. One of these people who reads the editorial section before the news section. Why the hell hadn't that occurred to me?

I tiptoe-ran up behind her and slipped her handbag off her arm in one fast sweep. She squawked.

"Just one second, please," I said. I dug a hand into the bag, pulled out her wallet, and jerked it open, avoiding her grasping hands and more squawks. "Janet Evans, Staff of the White House Counsel," I read off her i.d. card. *"That's* who you are. You work for Taylor's people."

"That's right. I happen to work at the White House. Now I'm warning you: give me back my things or we'll talk about this with the police."

I folded up the wallet and put it back in her bag and snapped it shut and gave it back to her. "That's just what *I* was thinking, Mrs. Evans. There's a police station right up the street. After you."

The woman's heavily-lipsticked mouth worked in the center of her chubby face, but only pieces of words came out. She looked for salvation over my shoulder, where running footsteps clop-clopped towards us. "The hell you think you're doing, mister?" It was Tough and Mean. He wore a salt-and-pepper crew cut and stared with that utter, writhing rage that you find among military people who lack an enemy to shoot.

"I just snatched her handbag," I said helpfully. "And Mrs. Evans wants to turn me in." I shrugged. "What can I say? Her good right. Let's go."

That got his attention. His hands dropped to his side where they clenched and unclenched in twitches like a camera shutter. He had a lean face and baggy eyes; in the clean light of outdoors, I could see the pallor of the meeting room ground deeply into his pores: a former Marine reduced to the battles of bureaucracy. His lapel displayed an American flag as large as a bottle bottom, as if a fatter pin denoted a grander patriotism.

"What are we waiting for?" I said, and pointed over the man's shoulder. There's the police station. That's why we set up our sting operation here. This way, you see, we wouldn't have to walk so far afterwards to do the formalities. Smart, huh?"

The two exchanged looks—the despairing looks of children condemned to eat their spinach. I felt sorry for them and eased the pressure—a little.

"Now look—before you do something stupid. If you come clean with me about all the bullshit that's been going on, I won't haul you up in front of a judge. But you *are* going to come clean. My friends and I set up that meeting in the passport section, and we filmed you, too. All three of you. So there'll be no weaseling out of anything."

"*Filmed?*" squeaked Mrs. Evans, entering the register of panic. "Oh no, oh Brad, oh my god! There's footage!"

"Easy, Janet!" barked the military man. "I didn't see anyone filming us, and we—"

I took out my cell phone and pushed some buttons. "Don't worry, I'm going to show you the footage," I said. "Now let's all go over to that donut shop down there and sit down and talk about this. Call in your guy tailing Big Throat."

We had to help Mrs. Evans, whose legs went watery. I couldn't blame her; I wouldn't want to be the start of a major scandal, either.

If they had done their work poorly, it was because it was against their principles. "Operation Questionable Honor"—Brad's splendiferous invention—was born of fear and executed without enthusiasm.

They needed donuts and coffee in front of them—and a glimpse of Stewart with his camera—before they loosened up enough to talk. The third man, who had tailed Randy, arrived ten minutes later. He was about forty, of an unhealthy yellowish-brown complexion, with a small head like a point atop his business suit and white shirt. Delwood Salter shook my hand, complained to the others, "What did I tell you? I knew it—I *knew* this would blow up in our faces! Right from the start! I just *knew* it!"; and walked out, where for ten minutes he paced back and forth in front of the donut shop window talking to himself and gesturing wildly. Finally, he got into a cab and went off to do whatever eased his wounded sanity.

No, they weren't spies. Mrs. Evans, the craggy Brad Bailey, and Salter were

Washington veterans with their pet projects. Brad Bailey was pushing to increase salaries for recently-enlisted soldiers so that they didn't need to apply for food stamps; Mrs. Evans was nursing through Congress a bill to create bicycle lanes along federal highways. They had never, ever thought that some day the White House that they had so much dreamed of working in would ask them to perform lie-detector tests and to spy on journalists. Little by little, Mrs. Evans talking and Bailey grousing about "need to know," the story came out.

The idea had originated with either Taylor's chief of staff, Jimmy Stork, or the White House Counsel, Cary Miles; in any case, both knew about the operation, and so did Taylor in general terms. Once the order came down to Bailey, he talked discreetly to people at the FBI, asking for help. They refused; they wouldn't touch the matter with a ten-foot pole.

"They *said* it stank Watergate to high hell. Really they hate Taylor, that's why," Bailey growled, his massive fists clenching again and again on the table. "Matter to them that he's the democratically elected representative of the American people? Hell it does. He can twist slowly-slowly in the wind, for all they care."

"Which really angers me," said Mrs. Evans. "Look, we *know* it's not legal—no argument there." She tore off a bit of her powdered donut, which she held between a finger and a thumb, and put it in her mouth. She had an upper-crust, arty, East Coast way about her. "But what happens if six months from now someone like you discovers that someone in our organization got too enthusiastic? And that someone paid off a few people in Frakes' organization and Gotchell's to create the scandals? *Then* where are we?"

"Right back in the shithouse is where," Bailey answered, thrusting his trigger finger at me. Then he counted to one on it. "By November fourth, this country had gotten itself two scandals in the hole. *We* got this presidency smoothly off the ground. Not too bad for a bunch of amateurs. That's what they *still* call us, you know. This after four months of the smooth-as- silkiest transition this country has ever had. We, I mean, y'know—me, Janet, everybody—till a week pre-election we were all planning to get back to our civilian jobs!"

"It was just a, a symbol," said Mrs. Evans. "The campaign, I mean. We were just trying to get a little campaign experience, make a few points for causes the main parties largely ignored. We weren't *supposed* to win!"

"And then we did!" Bailey laughed angrily. "Howinhell did *that* happen? Jesus H. Christ, Walker, everyone got scared shitless about this—still is. Even the president himself has mentioned it: What if it turns out that someone got the scandals arranged to get him elected? And what if that someone has a connection with us? Democracy takes one more bad bullet in this country, and all hell's liable to break loose!"

"Have you done checks on Taylor's campaign staff?" I asked.

"Everybody." Mrs. Evans wiped her hands on the paper napkin and took another careful sip of coffee. "Everybody, everybody. There's no evidence at all of anyone's connection with the scandals."

"Including the White House staff flutters: 'Did you—'"

"Flutters?" I asked.

"Lie-detector tests," said Bailey with another dreadful clench. He wore a three-piece suit, but the suit jacket sleeves were too short; his thick wrists hung out from them; one held a watch the size of a grenade. "'Did you play any part in the two scandals during the election?' we asked. Negative. Totally, completely negative, right down to the girl who did our hotel reservations. She does the vice-president's schedule now—great kid," he added.

Mrs. Evans again: "But even if it were a *distant* connection— an old friend of the president's, an associate's lawyer, whatever—it would throw this presidency under a shadow of suspicion. We're less concerned with Jover being caught with the false pass—that must have been his own fault. But what about the Frakes outtakes? That *couldn't* be a coincidence. But it's just that coincidence that shooed us into the White House."

Hence their mission. Since February they had been keeping tabs on the work of two writers researching the election: me and one other (who was about to finish his book, anyway). Except for an occasional look at our papers, they limited themselves to watching e-mail and, with a special program, monitoring what went into our computers; the program sent them all recently-opened files and e-mail every time the computer was turned on. Bailey alone had done the break-ins.

"I'm the one who had TSCM training in the Army," he said, which was apparently something to be proud of. "I got your stuff read and personally destroyed it all immediately. No records kept, nothing. The invasion-of-privacy issue got totally compartmentalized. Operation Questionable Honor never had any ambitions to keep permanent tabs on writers."

"And TSCM?" I asked timidly. "Just out of curiosity."

Bailey rolled his eyes. "Technical Security Countermeasures."

"Ah."

I never asked them what their plans were if they did find someone involved in sinking the campaigns for Taylor. I doubted that Mrs. Evans had the heart to take violent action, but Bailey I couldn't be sure about. Anybody who wore a lapel flag that big would happily martyr himself for the Republic.

Mrs. Evans broke off another piece of donut and deposited it in her mouth. "We had to do it all ourselves—the three of us. The Bureau wasn't going to get into a scandal."

"It wasn't going to save this *president!*" Bailey thumped his fists minutely on the table and glanced across the shop at the counter attendant, who had earphones in her ears. "I told the president personally that he should get his own man appointed to the Bureau, but he wants continuity. Continuity! Jesus H. Christ—everything in this administration has been sacrificed to goddamn *continuity!*"

"His own man *or woman,*" Mrs. Evans corrected him.

With strong front teeth, Bailey ripped off a chunk of a jelly roll and chewed it vigorously. I asked them about several people, some fictitious, some real. Rolf Obermeyer rang a bell, as did Phyllis Kirk; most of the rest did not. "How about Bert Macavee or Laura Prestini?"

Silence—neither embarrassed nor secretive—just dumb silence as if I'd asked them how to say *table* in Swahili.

"Well, you can end your investigation," I said several names later. "I've found the person who engineered the scandals, and it's no one connected with Taylor."

Mrs. Evans sighed with relief, but Bailey said, "Who? Who the hell did it, goddammit? He's going to get his miserable little legs broke in ten places!"

"Buy my book when it comes out," I said with a smile.

Bailey then gave me a speech, which I will spare you, about how if I made a public fuss about Operation Questionable Honor, it would start yet another scandal and "get the electorate's spirit crushed" and "hand our enemies a golden opportunity on a silver platter." To all of this, his fists played timpani on the tabletop and his shrieking coffee-breath bathed me. Keeping mum was a patriotic duty, he finished.

To his surprise, I agreed. My motives, however, were more personal than patriotic. These were good people caught in the giddy, schizophrenic eddies that any new administration generates, and especially an unprepared one like this. Their spying had done me no real harm—and the other writer was already sending chapters out to publishers (rejected far and wide, it never came out). The matter was nothing to me, but would have meant headaches for President Taylor. Far better, I figured, to bury it.

Bailey congratulated me on my decision, tears in his eyes. For her part, Mrs. Evans told me that if I ever needed anything in Washington, her East Wing office was open to me for as long as she occupied it.

So I asked for American citizenship for Naima. I did this not only for her; it also occurred to me that they would sleep easier knowing that I was grateful. Within a week I would send the applications and photos directly to Mrs. Evans, and ten days later—with the collusion, a hushed voice assured me on the phone, of Eminent Personages—Naima took the oath in front of a Saint Paul judge.

Which was just as well: the following day, she discovered that she was pregnant.

The three of us parted the best of friends—Mrs. Evans in particular looked refreshed—and we kept in touch during the entire Taylor presidency. Bailey and Salter still work in government; Mrs. Evans, who had a sharp idea of where the Taylor Administration was headed, left a year later to take an executive position with the League of Women Voters.

I returned to my keyboard and finished my book, now on my normal computer, for Bailey sent me a program the next day that nullified—or canceled or mugged or decapitated, whatever it is that computer programs do to each other—the one that allowed him to check my doings.

But all of that, as the Brits say, is by the bye. For our purposes in these pages, the episode put to rest the critical unknown: Laura Prestini had not been working for anyone, least of all the Taylor organization.

13 *The Saddest Election: Mitchell Taylor's Stumble into the American Presidency,* came out to wide acclaim in July and sold faster than the printer could ink the plates. Orders ran so high that I received a second, even more astronomical, advance—so much money that I felt sheepish looking at the numbers. Naima, however, was less abashed. She found us an eighty-five-year-old house overlooking a Saint Paul lake and set about decorating it—a sweet pastime for a pregnant woman.

I saw little of it. I started ten weeks of grueling book-touring, in which I did two hundred forty-seven interviews. But no complaints: for once in my life, I was solvent, interesting book projects came my way, and famous people put their manicured mitts into mine and invited me to eat at restaurants where getting reservations required divine intervention or rigorous voodoo. It was good fun.

It was the opposite of what Laura Prestini endured.

Her new nose must have been some consolation, I thought, as she marched from program to program admitting through her tears what a fool she'd been. Her nose was straight and slender, and together with her good clothes, a new hairstyle and smart figure, she could sit comfortably with coifed journalists. In fact, I seemed to see her more clearly, more in focus, on TV than I had in her apartment. She seemed well-seated, in her element. Her good looks only enraged the critics, however, who churned out rivers of cartoons, newspaper columns and commentary decrying her "contaminating an American election." Some excerpts:

A major-newspaper editorial: "Who did this poli-sci graduate think she was, striding the national stage, single-handedly keeping the presidential election fair and honest for all? All autumn long she traveled with a damaging tape of Governor Frakes in her suitcase, and never once, according to Sam Walker's careful account, did it occur to her to overcome her silly fears and throw such a campaign-decimating document into the back of a passing garbage truck."

Another editorial: "A middle-level campaign aide, Ms. Prestini had no business turning over a tape of any kind to the opposition campaign. Or helping the Gotchell campaign attempt to gain access to her party's headquarters to steal a damning Videotape. Good intentions, very bad deeds."

A syndicated columnist: "Fine and well. Let's accept for the moment Miss Prestini's (doubtful) theory that her boss, Phyllis Kirk, would have made a last-ditch effort to win the election by making public the key tape of Senator Gotchell seducing a young campaign aide. Fine. But you cannot—by any stretch of decency or benefit of the doubt—accept her turning it over to the Gotchell campaign. That kind of collusion between competing campaigns is precisely what gives third parties credibility when they say that Republicans and Democrats are two heads of the same horse."

And on and on. Lying on hotel beds from Burbank to Bangor, I watched her television interviews all along my book tour. (True to her dislike of print journalists, she refused all interviews with the print media, except women's magazines.) She never lacked perfect hair or her crucifix or a clean handkerchief, which she used to wipe her eyes when she cried, which was always.

Question: "And it never occurred to you, Laura, that the very existence of the Frakes outtakes was a threat to your party?"

Laura: "Well, of course, it *occurred* to me. But I'd put it in my purse immediately after the studio shoot, and then I found it in there again that night, and, gosh, every time I thought of tossing it out, I was just like seized by panic. It was like this, this phobia. What if someone happened to pull it out of the trash, thinking it was a porno film or whatever? I mean, I've seen homeless people going through trash cans, we all have." (Tears again starting to flow.) "Of course, looking back on it, that's exactly what I should have done."

Question: "So what's up ahead for you now, Laura? Will you continue to work in politics?"

Answer (with her teary giggle, a sigh of fatigue): "Would you, like, buy a used car from this woman? No, I'm afraid that's the last thing anyone wants. Who would hire me now?" (A hiccup, a wipe of the eyes before the next gush of tears.) "I fully recognize that it was all wrong, what I did. I just wanted to be sure it was a fair election, you know. I just never dreamed it would turn out this way." (Full-throttle sobbing.)

It was a nightly flagellation. I remembered Laura's remark about not eating any potato chips because she had told a lie—"creative penance." Perhaps the breast-beatings were her penance for warping the election.

Zack Stram's security video clip followed her everywhere and went through its motions like a pet dog with only one trick; no interview was complete without it. (A frame of it—the OutFrakes video lying cozily on that lacy, white bra—made the cover of a national newsmagazine when the news first came out.) Usually, the news shows allowed the clip to run an extra couple of seconds so that everyone could laugh one more time at Laura pinching Baronowsky's cheek.

But you had to give her credit: Laura owned up to everything, dodged nothing, never fudged facts, shouldered all blame. Her name instantly entered the national lexicon. To do something stupid and then apologize effusively for it became known as "to do a Prestini." This, of course, being too many syllables for the American mouth, quickly shrank to "to Prestini." For example, "If my stock investments turn south, I'll Prestini to my wife." She was even right in predicting the jokes made about her. "How many Prestinis do you need to screw in a light bulb? Two: one to screw it in and the other to apologize for screwing it in the wrong way."

For all of August, America's scandal month, no news report was complete without Laura. She was egged in San Diego, took a pie in the face in Miami. A madman attacked her in a restaurant two blocks from her apartment. Footage of her topless in a hotel swimming pool, where she'd stayed the night of an interview in Denver, showed up on the Internet. It lasted but five seconds as Laura emerged from the pool—the place was otherwise empty, the wall clock showing eleven-forty—and pulled on a bathrobe, but five seconds were plenty. Soon her full breasts were on display across the planet. Sheepish, Laura explained that her bathing-suit top pinched too much when she swam, and since nobody was around.... "Well, one more lesson in fame—or infamy," she sighed with a weary grin to the interviewer.

She showed up in a Columbus emergency ward four days after

this, and though the doctors swore up and down that she had foolishly taken a few too many pills for menstrual pain, the rumor persisted that she had tried to commit suicide.

Phyllis Kirk also fared poorly. As I said, I gave her version of events word for word in my book, but only a fool believed that she had simply thrown away the "Gotcha" Gotchell video: "I do not know where Laura's copy of the Gotchell tape came from; I do not. I threw away the one I had. I never made a copy, I never put one in the video library, I had no knowledge of it. Period." Her long-stemmed cigarettes and prune neck, however, turned her credibility into road kill.

Some scandal rag hired a private detective to put Phyllis' declarations to a vocal lie-detector test. The gumshoe, Solomon Ivories, paired her statements with others taken from speeches to shareholders in her company, and showed how the speech patterns were all different. "Ms. Kirk, I am very sorry to say, has failed my test miserably," he announced with sorrow in his voice that sounded much more like glee. I paid Ivories no attention—to the surprise of people interviewing me. I told anyone who asked that his test was a lot of squiggly lines from which you could extract the conclusion that you were paid most to find.

It didn't matter, though. Phyllis couldn't hold a candle to Laura, youthfully deferent, faultlessly polite, effortlessly groomed. Laura was ever-conscious of her error, delicately self-mocking, kind to one and all. One talk-show host gushed to her audience, "Our driver got sick on the way to the hotel to pick Laura up, and guess what? She put *him* in the back seat and drove here herself!" Laura could even chuckle about her underwear that showed up in the security video: "Yeah, well, what can I say? I like a nice, soft thong."

So, after the wave of editorial condemnation, the now-wait-just-a-minute crowd got into gear. First were feminist bloggers who noted that Laura was a woman and a young, attractive one—the kind that everybody loves to take shots at. Her videotapes mix-up was an honest mistake, and after all, she was a woman and a young, attractive one—the kind that everybody loves to take shots at. Laura denied nothing (unlike most men), and after all, she was a woman and a young, attractive one—the kind that everybody loves to take shots at.

It was, in fact, the women's magazines that first rose to really lionize Laura, mainly in the wake of the revelation, which Laura leaked, that a men's magazine had offered her two million dollars for a photo essay and that she had turned it down. Well, yes, the story was true, said a spokesman for the magazine, though Laura had been assured that she could wear a thong bathing suit. In September, I saw a women's magazine with Laura, gorgeous in purple, on the cover: "Laura Prestini's Winning Style" read the headline. In the article, the photos of her were stunning: pretty in simple blouses and slacks, with none of the thick sexiness of Brenda Taylor. "You might hate her politics," read the caption beneath her, "but there's no faulting Laura on details."

And slowly, across the country, as newspapers noted, she was cited by schoolteachers and parents and priests as someone who faced squarely what they'd done wrong, someone who for once wasn't rationalizing or covering up, someone who for once in our trashy public life actually apologized for what they had done wrong and ought to be forgiven. The tide was turning in her favor.

She hit her peak during her famous prime-time Halloween interview on *The Paula Everett Show*. Biting her lower lip, weeping with anguish, she blurted, "But you know? Sometimes…sometimes I wish I'd have kept the Gotchell video instead of recording over it! Sometimes, I wish I'd kept it, made copies, and sold them for a million a shot. I mean, I'm finished. I've had to quit my job at the PR agency, I need bodyguards which your network has been nice enough to donate for the moment, I keep my apartment rent paid by doing these interviews—I admit it, why shouldn't I? Where else am I going to make any money?"

Her voice warbled, Paula Everett clasped her hands, and the cameraman focused on the tears sliding down the interviewer's dove-smooth cheeks. "I'm a walking piece of history," Laura continued, "and it's not like Paul Revere and his famous ride or Washington on the Delaware or Neil Armstrong stepping on the moon. No, no—I'm that air-headed bimbo who destroyed an American election!"

Now Everett threw her arms around her and said to the camera, tears flowing like rainwater down rocks, "We'll be back—if we can—right after this."

They found it within themselves to come back after the commercials, and Laura ended the show, still crying, with a formal apology to the nation and Governor Frakes: "I want to apologize to everyone: to my party, to the people who worked so hard with me on the campaign, to Governor Frakes, to my family and friends for bringing this on them—I'm sorry, Mom and Dad—and especially, especially, especially to the American people for my slanting their vision of Governor Frakes, who really and truly is a great man. He should have been president, and all of this should never..."

She broke down crying and couldn't go on. Neither could Everett. The credits rolled silently over the screen, and the two of them, their heads together, shoulders shaking, sobbed right through to the fade.

And with that, Laura had won. It was all downhill from there, and from a very, very high point on the hill. Her candidness, the comic security video, her acute sense of guilt, her sweet face and figure— all of these dampened the jokes, fattened public sympathy, made America reconsider her. Suddenly, it was popular to object at the water cooler that, as one women's mag crowed, she was "America's Honestest Woman." Her new hairstyle—feathered and curled in just at the nape of the neck—became the new rage. Women ran to their hairdressers asking for a "Laura" (which, as one pro-Laura columnist noted, was a great improvement on a "Prestini").

By mid-November, she had written her own bestselling book— mainly to pay her security and legal costs (she had been hit by several nuisance lawsuits), though nobody blamed her for making a buck out of it. Her book briefly ran ahead of my own on the bestseller lists.

In December, she joined a New York public relations firm, though keeping her residence in Ohio, thus feeding political rumors which at the time seemed to me foolish. Her salary was well into six figures, which was good, because she still had legal debts. As she moved to the penumbra of the media spotlight, she was seen with a movie star. Blurbs about her in the People column of the newspapers inevitably began the same way: "Laura Prestini of OutFrakes fame..." She had paid a heavy price, but she had come out of the crisis intact and with prospects. I was glad.

I met Laura in person again, just after her move to New York: a puzzling encounter at the annual roast-the-president gathering of the American Press Guild.

I had been invited on the strength of *The Saddest Election*. So had Laura, though not a member and her book not exactly a glittering work of journalism: rather, a miracle of celebrityhood. Maybe it was the movie star that had wrangled the invitation for her.

President Taylor spoke last, and did justice to his former career as a stand-up artist and talk-show host. For twenty-five straight minutes he had the audience splitting its sides, me included. These were, you remember, still the glory days of his administration.

One joke stands out on the video I have of his talk: "You know," said Taylor, leaning one jaunty elbow on the lectern, "the way I won the presidency has really been an asset in my dealings with foreign countries. The other day I was in a meeting with a foreign, ah, *representative,* let's call it—a meeting that could best be described by the word 'tense.' This is a country which, to say the least, does not see eye to eye with us. And at one point, the gentleman, who personally represents the leader of this country, leaned over the sofa and looked me in the eye and said, 'Mr. President, you will need to be the luckiest man in the world to get away with a policy like that against my government.' I leaned over, too, looked this gent in the eye, and I said, 'Well, Mr. So-and-so, how do *you* think I won the last American election?'"

The audience roared.

"I mean, there are presidents who fall on the steps of Air Force One and others who fall into honey-traps, but who ever fell into a presidency?"

A little later, this: "But if I may…just seriously for a moment here…I would like to just put in a word for someone." He looked out past the dais into the dark hedges of dinner tables. "Is Laura Prestini here? Is she here? I'm told that she issss….Yes, Laura, would you stand up, please?"

Far to my right and in front, a spotlight swung and rested on her. She wore a tight-fitting evening gown, and I could see her thin shoulders and the small, straight back that dropped into the slim hips, and for a moment, I remembered her walking up the side aisle at Terry's funeral. *Goddammit, that was her,* I told myself. *I'm sure that was her.*

"Laura, I just want to tell you that your behavior in the wake of last year's revelations has been exemplary. You have behaved with candor and humility, and in general in a fashion that has been exemplary for young people everywhere in this country—and a not a few politicians, I might add."

Chuckles.

"You have publicly apologized many times for the mistake you made, you have stood tall under enormous pressure, and I just want to tell you, on behalf of the American people, that we accept your apology and wish you all the best. Let's give her a hand, ladies and gentlemen."

During this, I watched her back stiffen—proudly, as if she were receiving a medal. When he finished, she performed a shy, grateful nod of the head, then turned and with a faint sweep of a hand acknowledged the applause before sitting down again.

I also took a good look at Taylor. Stand-up guy that he was, he was measuring the applause, which sizzled warm and full (though if he hadn't had the TV lights in his eyes, he would have seen, as I did, several people whose hands remained in their laps: dour columnists, probably). It was then, I think, that he realized Laura would be a good name to have under his warm, cheerful White House roof. Three weeks before then, the first car bombs went off, and the military and National Guard needed important increases in personnel, and the YouthGo program was founded to encourage young people to enlist in the military. (It was that or an onerous draft, and the president knew where his support lay.) Taylor picked Laura for the job. In a gesture of humility, Laura accepted on the condition that her salary was not executive, but on the order of general staff.

My encounter with Laura:

The president finished and left, and the dinner dissolved into a sort of nightcap party as the crowd thinned. I kept an eye on Laura, and when she went to the restroom contrived to be there in the dim little hallway, ostensibly talking on my cell phone, when she came out.

When she saw me, a little four-piece chamber orchestra of emotions played in her eyes, and her hand rose to the chain around her neck. I noticed that the low neckline had returned to her repertoire after the months of TV demureness.

"Sam, it's *so* good to see you again!" It wasn't quite the set phrase of a famous person; she wasn't able to reach that register with me, and I was glad that she, too, felt how entwined our successes were.

She came forward and took my hand in both of hers and shook it. I made out the crucifix, the tiny earrings, the cool eyes which had visibly aged in the year since our interview.

"So am I." I tossed up compliments about her hair and nose. Then: "I'm glad to see you've gotten past the scandal. You've done pretty well for yourself."

She jerked backwards. "Well, what do you mean by that?" she asked.

Her tone caught me by surprise. It straddled puzzlement and offense, as if I might be accusing her of gaining her fame improperly. "Well, I mean, your new prestige, your book, the PR job. You've done well."

"Oh! Oh, I get it," she said with obvious relief. "Well, that's so nice of you, Sam! Actually, I'm just looking forward to getting on with my life now. Especially now that the president has, you know, sort of, *absolved* me. I feel a lot better."

"It was nice of him."

"Yeah, it just takes such a *weight* off my shoulders!" she said and laughed giddily. She might have been cured of cancer. "So I'm moving on now—you know, like Shirley Temple Black? She started life in cute little-kid movies, but by the time she retired, she was Madam Ambassador."

I remembered this same comment, word for word, that she had uttered on some TV interview I'd seen. "Well, Sam, I'd better be getting back. Hey, good to see you again!"

She placed a neutral hand on my shoulder and pecked my cheek, and walked off down the hallway.

Then something else occurred to me. I trotted after her. At the entrance to the ballroom, I touched her shoulder and said, "Laura, just one questions for the record—now that it's all said and done."

She turned. "Sure. What's that?"

"Look, I can't get this out of my mind: Wasn't that you at Terry's funeral?"

Her mouth hardened into a straight line I had never seen on TV, and she quickly moved around so that no one looking on might see it. "Oh, that's great, Sam," she said in a low voice. "You soften me up, then try to catch me off guard."

"*Catch you off guard?* That's....C'mon, Laura, that's not even—"

"How long have you been planning this, you bastard? What—you lean on your publisher to get you an invitation to this?"

"*What?* This is—"

"I told you I didn't go! Get it? You saw *someone else,*" she snapped into my ear. "Now don't bother me with that again!"

She stalked off into the crowd, and I stared after her—so long that suddenly Naima was at my side giving me back my drink and asking me what I was looking at.

"A ghost," I said.

14

America hates a traitor, Laura had said of Terry Letizzle. I wish I had reflected on the conviction in her voice.

For the one who took the hardest blows from *The Saddest Election* was neither she nor Phyllis, nor Gotchell, about whose busy sex life my book revived questions; but Terry, if only because he was no longer around to defend himself. His mother tried to at one point, but made a pitiful, pleading, teary hash of it that is better forgotten.

Terry was derided for flubbing Laura's directions on the security pass (though one columnist thanked him), and crucified for being a turncoat when Laura mistakenly slipped him the Frakes outtakes. Every single official on the Gotchell campaign denied, with greater and lesser plausibility, ever seeing the Frakes video or deciding to leak it to CBS (I never mentioned Obermeyer by name until this addendum), and the producer has never revealed his source. So Terry was credited with running to the producer himself.

Without citing Rolf Obermeyer, I pointed out this error whenever I had a chance—to no effect whatever. The eternally replayed sequence of him coming on stage with the video tucked under his arm had turned him into a ghoulish abstract, like a pop tune beaten to a pulp by constant radio play.

You could say anything you wanted about him. National newscasts named him "Mr. Letizzle"; the ladies-talk-show hosts who held Laura's hand called him Terry," with a sneeringly plosive T; the print dailies gave him a plain "Letizzle," and the print news magazines tut-tutted with "Traitor Letizzle" and "Scam-Artist Letizzle." The tabs, as always in a class by themselves, raced to outshout each other: "Laura:

Tizzed Off!" "Tizz the Reason to Be Sorry!" "Terry: Was he Tizzled by CIA?" Under the latter headline, the CIA was accused, for several editions running, of having murdered Terry and made it look like a suicide.

His ethics being too deep a subject for them, his sexuality was called into service, and a pliant Columbus video club furnished a long listing of his video rentals; it consisted half of action films and half of porn, with a clear leaning towards sado-masochism in which young women took the worst of it. The listing poured gasoline on the women's-mag fire. I hoped Senator Gotchell would make some kind of comment on Terry at this point, if only to say something about the stupendous populations of skeletons that some closets hold; but that would have reminded the world too much of his own.

So for the sixth edition of *The Saddest Election*, I decided to write a sympathetic prologue about Terry: that he was a green kid dazzled by the proximity to power, but all the same a hard worker loyal to his candidate and silent about the latter's sexual gambols. (How Terry must have pined for the girls who grinned their ways in and out of Gotchell's bed).

I wouldn't defend his taking advantage of Laura's mistake: he should have known what the campaign brass would do with the OutFrakes tape; that didn't require genius. But I would remind everyone that Terry had only brought the video to the campaign bosses; *they* were the ones who went public with it.

My putting the emphasis on Terry was also a jab at my New York editor, Walt Greene-Halver. He wanted a prologue for the sixth edition, though he had quite a different one in mind.

"Thou seeist where I'm coming out on this, Sam?" he said, raising his hands and framing the august air of the Ritz with forefingers and thumbs like a movie director. Though British, he had a very American sense of the bottom line. "A nice, softball, looking-back-on-it-all reflection, burnish our public image a bit, give us a spot of *gravitas*, and at the same time dash a little mustard on sixth-edition sales."

I murmured that I was awfully busy on a new project—an overview of Kennedy foreign policy, which would come out two years later—and Walt added, looking sadly into his Marques de Riscal 1991, "It's a risk putting out a sixth, anyway, Sam." Which, as he well knew, was preposterous: the fifth—huge—edition was selling steadily.

Janine, the editor who had worked on the text—and with great skill—was also there. She stretched backward and let her long, gray, stiff, tobacco-smelling hair hang over the floor and peered through window-sized glasses at the ceiling. "You know, Sam, it's little things like this that make a big difference when negotiations for future projects come 'round. I mean, look at it from a publisher's point of view. Every print run—every book—represents a risk. What does a publisher have to work with at the end of the day but ideas? Ideas printed on well-bound, high-quality paper. That's all we offer the public: pretty ideas."

It was not a subtle hint, and I figured I'd better keep everyone happy and write the prologue, though *our public image*—what there was of it—was just peachy as far as *we* were concerned, *gravitas* included.

Still, the prologue turned out to be a salutary exercise indeed, for it was in doing the research that I discovered that *The Saddest Election* was all wrong.

On a warm, heaving, late-afternoon in late March—remember that we are now eight months past the original July appearance of *The Saddest Election,* and into the second year of the yet-to-crumble Taylor Administration—when the air blew along in bales over the endless green yards of Ohio State University, I ended the day in Rutherford's Tavern, a cozy, wood-lined beer hall just off campus; Terry had mentioned it in my interview with him. Every Friday at five there was a political-science cocktail, and according to five or six people that I had interviewed in the past two days around Columbus and the OSU campus, Terry had always been the first to show up and the last to leave, and contributed more than anyone else to the collection box for the drinks. He had even made it a condition of employment at his last job at the golf shop: come hell, high water, or clearance sales, on Fridays he knocked off at four-thirty.

Ethan Hopkins, one of Terry's professors whom I'd been interviewing for the prologue, had invited me to the cocktail hour, though he told me not to expect much political chatter at that time of year. I didn't. It was the Friday before Spring Break, and the campus was emptying out. Its remaining life-forms consisted of ponderous professors in wrinkle-free plaid shirts and crabby janitors who threatened with citizen's arrest anyone who placed a foot on their dry-waxed hallways. Only the foreign students with nowhere to go hustled lonely across the lawns and sat still as reptiles in the library carrels.

Hopkins and another poli-sci professor, Chad Dawson, were the only two who showed up for the cocktail—demarcated by a tattered, stained strip of red-white-and-blue bunting along the right half of the bar. Rutherford's was dim and quiet—part bar with stools, part booths, mercifully free of music. The three of us spent a cheerful, noisy hour hashing around OutFrakes, President Taylor, and national affairs in general, especially the car bombings.

Professor Ethan Hopkins was big, bald, and shaggily bearded, threw his arms about a lot when talking, and had strong and conservative opinions about everything—to him Laura Prestini was "an American Gandhi"—except his appearance. His tie, to take the most discreet example, did not reach as far down as his belly button, and its extremes caught on the wrinkles of his shirt so that it looked like a clock stuck a few minutes after seven-thirty. A single greasy lock of hair wagged over his forehead, and I wished he would either cut it off or paste it back.

Assistant Professor Chad Dawson, on the other hand, was short, compact, intensely logical, about twenty years younger than Hopkins. He argued his points jabbing his forefinger from the waist as if it were a corkscrew that he wanted to twist into his opponent's belly.

"And this is really the most salient sign of a political amateur," he said of Taylor. "This constant striving to appear calm, organized, at ease in the job. The John Wayne toughness. The endless stream of jokes. But I've heard that *inside* Taylor's White House, it's a madhouse—as bad as the stumbling takeoff of the Clinton Administration. Taylor has no control over his people *or* his agenda; it's guerrilla warfare." An acid smile. "But Taylor's approval ratings are still in the fifties, so what's it matter?"

"Half of that is due to his daughter," I added, and they nodded. Her second action film, complete with bare-all sex scene, had just come out; only the first whispers of her drug habit were appearing, still easily swept aside.

"And when that half gets old, and people get a little tired of presidential *style*, the best joke-writers in America won't be able to save him," said Dawson, and you have to admire his foresight.

"Well now, Chad, he's still trying to get into his stride. I'll bet Laura Prestini will be seen as his turning-up point, now that she's heading up YouthGo."

"She certainly turns my point up," said Dawson with a grin.

Hopkins cut him dead. "Chad. Laura Prestini is a national hero. I won't have her talked about in those terms. On your own time, fine, but not while I'm around."

"Ethan, it's only—" Dawson started.

"No, no, not this time. One has one's saints and one doesn't like to see them turned into cheap sex dolls. When was the last time you heard of someone giving the other side a hand? Of trying to keep an election clean? Of keeping the dirty fingers of *her own campaign officials* off material damaging—disastrous—to the opponent? She didn't blow the whistle or go running to the press, you know. She just quietly removed it from the campaign library." He toasted. "America's honestest woman for president."

"Well, Senate," Dawson said. "*If* she promises to vote more money for university research. Sam, what say ye?"

Luckily, Dawson caught me in mid-slurp of my beer. I didn't want to rain on Hopkins's infatuated parade, but Laura, for my money, had made too fast and—with YouthGo—too sweet a run out of being the prodigal daughter. Celebrity galas were one thing; a West Wing pass was another. "Make it state congress," I said, "and we'll see how it goes."

"No, no, no, no, no," Hopkins scolded. "You're both prejudiced against her. Laura is an original. Unless I'm way off, Laura is the new hope for this country. And just to show you…" He drank beer and worked the foam from his mustache into his beard. "This was what I was about to tell you, Sam, when you asked me if I'd ever seen the two of them together, Terry and Laura, that is. But I was interrupted by this, this, this"—his big face broke into a grin and he grabbed Dawson's arm—"this most excellent friend and perspicacious observer of American politics, Professor Chad Dawson."

We all raised our brews.

"Laura and Terry," began Hopkins again. "Haven't told anyone this. Bit gossipy, I suppose, but it's ancient history now. And illuminating. Now, this was long before Terry's suicide or your book, Sam, or anything—just a few weeks after the election, actually, the two of them just home from the campaigns."

I reached for my notepad. Laura had told me that she had never spoken to Terry again.

"For some reason, I got here a little early for the poli-sci TGIF, and just sat down in a booth and read for a while. And the next thing I knew, Terry and Laura Prestini were there at the bar, sort of quietly arguing. It seemed to be some kind of falling-out or something personal, so I didn't listen much, but the gist of it was that Laura wanted to buy him a drink and bury the hatchet. And you know—"

I interrupted him. "Wait a minute here, Ethan, wait a minute. Did you say *she* was trying to buy *him* a drink? When the election was already over?"

"That's right. Strange, isn't it? After what Terry did with the OutFrakes tape? But it just goes to show you the rare kind of a person Laura is: forgive and forget, water under the bridge. Which is basically—"

"Sam, what's wrong?" Dawson laughed. I must have looked pretty shocked, or maybe my hair was stretching for the ceiling.

I scooped deeply into self-control. "You're sure now?" I asked Hopkins. "*She* was inviting *him* to a drink?"

"Of that much, yes."

"All right," I said carefully. "Did they have the drink or not?"

Hopkins vacillated a moment, looking at my notepad, and I was afraid he would clam up, but he didn't.

"No. Actually, Terry was very rude to her. Not that he yelled at her or anything, but he turned his back on her. Laura ran around the other side trying to reason with him, and he just turned away again. He wouldn't even listen, that rascal. Then a few other people started arriving for cocktails, and Laura left—holding back tears, *I* thought. She was hurt. It was none of my business, of course, so I didn't stick my nose in. Wish I'd chewed him out good, though, now, treating Laura like that."

I scribbled every word of this.

"Why should Laura be so eager to make up with Terry?" Dawson wondered, taking the words out of my mouth. *"Terry* is the one that took advantage of Laura's video mix-up."

"No, no, no," Hopkins objected. "Laura is that kind of person. I only talked to her here on a handful of occasions—which I regret now—but I've seen her enough on TV to know. It was all over, and she was letting bygones be bygones. That's what I call character, by God, and I'm not afraid to say it."

I was hearing Terry: *She can take her bygones and shove them up her tight little ass!*

"And Terry was obviously furious with her, huh?" Dawson said.

"Yes, indeed, but, oh, who knows? Maybe he was having a bad day," Hopkins said with the irritation of a man who sees his opinions disturbed. He changed the subject to his specialty: environmental policy.

We chatted a bit more—though I hardly paid attention now. A sort of hot panic was spreading over me, as when you're sure you've left the bathtub running back home. But in this case, what was running were all those little doubts and loose ends that had fretted me, the armchair-detective bloggers going over my book and pointing out one inconsistency after another.

For example: Why did Laura put that video box on the counter when she exited through the metal detector? There's nothing in a video box that would set the alarm off. Another example: Phyllis Kirk said that, in the "Gotcha" videotape, the view of Gotchell and the woman was from down the hall, parallel to the dressing-room doorframe. But Laura had described the view as looking *into* the room: *You can make her out in the back of the room.* How could that be? Another: When Laura opened her suitcase in the security video, the Squeel-EE suitcase alarm should have been visible because one of its clothespin arms had to touch the top of the suitcase. It wasn't.

And now this: Laura's clear sense of having wronged Terry. By the time we left Rutherford's, I felt as if floating in a pool of lightly electrified water.

Dawson went his way; Hopkins offered me the benefit of his car's air-conditioning to my hotel. Even in a March twilight, the wet heat was sticky. On the way to the car, we passed a household appliances shop, and Hopkins halted: "Look, there she is."

The doorway of the shop was surrounded by a display of perfectly square, smallish television sets; two columns of six sets flanked the sides of the doorway, and a row of six more sat high on a plywood bridge between the columns. Laura was talking earnestly into the camera, seated on a high glass stool with her legs crossed at the knees. She had a new "Laura" hairdo now: lightly permed and falling in feathered layers to her shoulders, a dark backdrop to her usual tiny earrings—pearls, it seemed. Behind her stood an American flag.

"…Because with the country under attack, *your* support, *your* hard work is needed more than ever," Laura was saying. "There are hundreds of crowded areas to patrol, Internet viruses to guard against, and hospital emergency systems to stock and maintain. So, please, if you're between eighteen and twenty-five, enlist. In the Army, the Navy, the Marines, the Air Force or National Guard. It's the best way for you to tell our enemies that this is a great nation."

The camera closed on her, and she leaned forward, her cross swinging out between her lapels. "And *I* know as well as anybody that this is a great—and great-hearted—nation."

The ad ended, the cross winking at us in the studio lights. A game show appeared; we walked on, Hopkins drying his eyes.

"More power to her, Sam, more power to her. Nothing, but nothing, is worse in this country than looking stupid. Americans are willing to overlook handicaps, social class, racial background, crimes of passion, bad upbringings—you name it. But not looking like a fool. And Laura Prestini admitted her foolishness to the whole world— let it all hang out, as we used to say. 'I did it, I'm sorry.' How often do you hear those words in public life? And then…she *overcame* it. That is truly, unquestionably, an achievement. For her and for the country. Did you hear about her new book for kids? *Standing Tall*?"

"Not much."

"It's a kids' story on what she did and her mistake and how she went around the country explaining to everyone what had happened and apologizing to everyone. The first print run was the biggest in publishing history. Come summer, it'll be the most-read children's book in the country. And it's not like Laura is making bucketloads off it; three-quarters of her royalties are going to the Victims of Terror Fund." He laughed. "I'm going to buy ten copies and give them to my Ph.D. candidates!"

"I'll have to pick up a copy," I muttered.

Hopkins dried his eyes again. "What a great country this is!"

Me, I was not pondering the greatness of the country at that moment, but Laura's cross on the chain.

Laura's faith.

Winking at me.

The truth had hit me before I even realized, like those fat, wet Ohio breezes that come and go and leave you dripping with perspiration. I knew; I saw it all. From the note flapping on my windshield to Zack Stram's videotape, to the expense sheets, to the Squeel-EE, the suitcase lifted, the guard pinched, the nose fixed, the hair styled, the video on the bra, the boobs at the pool, the tears streaming, the tabs crying, the hacks blabbing, the priests howling, the zines, the books, the fans, the fun—yes, the fun, a demure wave to the audience one minute and head of YouthGo the next, and at general-staff wages just for that grace note of humility. What the hell? It was a lot further than Phyllis Kirk had ever got.

Yes: under the hot, grinding quiet that precedes nausea, I saw her whole scheme. I had a new topic for my prologue.

15

How had she done it?

Right in front of everyone. The famous scene in Frakes campaign headquarters when she'd pinched the guard—that was the key.

I flew back to Minneapolis. By accident, I got off the plane in Indianapolis—I was just that lost in thought—and it was only a kind flight attendant who let me get back on. Once home, I put on my copy of Zack Stram's video. Actually, by that time I didn't need to; the sequence ran smoothly through my mind, now like an alarming organ note rising higher and higher and higher. Watch it on the video clip included here on the website.

Here is Laura, still a sweaty campaign hack, still when her tight slacks and cleavage are an honest-woman's vanity, her spite against the bad joke of her nose. She steps up to security and shows her pass to the guard and signs in. She asks the guard if she can just leave her suitcase and purse there while she runs in, and the guard, happy to please those curves, agrees.

Laura pulls out her key ring and coins and a few other things and steps through the metal-detector and hastily collects them again; again we are reminded that she has a plane for Baton Rouge to catch: wouldn't it have made more sense to leave them on the counter for a moment? And off-camera she goes while Baronowsky, Zack's "dumb poh-lock," watches her southern delights sway away towards the campaign video library.

After the one-minute interval—how could it not have hit me the first time around?—Laura comes back and dumps her stuff on the counter again: videotape, the coins, the Squeel-EE infra-red beamer, and the keys.

The keys. Laura had been on the campaign trail for weeks at that point. What did she have to lock or unlock? Not a car, not an apartment. And even on the distant, black-and-white security camera, it is clear they aren't little suitcase keys; they're far too big, more like house keys. Besides, hadn't she told me that she had left her keys with Henry the green-thumb neighbor?

But she needed those keys for the next sequence, didn't she?

For here she was, back now with the video box. She steps through the metal detector again, and twists back to pick up her things again. Why such heavy choreography? Because the video box did not contain a videotape at all, but something metal, which would set off the metal detector. Yet Laura needed something metallic to put on the counter *with* the video box; putting *only* the box on the counter might look odd because a videotape has no metallic parts for a metal detector to detect. But this is no ordinary video box. Inside it lay not a video cassette but the Squeel-EE alarm, that nemesis of baggage handlers, its clothespin teeth just waiting to clamp together and release a shriek that could split concrete.

Not today, however, and not for Laura. Today it is merely the last bit of evidence that needs to be evacuated from Frakes campaign central. It has weeks ago done its job.

Why? Because Arnold Jover, he of the poorly-forged security pass, just might have slipped by those lazy security guards and got his hands on that video box, thinking as any fool would that it contained a videotape and not a Squeel-EE. And poor Jover had good reason to try a grab: this video reportedly showed his incontinent boss, Alan Gotchell, doing what came naturally with young women. At that point the die was cast. Either Jover opened the box amidst the video shelves of the library—*EEEEE!*—or he slipped it under his well-tailored suit jacket and walked out through the metal detector, which would have detected the Squeel-EE alarm. The guards would then have taken a good look at Jover *and* his pass. And very much *up,* as they say, would have been the jig.

Back to Laura. Once through the metal detector, the only matter left was to deactivate the Squeel-EE alarm and put the video box in her suitcase, which of course she did with the greatest panache, having studied the camera angle in the Jover-arrest video; it was the same camera.

Just for the record, let's go over the ground here.

Laura displays her left profile to us and lays her suitcase down flat on the floor. She places the video on top, on its left corner, where we can all see it. She opens the latches, and, may I add, without the aid of any keys. From her right jacket pocket, she takes out the suitcase-alarm deactivator, kindly puts it in her left hand for us to see, and aims the beam. She and Baronowsky flinch to the all-clear beep of the Squeel-EE alarm. And only a carping bastard like me would suggest that the alarm is not in the suitcase at all, but *in the video box.*

Why carp, when—up goes the top of the suitcase—Laura is cheerily revealing her fine and sensual taste in lingerie? Dark colors on light, light on dark so that even a distant black-and-white security camera picks up the nips of frill, the dashes of lace, the festive bias towards the "nice, soft thong." Even the black OutFrakes video nestles in the white divot of a half-moon brassiere. The Squeel-EE alarm appeareth not amidst these visions of sublimity, but who cares? Bliss is indeed ours until Laura closes the suitcase. She caresses the guard's cheek, to our delight pinches it, and glides off camera, stage left. Our cup runneth over.

Within an hour of my talk with Dawson and Hopkins, I had put on hold the entire Kennedy project—interviews, pending leads, everything—and moved fully into a revision of *The Saddest Election.* I told Naima not to trouble me about meals, pulled my *Saddest Election* files and notebooks out of the basement, and got to work. She thought I was crazy; at the moment I probably looked that way.

And the first thing I looked into was that damn set of keys. I took out my own copy of the Zack Stram's security video and watched Laura again, stopped the tape and knelt in front of the screen and counted the keys: six, on a plain, unadorned key ring. I remembered Laura's September expenses sheet and got out my copy—I'd kept one of both hers and Terry's—plus a copy of that long receipt from a department store in Toledo, Ohio, where she'd bought them. Just as I'd figured: the date on it was two days after the reporter crisis in Indianapolis. And was it just a coincidence that she buried the keys in a list along with toothpaste, gum, the Squeel-EE, Post-its and some twenty other everyday items?

Three copies had cost $1.89, and the other three, $1.79. What could possibly account for the ten-cent difference?

I found the answer just ten minutes away, which was early recompense for all the miles I would cover writing this addendum to my book. The department store chain had a branch at the shopping mall near my house, and the key-copying section had its prices listed on a sign as broad a basketball backboard. Normal metal keys, it proclaimed, (now) cost $1.89. Colored keys (now) cost $1.99. The polite kid behind the counter, whom I recognized as the star quarterback of the local high-school football team, informed me with an embarrassed grin that with the purchase of two copies or more, you got a free key ring, which that month featured a photo of Brad Pitt.

So was I really looking at three colored keys and three normal ones on Zack Stram's black-and-white security video? I went home and looked again. Hard to tell. I took the video and drove through midnight streets to the U of Minnesota campus, to one of those vaguely bohemian 24-7 shops that can copy your thousand-page thesis in the blink of an eye, develop photos, and turn data into anything animal, mineral, or vegetable.

I got more than I'd bargained for—much more.

Naavy Thao, a Cambodian-American who was financing her major in Music Therapy by tending the midnight needs of anxious grad students and deceived writers, looked through the video footage several times before choosing a frame to work on: the keys when Laura was about to enter Baronowsky's metal-detecting arc for the second time—that is, on her way out. For nearly an hour, weaving her head to speculative Keith Jarret on the stereo, Naavy played with the contrast, focused and refocused, and finally blew the photo up to fifteen inches to get a good image of the tints of the keys.

Fine work: you can see the results here on the website. Splayed out nicely, the keys clearly consist of three colored and three plain, just as on the receipt. But that was not the reason that Naavy won a sudden, one-time, thousand-dollar contribution to her education. Best and most beautifully unexpected of all, the keys had the exact, same indentation. All of them. Naavy noticed it first, largely because of the two very high gouges in the teeth that make them look slightly bucktoothed.

What Laura had dropped on Baronowsky's counter were six copies of the same key: a theatre prop, just as I had predicted.

W hich I might have figured out myself, I reflected as I now crisscrossed the country, running down loose ends. Laura had carried no keys on the campaign trail, so what was she supposed to do when she needed a bunch of them? Swipe someone's keys? Risk borrowing on a flimsy pretense that someone might remember? Instead, she'd got hold of one key somewhere and made copies, never counting on anybody like the tenacious Naavy Thao to blow up them to fifteen inches.

I had keys; now I needed people. I hunted down security guards from the Frakes organization and people who had attended the third debate and others who had attended Terry's funeral. I called Frakes campaign staffers and banged on their and others' doors, some of which opened.

One that opened—in early April—belonged to Arlen Barrington of Ohio State University, Laura's funeral-hour alibi.

I was curious to talk with Barrington, not only for what he might tell me but for how he would tell it. I doubted that he had drawn any connection between Terry's funeral and Laura; months had elapsed between the funeral and my book's publication. But he had surely wondered what Laura had really employed those hours for. To keep one client at bay while attending another? Or to keep a boyfriend at bay during a dash up a sexual side street? Surely he would remember the favor of covering for her; I hoped to get more detail.

I didn't find Barrington at his office, or even at Ohio State's Athletics Department, where he had been director of operations for the football team. The past several months had been a fine period for him. He had married his second wife, who, from the Internet photo I saw, was at least fifteen years younger. He had also leapt to director of operations for an East Coast pro-football team. (That was why the name had rung a bell at Laura's apartment. Until about ten years earlier, he had played running back for the Green Bay Packers—a huge star, according to Randy Nuttle, who laughingly filled in my spotty pop-Americana.)

In northern Florida, I finally found him at his posh, new Swiss cottage that looked on an artificial lake. The smooth asphalt driveway that led to this sweet hideaway was flanked by plains of mown lawn and classical statues on pedestals—a stab at culture, squelched by the football-motif barbecue pavilion: referees who signaled touchdown at each corner and held up half a football, complete with black letters that read, "Official Size and Weight."

The reason for this cultural disparity was apparent to me once I reached the living room: I had entered a domestic war zone. On one wall hung a rectangular mirror in an ornate, gold-leaf frame; on the other, a frameless mirror shaped like an S. A good oil painting of Broadway in the rain squared off against a framed poster of Michael Jordan, complete with autograph. Worst of all, the sandstone plaque over the fireplace had their initials, but the E (for Eva) was a Gothic italic that stabbed toward the Roman A (for Arlen) like an angry baseball manager in the face of the umpire.

Barrington delayed his entrance long enough for him to assume more importance than me, so I widened my horizons with *Trash Talk with Al Smokel (as told to his tape recorder),* which I found on the coffee table beside *Ten (Non-Violent) Days to a Better Marriage. Trash Talk* was autographed, made out to "The Ringer" by "The Smoker."

"Sports are like a washing machine you know," Smokel pontificated to lead off Chapter Two. "It has like these cycles, tumble dry spin heavy dirt light and perm press. That's one thing, you just gotta get used to as a professional athlete like. I used to think it would be like one great long ride, practice by day girls by night but no that ain't it at all no way."

"Al's a great guy. Ever read that?" Barrington asked, creaking into the room on historic knees. He wore a silk polo shirt of explosive orange that was meant to billow but had little billowing space around that bass drum of a torso. He seemed to be as deep as broad, and the cocktail glass in his hand tiny like the helpless blond in *King Kong*. His neck was thicker than my thigh. Not that he was overweight. He was quite trim for a man that size—though I bet the effort to keep his figure was Herculean.

"No, I guess my reading tastes run to—"

"Yeah, history, right? You sure did a history job on Laura. Arlen Barrington." This was his introduction, and it took me by surprise. I tried to understand his mood as he crunched my hand, clammy from the icy drink. Friendly? Unfriendly? I couldn't tell. It didn't matter, however, for he admired me: "Gotta hand it to you, Sam, you sure sold a goddamn lot o' books, and at the end of the day that's the name of the game."

"Well, this game has a lot of names," I replied dimly.

Barrington might not have heard me. He stood back from me, hand in his pocket, head back as if looking at me through spectacles. "Hey, tell me something. Who sold more books, you or Laura?"

"No idea, really. I was on the *New York Times* Bestseller List longer, so I would imagine that I did. Of course, hers had a sharper—"

"Okay, but how many did you sell? Total, like."

"I don't know the latest figures. They only come out every three months."

He wouldn't stop till he had hauled this ball-carrier to the ground. "So what was the *last one?* C'mon, how many?"

I threw out a number. He weighed it, tipping his head to one side and another, and considered it sufficiently hefty. "Wanna drink? Sit down. God, it's dark in here. People always closing the damn drapes. God damn, let some sun in. Why we come down here."

He crossed the room in three strides and yanked open the floor-to-ceiling drapes. Then he stepped aside to see if I thrilled to his marvelous view, which included not only the lake and a horizonful of pine trees, but the sumptuous carpeted dock with sumptuous full bar and sumptuous Latina wife in a bikini. Two other women, neither yet twenty-five, were also lying on the dock; and something collusive in the tilt of their heads and artless, straight-armed poses suggested that they were friends—*her* friends, and ever less his.

I gushed about the view because that was what he wanted, then asked for a beer.

"Beer? Nah—lemme make you something. Whaddaya say to a G and T?"

"Sounds great."

He sighed. "Yeah, great view, great house, great wife, great life," he recited, going to the wall where Jordan hung. He flipped a switch: motors whirred and the wall swung. It was now a bar.

"So what's the point of all this—Laura?" he asked. "That's a kind of over-and-done-with deal, isn't it?"

"Well, I'm doing a prologue to the book for the sixth edition—mainly short profiles on the people involved: Laura, Terry, maybe Phyllis Kirk. Who they were before the book, what's happened to them since."

"Everybody knows that about Laura—America's honestest woman," he said with a shrug. He smiled sideways at me. "Sure you didn't just find yourself with a good excuse to talk to a famous athlete?" He laughed shortly and went back to the bottles, which he handled swiftly, the way a sales rep handles samples, uncapping them, tilting them, shaking out the contents. "Guy showed up here a few months back—reason I ask. Said he was doing a story on Swiss architecture in Florida. Yeah, sure you are. Showed him the Swiss door and closed it behind him. Don't get me wrong, Sam, I don't mind helping a guy out—but he's got to prove himself first. Like you."

"Well, I sure appreciate your help."

Then he looked at me, hands still. "Sam, I can talk this way, can't I? I mean, you've been in *People* magazine, too, right? In a different sort of field, but you're one of us, too."

I flipped the first answer off the top of the deck: "Sure you can. I wasn't born yesterday, either."

This pleased him. He aimed at me and squeezed off a shot on an imaginary pistol. "That's the stuff." He returned to the drinks. "Hey, stick my name on the back cover if you want—you know, 'including an exclusive interview with Arlen Barrington.' Fine by me."

"Thanks. Very nice of you."

"Anytime." He placed a lime in a sort of miniature guillotine, slapped a switch and cut off a perfect slice. "That's all right. You know, us athletes, we're sort of like modern saints. I mean, athletes, movie stars, some singers—although they're kind of fading now—celebrities, big names. We lead this country. People, they ask us for advice, they take down every word, they practically *pray* to us."

"I never thought of it that way," I said, taking the drink he handed me. It was strong, but well made.

To a progression of squawks from his joints, he sprawled on the sofa sideways in a running position. One arm lay extended along the back of the sofa. The other cradled the drink in his lap like a pet kitten.

"And you know, Sam, I'm proud of being part of that," he went on, referring, I supposed, to the firmament in which his star shone. "I'm proud to be a leader in this country. And I'm a very proud man." He raised a disclaiming hand. "I'm just one of them, make no mistake about it. But I'm proud of *us*. We're taking this country through some tough times—terrorism, security-slash-war issues, the economy looping around, all that. But hell, I think you'll agree that America is just getting better and better on a daily basis."

He went on. With a jolt, I realized he was already in interview mode, not waiting for questions, just giving the visiting journalist his allotment of material for an article. It took me some work to swing the conversation around to Laura.

"Okay, Sam, but let's get one thing straight up-front-and-personal where the subject of Laura is concerned, okay?" He craned his head towards my tape recorder on the coffee table. "There was *nothing* between us, okay? Planning the Buckeyes' souvenir package, ah, pro-mosh stuff—the usual. A little lunch now and then." He sipped more, glancing past my shoulder out the window. "And Laura was great. Now and then, I'd say she hit outstanding."

"She's had a hell of a career," I said.

"And worked for every goddamn bit of it," he retorted suddenly, as if daring me to deny it. "Ya see, most people's problem is, they don't want it enough. You gotta want it, Sam." This with great conviction, so although I was recording the conversation, I displayed Awed Reverence and wrote it down.

"Laura's always done what she had to do: the boobs, the nose. Did wonders for her. She did her chest not long after she started with us—ya know, OSU. Outstanding. Half my offensive line was in love with her." He looked past me to the dock again. "She's totally religious, too, know that?" he added. "Has a really real sense of the Lord."

"I take it you two were pretty close, then," I said.

"Yeah, we were like brother and sister back then. During the season, mainly. I mean, PR—that's bedrock. But just that, right? *Brother and sister."*

I now displayed Pious Understanding. "Look, the reason I ask is this. It's kind of a strange thing, but I talked to one of the owners of her company—back in the Columbus days, before she became famous—and he was clearly kind of resentful. I finally asked why, and he said that he never caught her red-handed, but he had the feeling that Laura was slacking off on office hours. Instead of doing her work, she'd be getting a massage or something."

"Impossible. Laura Prestini is America's honestest woman. She has solid, Class-A, one-hundred-ten-percent credibility. That's why she owned up to everything and more when your book came out."

"That's what *I* thought," I said. "But he told me that he accused her to her face once, and she told him that on some occasion or another, she'd been with *you*—on business, that is. She told him he could call you up and ask if he didn't believe her."

Barrington watched me. "So what's that got to do with the tea in China?"

"So Laura never asked you to cover for her for some kind of—"

"You think I'd tell *you* that?" Barrington said incredulously. "One: even if I could, I would never betray Laura Prestini. Walk on hot coals first. Two: even if I wanted to, how am I gonna remember one particular morning years ago? That's not even a possibility."

"All right." I looked at my notes. "Well, did she ever ask you to cover for her? On anything?"

Barrington was clanking the ice in his glass, trying for a last sip. With the other hand, he waved down my questions. "No, no, no. No comment on all that. Promise is a promise."

So: a promise had been made.

Barrington realized this too, but late. "You writers are all alike—always lookin' for dirt!" he chuckled. He again raised the glass to his mouth but only made noise sucking on the ice.

"Well, aren't we having fun!" said Eva Barrington with a barbed tone. She entered wearing only her string bikini, which suited her wonderfully well, though a woman with her curves would shine in a nun's habit. With a secret look I confirmed that she'd had a bathrobe on the dock with her.

Barrington's eyes had tightened a fraction in alarm. He introduced me and said I was "a reporter"—but Eva remembered where she'd heard my name.

"Did you know that *Arlen* used to know Laura Prestini?" she asked me. We were all standing now, and she reached her arms luxuriously up and behind her, grabbing Barrington by his pipeline neck and jerking him forward over her shoulder.

"Well, no, I didn't," I said because Barrington was wagging one finger in the air behind and above him, an awkward movement that caused his shoulder to creak. "Actually, I'm here on something completely—"

"Yeah, he knew her—biblically, though before me," she went on, arching her back and daring Barrington to fondle her breasts. But he couldn't with me there.

Her prisoner, Barrington chuckled, embarrassed.

"Arlen likes 'em young and hot, with big, big boobs." She moved her head to him. "Don't you, hoh-ney?" she asked with a dash of Puerto Rican syrup in her voice.

"So much for full-disclosure-slash-privacy issues," griped Barrington.

She released him. "'Full disclosure' means introducing all house guests to each other *and* saying why they're here. This includes, of course, when Laura made use of one of your apartments in Columbus when the storm broke over her."

"Which I told you about." To me: "We were dating at the time."

"*Yeah, but after* it came out in the newspapers."

"The *same day* it did," Barrington insisted, and it was easy to see that they were already taking their first steps down the hoary halls of litigation. "Hey, *someone* had to face the press for her. Laura Prestini is an old friend of mine!" This with genuine feeling. "We had a talk, we called out for Chinese, I calmed her down. She was a mess. We put together a statement, and I called the media and gave it to them for her. *Nothing happened*."

"And I believe you, darling." She kissed him on the nose and went to the bar. "I believe you."

But of course she didn't, and neither did I, mainly because it was such a smart move on Laura's part: to use a celebrity to blunt the initial charge; I had forgotten all about Barrington's little cameo. I later read the *Columbus Dispatch* news article; in the four-paragraph statement, Barrington had used the word "feel" eight times, "confident" three times, and "soul" twice:

"I feel extremely confident that Laura will come out and meet these challenges and move on to a better plane of living in the shortest time frame possible," he concluded. "She has an unparalleled faith in the Lord and stiffest damn upper lip that ever came down the pike. After a period of well-deserved rest and reflection, I feel confident that Laura Prestini will beat this thing, and America will be grateful for her efforts."

Prophetic, that.

The domestic sniping continued for a time; I won't waste more ink on it. Soon Barrington was walking me to my rented car, knees creaking with each step as if griping to each other. He still had the empty glass in his hand. It was full of ice and would not stop rattling.

"We're, ah, we—Eva and me—we're working through a lot of challenges, you know, Sam, so you'll take that into consideration, right?"

"My business isn't scandal." This surprised him—he didn't seem to believe me. "But I wish you'd have been a little more up-front about Laura."

"Yeah."

I stopped and faced him. "I still do." And if Barrington wanted to take that as a threat, fine by me.

"Yeah." Again he tried to get more alcohol out of his empty glass, tilting his head back till the ice fell on his nose. Then he looked over the grassy plain down to the road. The poor saplings on it listed one way and another like seasick passengers. "Look, she did call me once to ask me to cover for her, okay? But this was long before—months before—the scandal over her broke. Call it, yeah, call it after Easter last year. I told her about doing the egg-hunt bit with my kid from my first marriage."

That placed it within weeks of my interview with her and Terry's funeral.

"But get this straight: it wasn't anything about goofing off on her company—Laura wouldn't do that. She needed..." Barrington thought, jiggling the ice in the glass. "Yeah, it was something like... something about—yeah, that was it. She wanted to show a prospective client how important she was, so she let something slip about me. That was it. Something like, 'I know we're just a small PR agency, but look, I just had a meeting with Arlen Barrington at Ohio State just the other day.' You know—impress the guy. Thing is, she thought the guy just might call me and check it out. Now, can we leave it at that?"

I said something agreeable, yet thinking what a fool I'd been to assume she would use some standard excuse. Of course: she would exploit his vanity.

"When she asked you this, was it in a phone call?"

A puzzled, what-difference-can-it-make flap of the arms. "Yeah. Right. A phone call."

"Morning or night?"

"First thing in the morning—before I'd even left the house."

"And how long before the call was this appointment with you supposed to have been? The day before? Two?"

"No. A few days, maybe a week," he griped. "Okay? Are we down to closure issues here yet, Sam?"

His answer fit perfectly with Terry's funeral. I thanked him and got into the car, swung round the circular driveway and drove away. On the side of the house, I saw two servants doubled over with laughter, hands tight on their mouths.

I did, by the way, "leave it at that." But in checking my story one last time before publishing this account, I discovered that, not three weeks after my visit, the Barringtons filed for divorce, complete with press statement, which said they had broken up after "seventeen months of relationship"; as if "relationship" were another cocktail that could be mixed and drunk in the quantity one desired.

From the far end of the driveway, I glanced in the rear-view mirror, and he was still looking after me—an orange blot against the cottage, hands at his hips, torso thrust forward, disgusted as if he had fumbled the ball to the other team. He flicked his wrist—the ice burst out of the glass and scattered over the lawn—and with a long roll turned back towards the chalet.

And it struck me as never before what a desperate, hungry lot are people who measure their lives in glory, whatever its mode: victories, applause, earnings, dropped names, bedded women. It's meat and drink—it's survival itself—to them, and the rest of life is a niggling, tiresome trifle, like doing a tax declaration or getting over a cold.

That, I think, was what I really learned from Arlen Barrington:

how much Laura cherished her star.

16 Barrington's information was a good lead—and interesting in that Laura had obviously called Barrington the morning *after* I'd spoken to her; it meant that she had not bothered to prepare an alibi beforehand, and figured that she had gotten away clean from Terry's funeral. No wonder she'd been so shocked when I'd asked her about it.

Was it Barrington who tipped Laura to my new investigation? I'll never know, of course, but it was not long after my talk with him that I learned of a quiet campaign against me by Laura and her people. For now she had "people," had them in the sense that a corporate exec or a pop-music star or the Wicked Witch of the West has them. And they formed a little government around The Great One. This government had its army and its spies and soldiers. The Great One rode above the fray.

My second clue that something was up—I'll get to the first one in a few paragraphs—came in the form of a sudden, mid-April media barrage about Laura. By then she was planning a run for the Republican nomination to U.S. Congress—had all but announced. Polls already showed that she was a shoo-in for the party nomination in the September primaries; and against any of the top names of the other party, she could go head-to-head. Female voters especially considered that any woman worth her bra trusted Laura more than a man. (Someone asked ex-Governor Frakes to endorse Laura's candidacy. He answered, to the unbroken rhythm of his pruning saw: "God strike me dead before I endorse Laura Prestini for assistant dogcatcher!" He was quickly labeled a bad loser.)

Again she was making the rounds of the women's talk shows, where the emcees hailed her as something of a sage. And she was. She talked articulately about employment problems and makeover solutions. The women's weekly mags were quick on the uptake and had her on their covers by the end of the month, with the monthly rags chiming in by May. The photos of Laura in her "Columbus residence" showed the bookcase, though I noticed that the huge crucifix had been carefully cropped out; no use troubling the readers with that. I could see just the toes of Christ's bloody feet behind Laura's head as she sat in her maple-wood block.

The ostensible reason for all the attention was that she had changed boyfriends and was now hanging on the arm of Heath Matthews, a photogenic film director universally described as "the hunkiest thirty-something in America"; his new weight-lifter movie, *Ripples,* had just come out, so the publicity suited both of them.

And Ron certainly did his part to deepen her image, saying, "Laura knows everything going on in this country: politics, trends, clothes, women's issues, everything. You can spend hours in the deepest of conversations with her."

Her out-of-the-blue media blitz was good news, though, in one sense: if Laura felt vulnerable, I was on the right track.

Now the first clue. It arrived a week after my interview with Barrington and courtesy of Rolf Obermeyer.

In case you don't remember from page one, Rolf was the chubby, chain-smoking Gotchell staffer who confirmed for me that Terry had received the tape at the debate, and that Gotchell had chased skirts all campaign-long. We had kept in touch. I had sent Rolf an autographed copy of my book and had lunch with him now and then; we lived only a few miles away from each other. He had since tied up the loose ends of the Gotchell campaign and was organizing an upcoming gubernatorial race in Minnesota. While I was out grasping for clues all over the country, he had come to my house and left a message for me to call him "only from a land-line telephone and not your own." Clear instructions; I followed them.

Rolf came over, hauled me into his car and down a few miles to the ugliest pool-table bar I'd ever been in. There he ordered a pitcher and enough peanuts for a herd of elephants, threw a twenty at the waitress and shooed her away. He loosened his collar and tie, and the blubber of his neck fell with a bounce and settled in an even roll, like a neck brace, between his head and shoulders. He downed a river of his beer and accommodated his lard to the filthy, beaten pine of the booth.

He announced: "Sam, now is the time for all good men to come to the aid of their friends who are about to, ah, get poleaxed off the public gangplank—to put it in the best of cases."

"The best, huh?"

"*The* best—that is in point of fact the operative watchword here,

Sam. Caca in the superlative is another, I might add. Would you kindly give me some kind of, ah, general, half-ass blurb on the, ah, call it the whys, whats and wheres of your latest project? Just a five-and-dime teaser will do here."

"Well, I'm a little reluctant to go into detail on works-in-progress, Rolf. Not out of superstition or anything. Call it my loner streak. Can I ask why?"

Rolf rearranged his volume to evoke sincerity. "Look, Sam, I'm a helluva far cry from the kind of guy that goes around nose-sticking into the business of his fellow man. But about a week ago I ran smack into the distinct impression that you are about to, ah, suffice it to say, get your sweet ass drop-kicked over the goalpost of life, if you don't mind me speaking vernacular here."

I drank some beer and digested this. At first I wondered if my digging into Kennedy's foreign policy had stepped on any professorial toes. It didn't occur to me immediately that he was referring to Laura. How could it? At that point, I'd been going on her for less than a month, and I hadn't published or said a word. Then Barrington staring after me in his orange shirt bloomed in my mind, and I began to feel uneasy.

"You mean what am I doing *now?*"

Rolf rolled his eyes. "Correct, Sam. Call it, ah, your basic 'now' in real time."

"Well, it's a theory I'm working on," I admitted.

"Which unless I am off ground-zero dead center, has to do with a roughly female eight-hundred-pound gorilla. Is that ballpark?"

What had he heard? "This is between you and me, Rolf, right?"

Rolf and his beer nodded.

Two pool players and the little crowd that bet on their game were arguing: one player accused the other of grazing a ball with his hand while shooting. We watched while I thought of an answer.

"Laura Prestini," I said. "I think my story about her was all wrong."

"Wrong." Rolf watched me a moment and tested the word again. "Wrong. Now Sam, are we talking *wrong* as in, ah, 'Two-and-two-is-five wrong,' 'send-in-the-lawyers wrong,' or, say, ah, say, 'If my wife catches me, then it's wrong'?"

I cracked a few peanuts before answering, and not only because the distinctions were fine ones. I decided to tell Rolf, just to hear myself say it out loud.

"I think she planned the whole thing, Rolf: set up Terry on the security-pass thing, planned for me to see her on that security video, planned for me to write my book, planned to make a national tour apologizing, become famous, and work into everyone's sympathies. And I don't think she mixed up the videotapes. I think she passed Terry the Frakes outtakes on purpose. First she sank Gotchell and then she sank her own candidate."

"You mean she *shafted* a whole American presidential election? She took us all for a ride with the crying-and-bawling bit?"

I raised a finger. "We're talking *theory* here, Rolf. For the moment, strictly theory—I'm still researching. But I think I'm right." I gave him a short account of Laura's use of the key copies and the video box that probably held the Squeel-EE.

"Doesn't sound theoretical to me," he muttered. "Sounds pretty goddamn hands-on, show-and-tell, shove-it-up-your-ass-and-tell-me-if-*that*-feels-theoretical."

"It was a lucky break. I was only looking for—"

Rolf's growl came from deep in the chest. "That motherfucking sweet-tits!" He looked away, then back at me, the flab of his neck wobbling. "That *bitch!* You know, I always thought she was just a little too, too…Girl Scouty. That and taking that cushy YouthGo job for the janitor's salary, which she doesn't need anyway after writing her book. But scamming a whole U.S. presidential election— fuck! I spent seventeen months—*seventeen fucking months*—on that election even before New Hampshire! I had twenty guys just… *fuck!*" He snatched his beer and stuck it into his mouth before he lost control.

This for half a minute.

"Not to mention nine months post-election with the whole damn staff sending out résumés day and night," he went on. "Try running an outfit that's sinking under your feet—lotsa fun." He huffed. Yet Rolf's many years in politics have taught him to stifle his anger. In a second he was back to normal. "What else you come up with?"

I told him about Terry Letizzle's funeral and my seeing Laura there. Rolf needed a couple of seconds to recall, digest, calculate; after all, it had been ten months since the publication of *The Saddest Election*.

"Thing is," I summed up, "I didn't get that good a look at her, and I couldn't be sure, and when I asked her, she denied it. At the time I didn't worry because it didn't make any sense—I didn't see any motive in it."

"What motive?"

"Well, not to go into it too much." I drank. "Guilt. Her scheme drove Terry over the edge."

"Guilt? After what she did?"

"I think that's why she took on YouthGo for nothing, too. She's making up for screwing the whole country."

"Or to continue her goody-two-shoes bit."

"No, I really think it's guilt. Somewhere way back the idea got planted in her that any bad deed could be atoned for—and *had to be* atoned for." I told Rolf the story about the vinegar potato chips that Laura wouldn't touch because she'd told a lie.

Rolf thought this over and shrugged. "I don't give a shit. She's still a bitch."

"Anyway, that's what I'm up to," I said. "I'm looking for some kind of confirmation. If I can prove her at Terry's funeral, that will strengthen my argument that she planned the whole thing."

Rolf blinked twice. "Ah, Sam, can you just, ah, put the magnifying tool on that one and click a few times? Not quite following the line of your snowdrifts here."

"Look, everyone thinks it's *Terry* who screwed *her,* right? Look at the official story: Laura gave Terry a description of her security pass so that he could get into Frakes headquarters and get the 'Gotcha' Gotchell sequence out of the video library. She was afraid that Phyllis Kirk would use it against your candidate."

"So was Terry. So was I, so was everybody."

"But the scheme didn't work because Jover got caught entering. So Laura did it herself, right? She flew to Columbus on the day of the third debate, snatched it, pinched the guard, and ran for her plane. Backstage at the end of the debate, she passed it to Terry. We saw Terry with it under his arm. And then Terry, the official story goes, saw that Laura had passed him the wrong tape—the outtakes of Frakes cursing the Medicare crowd. But was Terry grateful to Laura? Did he toss the tape down the sewer? No, he ran with it to the campaign managers."

"And Terry turned into the new Benedict Arnold in every tabloid from here to eternity."

I poured more beer over my hot tongue. "Logically, Laura should be pretty damn furious with him—just as she told me. And yet the opposite is clearly the case: Laura went to Terry's funeral. Before that, she even tried to apologize to him in person."

"*What?*"

I told Rolf about what Ethan Hopkins saw at the poli-sci cocktail hour. "See? It's *Laura* who felt bad—guilty. What I have to do is prove it."

"Yeah. Right—now we're throwing a little more flame and less heat here, Sam." More suds. "But you *have* pretty much all you need, don't you? I mean, if this OSU professor is saying that they were trying to bury the hatchet over something, and Terry wasn't going along with it, I'd say that's pretty good."

I scowled. "No, that's just one guy vaguely catching one conversation. Good for confirmation, not the main thrust. But with that—*and* I have Terry on tape saying that he turned his back on Laura and told her to shove her bygones up her ass, which was obviously the little scene Hopkins saw—"

Rolf's beer hand fell back in mid-upswing. "*Really? You have that?* Hey, that's good!"

"With all that *and* Laura at Terry's funeral, I have my argument that she ruined him—very much on purpose—and Terry took it harder than she'd ever thought and ended up shooting himself."

"Because Terry knew that the story was going to turn him into media cannon fodder."

"And she felt responsible. More to the point, she felt guilty."

"Yeah, I get it now, yeah." Rolf pulverized some peanut shells and ate. "One thing: when you asked to interview her, you think she knew that you and Terry had talked?"

"She knew I was on the story. When I called her to set up the interview, I had the feeling she was expecting me."

"When you called, how much time passed between the call and the interview with her?"

"It was the next day."

Rolf laughed. "Ambitious twenty-something like that? Runs a PR firm? And she didn't say 'take a number'? When there was nothing in it for her?" He nodded. "She was expecting you, Sam."

We watched the pool players, who had all taken back their money and started a new game, jaws grimly set. The accused player piously refused to break and insisted that the other step up to it. I wondered again—yet again—how I hadn't thought of the guilt before; that huge, ugly crucifix in Laura's house had said it all. "So why is it time for all good men to come to the aid of their poleaxed friends, or whatever it was?" I asked.

"Oh, yeah," Rolf said heavily. "Because Laura's trying to get you, Sam."

"To get me—as in 'to destroy.'"

"To variously destroy, trample, discredit, and/or get ejected from the game of life. She's sicked her goons on you. They're running a smear campaign at full speed, every gun blazing."

"Me?" I laughed. "I don't even jaywalk—what's to smear?"

Rolf laughed. "Sam, you are just a teeny-tiny little bit born yesterday, know that?"

"My mother says that's my best quality."

"Sam, smear campaigns work best on jaywalkers. 'Cause people have dirty little minds, in point of fact. Her boys are sharpening their knives as we speak."

"That so?" I said casually, and I could hear the fear in my own voice.

"Here's the skinny." He poured a new beer to lubricate himself. "Went to a cocktail party a couple weeks ago in Nebraska—trying to get their Senator Ricks to, ah, swing up to Minnesota in September and promo my gov candidate. Sally Visterman—Minnesota Secretary of State? She's a little teeter-tottery in a debate, but she has a mind like a bear trap and a heart like syrup over pancakes."

"Sounds good."

"Anyway, I heard about this wing-ding at the house of a rich old dame who bankrolls half the party in Nebraska, and I go down to Lincoln. And I'm slowly, ah, call it, elbowing my way past diamonds and silk ties, and I hear your name."

"I'm honored."

"Not when you hear the, ah, reference material." Rolf slurped beer and slapped his mouth dry. "I'm standing behind this greasy Hahvahd shit whose shoes cost more than my house. And as he tells it, you, ah, allegedly tried to pull Laura's pants off after your famous interview with her."

"Oh really?"

"Yeah, except that as per the story, now, Laura wasn't having any of it, and you—ah, per the story allegedly goes here, Sam—ended up offering her an exchange: you'd water the story down or do a remake altogether, if Laura, ah, pardon the vernacular pun here, took a quick trip to the moon with you."

I moved more beer to my stomach. "And Our Lady of the Virtuous Tears said no, I suppose."

"Affirmative. Which is why you, ah, jumped right in and published your account in an 'as is' fashion, and accentuating the gory Ds to boot."

"I see." More gulps. "There's nothing like—"

But Rolf was holding up his chubby hand. "Hold on. There's more. I heard the story again during the wing-ding, but this time it was standing in a circle and came from a guy named Duane Hale, who just kind of barged it into the conversation. You know, like one minute we're talking about subsidies for daycare providers, and that reminds good ol' Duane of the time that Sam Walker tried to tiptoe through the Tupperware with Laura Prestini? A prop of nothing?"

"*Apropos* of nothing," I corrected him.

"Uh-huh. Heard of him?"

"No."

"Neither have I. I had this itch about him, though, so I threw out a few lines once I got back here. Turns out he's head of Laura's campaign staff. Unofficial and undeclared, of course."

"So she's spreading a rumor about me."

"She doesn't need to anymore. It's swinging across the grapevine faster than hotcakes. It's already on the blogs. You can—"

"That's Laura's m.o., all right, no question about it. Just like the rumor about the Gotchell tape of the senator and the girl in the dressing room." I took out a notepad and pen. "Half the reporters I talked to in the campaign said they'd heard it from Laura. Get it, Rolf? It was *only* a rumor, and if she wasn't the one who started it, she sure gave it a good hard shove to send it on its way. And why not? She knew that in no time everybody on the campaign trail would be passing it around. I'll bet the tape didn't even exist, but she needed to provoke Terry into trying to make a grab for it in Frakes campaign HQ."

Rolf cracked more peanuts. "Sorry to slip you the one-eighty here, Sam, but, ah, didn't you say in your book that Phyllis Kirk saw it?"

"Damn—that's right," I said, stung. "She's the one who first received it."

Rolf nodded. "That one sounds like a lost cause on this side of the table here, Sam."

Rolf and I talked longer—to the effect that Laura knew how to play to the gallery and that I had to be careful—but most of the time I was mulling my theory about the Gotchell tape not even existing. It was just fit too snugly, smelled too much of Laura; the well-timed lie was, besides that great figure, her best weapon. And yet: Phyllis had seen the video of Senator Gotchell and the girl—seen it at her leisure in the calm of her home; she had even described it to me.

Rolf was looking away at the pool players, silent. And to my shock, I saw him wipe away a tear. "That poor shit. You can't imagine how many times I've thought of him, Sam. That poor, dumb bastard, sitting on his bed after you left and knowing the whole U.S. media was going to string him up by the ying-yang. All he ever wanted to was be a hero."

"Terry, you mean."

Rolf nodded and looked at me. "Fuck. Even if he did go to the top boys with that tape of Frakes. What was a foot-soldier like that supposed to do? Sit on it?"

"He didn't sit on the chance to get Gotchell's 'Gotcha' tape," I added. "He went to the top man in Security, Jover."

"Damn fucking right, Sam. He didn't try to buck the system, he went through channels, he followed the rules. Hell—Bill and Milt and the rest of the campaign brass were saying it all year long: anything out of the ordinary—offbeat local issue, pissed-off contributor, interesting photo op, whatever—all that had to go top level, and heads would roll if it didn't, boy. Fuck no, Terry just did what he'd been told. The high llamas were the ones to make the call. Terry even told them that maybe this wasn't all that peaches-and-cream ethical."

"No kidding? He did?"

Rolf raised a hand. "I only heard the full fuckwad from Milt later on, actually, Sam. At that point, when they started discussing what actually to do with the tape, I was out of the room on my cell phone."

"Well, you can be sure it'll get into the next edition."

"Good—do that." He lifted his beer but didn't drink, too busy scowling. "And from what Milt said, once Terry'd said his Political Ethics 101 piece, they patted him on the head and sent him away to brush out the senator's suits. And Terry wasn't too happy about it."

"Jesus."

"Milt thought that was a laugh, the bastard. But you know how those guys are: my SUV's bigger'n yours any day, so fuck off."

"He never gave *me* the time of day, that's for sure. He's working on Wall Street now, isn't he?"

"Office bigger than Machu Pichu. And he was going to be Gotchell's chief of staff. Let's hear it for American democracy, huh?" Rolf looked away and squashed another tear. "They could've stroked him a little, y'know. Terry, I mean. They could've told him he'd just won Head of White House Internships, with trolling rights to boot. Did they? Like fuck. No wonder he ended up on the wrong end of his own gun."

A s I said earlier, I soon began to see magazine covers with Laura on them, but if you wanted to see the crease of her bosom, you had to buy the mag and open it. (When a reporter asked her that spring if cleavage was a proper image for a White House executive and possible congressional candidate, Laura just laughed it off: "I suppose some of the pictures *are* sexier than normal, but heck, I'm trying to get American young people to sign up for the fight against terrorism. I need every weapon I can get. Besides"—a giggle—"I never heard the guys complain.")

The magazine covers held a secret message for me: *Who's going to believe you against me, Sam? I'm America's Honestest Woman. I'm the woman you see in the People column every week. If—when—I let slip that you leveraged your story to get me into bed, people will believe me. I'll let it slip and my eyes'll go watery and I'll grasp my cross for the Lord's support as I remember that terrible, terrible moment. And people will believe me. I'll kick your public ass to a bloody, shapeless pulp.*

The blogs were indeed picking at the story about my post-interview indiscretion with Laura. A reporter called to ask about this, and I told him to shove it. Nobody seemed to consider that a

woman with a gob of surgical bandage around her nose is not exactly Playmate of the Month material.

I didn't have much time left.

17 I started talking to everyone who'd been at Terry's funeral—Terry's mother gave me names and addresses—flying
around the eastern half of the U.S. The truck bomb on the
road to Atlanta's airport missed me by one day.

To make a very long part of my story very short, the effort was
fruitless, unless I count the excellent German chocolate cake served
me by Terry's Aunt Grace, who lived in a lovely old town near
Chattanooga, Tennessee. Nobody had more than a hazy recollection of a woman in the back of the church; most had assumed that
she was there praying for another reason. Not even the grizzled, old
priest, Reverend Joe Mills, who had been facing that way, could con-
nect the face with Laura Prestini—who wasn't famous back then, let's
remember. Still, it's worth noting, as our spotlight passes over him,
that the distant woman's hunched shoulders and lowered face had
made the same impression on him as on me:

"Yeah, sure I remember her. Sat way back from the rest, almost
like in disgrace. I wondered if it wasn't some old girlfriend and
Terry'd been dumped by her or somethin'. Funny thing was, she
seemed to be the one most aggrieved by Terry's passing. Glad to see
it, I'll tell ya that—real glad. Known Terry since he was a fifth-grader,
ya know—first in Akron, then here. Not a bad guy, just never grew
up, that's all; decent woman and a couple o' kids woulda jerked him
up straight. Bad luck....Anyway, most everyone else was there out
of obligation to the family, you can always tell. But that woman sit-
tin' way back there grippin' the edge o' the pew, now that was somethin'. Left towards the end of the service, ya know. Looked up, she
was gone. Forgot all about it till you brought it up, tell you the truth.
But I got the impression she was just shocked as hell."

Interesting, but that was no connection with Laura, either. I
pressed on.

From the funeral list, I was down to a cousin and one elderly
great-aunt. Had they by any chance taken a good look? Did they remember anything? Had Terry by chance mentioned Laura? I was at

the end of my rope. After many tries, I finally got together with Betty Stuymenn, who lived in a suburb of Cleveland. Betty was Terry's cousin, the daughter of Aunt Grace. She had known Terry through the years—a summer or two when they were young, since then the odd Christmas or Thanksgiving dinner. I had been trying to meet with her since the first week that I had turned my attention back to Laura. She had canceled the interview twice, then been on vacation, then canceled again. But finally we had a firm date, and I intended to keep it. I kept my cell phone turned off, hoping that this would discourage another cancellation.

I arrived at the airport and rented a car and after much hassle found her house. The housing development's streets were so new that the car's directional advisor could do no more than get me to the correct turnoff for that area. After that, I had to ask directions four times; nobody in the area knew the streets, either. Finally, a gas station with a convenience store loomed up, and the two attendants, after messy bickering, roughed out a little map for me while I calmed my neglected stomach with a ham sandwich and a can of "the greatest thing since the slice of bread." It turned out I was just five minutes away.

I suppose that every residential area was at one time or another a new housing development, but this one looked as if eternity itself would not relieve the warehouse-district desolation that the bulldozers and buzzsaws had left behind. Warehouses, in fact, seemed to have been the architects' inspiring motif.

The bloated houses—painted pearl-gray, tan, or bone-white—crouched away from the streets behind menacing three-car garages as faceless as hitmen. The roofs all had the same dark-gray shingles, the window frames the same white PVC, the lawns the same crumbly bulk-rate sod that begged for water. Each front door had the same brass-plated knocker, each lawn the same luckless sapling stuck in it like a straw in a milk shake. Between the loops of houses—forming one damnable cul-de-sac after another—stood play sets for the local children and sandboxes for the local dogs. Just to look at it all, you thought of housing starts and man-hours.

Betty lived in one of these, at the entrance to another cul-de-sac, and I supposed that she worked a strange workweek or was on vacation because it was a Wednesday at around noon, yet her car was in the driveway and a kid's scooter leaned against the wall of the open garage. I got out of my car and noted the only signs of life on the street, and almost the entire area: across the street, a child of about five scolded her two dolls lying on the grass for "messing around when you should be sleeping"; at the back of the cul-de-sac, a guy in a business suit—an expensive, well-tailored one, as if he were a sales rep—stood looking into the engine of his car and talking on a cell phone. It was a warm, humid May day—perfect for a breakdown. I wished him a clever mechanic.

A grandiloquent doorbell worthy of Xanadu announced me and soon the front door opened with a sucking sound—all that PVC, I supposed. Betty stood there expectantly in a barrage of frosty air from the air conditioner. She was about thirty-eight, had a broad figure and mannish shoulders that her skin-tight, pink T-shirt ("Cheerleader Squad—Lieutenette") displayed in detail, down to the floral pattern of her bra. The shirt was at least a size too small, and she should have taken it back. But I spied a small cut in the crew neck in front, and figured that it was too late.

What else? Blondish hair grown past the shoulders and blown dry at full gale to hold a hairstyle that was too young for her; a big face with a slim, pointed nose that poked forth like a beak; good lips painted in the same too-bright red as her nails; broad, gray teeth that needed a dentist. I promised myself to make this a fast one.

"Hi. Betty Stuymenn?" she said as if she herself didn't know, and stuck an arm straight out to grab mine. "And you are?"

I mustered patience and told her. We had already talked on the phone ten times.

"Oh! Right! Sam!" she cried. She clapped her hands once. "All right. *So!* Ah, great to see ya, come on in, let's get ya settled."

I stepped into the chilly house. The foyer had a high ceiling, as my own house does, but this one was formed by planes of Sheetrock from which the gold-plated chandelier did not distract the eye. She moved ahead of me into the living room—I noticed that the back of her T-shirt had a corresponding small cut at the neck; maybe she'd botched cutting off the clothing tag.

She swung around so fast that I flinched, to my embarrassment. "First, what would you like to drink?"

"Nothing, thanks. Like I said on the phone, this will just take a few minutes. If we could just sit down so I could write on my pad here..."

"Oh! Fine. That would be perfectly fine." I seemed to have solved a hospitality problem for her.

The population of the living room was three: a sofa facing the fireplace and, beside it, a small table that strained to hold the corpulent lamp on top. A moving-company's box formed the coffee table and on top of it lay a scandal tabloid whose headline I itched, as always, to read; but it was covered by a coloring book and a magazine that followed the reality shows. And there was a television, of course. It stood atop the fireplace on a broad mantelpiece set into the wall where the chimney should have been. The cozy, gray logs in the fireplace were therefore false; the switch beside the fireplace turned them on.

Betty sat at the other end of the sofa from me, leaned forward enthusiastically, elbows on her powerful thighs, these outlined by warm-up pants. Now and then she slapped her hands together lightly. I sat hunched over my notepad, flipping through the pages to find a fresh one. It was a practice I had picked up early in the campaign. People often asked me what I had written on the same page as their page, or took poorly the fact that their testimony was crowded together with that of the riffraff.

"Sorry this is so, like, barren? Like I'm recently divorced, and I'm just kind of now fillin' this place out?" She was one of these annoying people who spoke in questions.

"Starting over, huh? Well, you'll get it shipshape pretty soon."

"You don't use a tape recorder, do ya?"

"Not when the quotes aren't important. I just need a few facts, though—"

"Oh, that's good," she said and clapped her hands once. Then she needed to explain herself. "It's just that I hate being tape-recorded."

Which was obviously bullshit, and I wondered why the hell she was so apprehensive, almost giddy. Betty had always struck me as a person who didn't intimidate easily. She was, in fact, a sales manager—for a firm that provided soap and other complimentary articles to hotels; I knew this from my phone calls to her.

She shifted her big shoulders. "Hey, did you fly all the way out here? You know, just to talk with me?"

I had a standard lie for this question: "Actually, I have to check out two more leads in this area."

"Oh, you have to go soon? I was kinda hopin' you could stay. Like for lunch?"

It crossed my mind that she was making a pass at me, and I doubled the guard. I said that I had an interview later on with another person and had to check out some facts. With relief I finally found clean pages.

She thought over my answer and said, "Still—you must have some real bucks."

I smiled. "I got lucky on *The Saddest Election.*"

This seemed to strike a chord in her: "Yeah, that's what it is, all right. You get lucky, and the rest's history. Ya know, that's what you see, like, with all these stars?" She jerked a thumb at the TV. "Anybody who gets into the news, almost automatically like, he's rich. I mean, somebody oughta do a study of the income brackets of people who get on TV. I mean, not just people ya see in the crowd at a football game, ya know. That doesn't count. But I mean, like, people ya see regular-like talkin' on TV? Even people who get interviewed, like you? It's like they're all millionaires."

"Before I published my book, I had to make a chicken last a week."

Her hands, casually linked between her knees, fell apart. "Yeah? A week? How'd ya do that?"

"Lotsa rice and noodles."

"Yeah. Fill it out—good idea. I'd really like to be on TV, even if it's some stupid reality show? Or a game show, maybe? That'd make people stand up and listen, boy. You didn't meet anybody out there in television land that does reality shows, did ya?"

She went on, hands slapping, her pointed nose flattening and unflattening on the Ms and Ns so that it gave the effect of a bird pecking. I wondered about the child who owned the coloring book. She'd finally loosened up; I moved into my interview before she froze up again.

As always, I mixed the key questions into a general review of her relationship with Terry before he died. She'd seen Terry in Columbus at his last Christmas, to which Terry's mother had invited Aunt Grace and Betty, "since I'd just separated from Winston, ya know."

The answers to the important matters were no: no, she hadn't noticed anyone at the back of the church during Terry's funeral; no, she hadn't seen anyone resembling Laura hanging around outside before the service ("Whaddaya mean, someone who looked kind of like Laura Prestini? Hell no. Heck, after the turncoat job Terry did on her?"); no, Terry had never mentioned Laura, not even at Christmas, when to his proud mother's prompting he had recounted his adventures as Senator's Gotchell's assistant. "After a while, we had to, like, change the subject on him? 'Cause like otherwise Terry woulda talked till the turkey was cold?" Another clap of the hands.

Equally important was my clear impression that she was telling the truth and hadn't rehearsed her answers; for it had occurred to me that the long arm of Laura Prestini, or her fluent hatchet man, Duane Hale, might have arrived ahead of me with a better story and a more lucrative offer. But no: Betty answered naturally, even her anecdotes about Terry.

"Ya know, it's like I never really saw that much of him? I only went to the funeral to do a favor for Aunt Emma—his mom." She laughed. "He always wanted to dance with me—well, with all the girls, ya know? At weddings, like? We'd all say no to him, though, but he'd keep asking anyway. It was pretty funny."

"Persistent, was he?"

"Yeah, lemme tell ya. Once at this wedding—we musta been in high school or something—he offered this one girl five bucks. My sister Hannah? You interview her?"

"Two weeks ago." Another wasted flight—to Springfield, Illinois.

"She's like max-sexy, don't ya think? Always has been. Flight attendant—guy in every airport." A chuckle and a clap. "Well, Terry gave her five bucks. You know—to dance with him? So she takes the money and dances half a song with him and then runs away. And Terry spent the rest of the evening tryin' to get his money back from her. She told everybody about it later on—it was pretty funny."

I wondered if anyone in this vale of tears had ever given Terry Letizzle an inviting caress, or just an even break.

I finished scribbling and thanked Betty for her time and got up. I didn't have to get a jacket or anything—though I would have been grateful for one in that icebox of a house—and began shuffling towards the door, when:

"Hey, Sam, like, could you help me hang somethin'? Like, a curtain bar? I mean, since I helped you out here?" she added. Ten minutes of interview equaled one hanging job, in Betty's book.

My heart aching for the warmth of the street, I said yes.

She led the way to the stairs, which were off the foyer. "It's up here. Ya see, I'm like divorced? It'll just take a sec."

"My pleasure." And up half of those stairs I trailed the well-kept roundness of her behind in the gray track-suit pants. Much was my enjoyment diluted, though, by the five-alarm panic bursting in my stomach: upstairs rooms have beds.

The stairway rose beside an ugly, narrow, two-story PVC window that looked on the street. Three or four steps up, I looked out; I was hoping to be distracted by something and exclaim, "Hey, what's that?" or "Isn't that interesting?"—anything to hold things up. The five-year-old was still sitting, legs flat on the shadeless grass, beside her dolls eating a wedge of sandwich that she held in both hands. Someone had rubbed white sun protector on her nose. The busted car in the cul-de-sac was gone.

Which struck me as strange: no tow truck had passed. I'd been vaguely on the watch for one from the living room.

My feet thought faster than my brain, and stopped dead on the stairs. Of course: the neighbor lady across the street was home, and she would make a much more credible witness, wouldn't she? There would be no need to explain why the sales rep had just happened to be there.

"Betty," I blurted, "hold on."

"Yeah?" She stopped near the top of the stairs and turned.

"There's something you ought to know. Just before I came here, I stopped at the gas station—the one up by the county highway? And I asked directions." I pulled the map out of my shirt pocket. "See? They drew me a little map. And while they were drawing the map, I was eating a sandwich and drinking a root beer. And the receipt for them is in the bag in my car—business expenses, you know. And on the receipt is the exact digital time of purchase, which can't be twenty minutes ago. And right now, I'm going to get back in my car and drive back and talk to those guys again, to be sure they remember me, and I'm going to buy something else and get another receipt with the exact digital time. And in between those two times, I have a page of notes I've taken with you, so I can account pretty exactly for the last twenty minutes of my life."

Betty stretched really, really hard for the casual note. "Yeah, so?"

I didn't even bother to answer. I was hanging over the abyss. I needed to put the fear of God in her, and I had five or six sentences to do it in. "You see what they're doing? They're tricking you into getting me in trouble. Thing is, they don't know I'm on to them, and I'm being real careful about every interview I make—even with Aunt Grace."

"You didn't tape the interview," she challenged me.

"Tapes are worse," I shot back with a security that amazed me. "Because tape recorders turn off and leave a jury wondering what went on afterwards. My lawyer told me not to carry one even in the car."

"Look, this is, like....I don't know what you're talking about."

Always the cliché. I pushed on.

"Not that your friends give a damn what happens to you. What they want is to get me in the news on some kind of sexual assault charge—just the suspicion is good enough. Later if I sue you to high heaven for defamation, well, that's *your* problem, isn't it? They've given you false names, paid you off in cash. But once they hear there's trouble, you'll never find them again no matter how hard you look."

"What...friends?"

"The ones who put those little cuts on your T-shirt so that it'll tear easier right down the middle. Makes it a lot more convincing when you run out into the street screaming."

Betty tried to say something but nothing came out. "So why don't we just call it a day, okay?"

Avoiding touching the banister, I turned and walked back down the stairs. "Surely you've already gotten a part of the money—they wanted to show you they were serious, didn't they? Well, don't give it back: you've earned it fair and square. I got lucky and spotted the scam, that's all; the guy with the break-down outside isn't there anymore, y'see."

When I reached the front door, I looked back and saw Betty at the top of the stairs, slowly, slowly sitting down till, the last few inches, she dropped with a thunk, her face between muscular hands.

"Betty, I didn't say that I was going to sue you. Just forget the whole thing."

An unhappy laugh perked out between her hands. "I'd rather you did sue me—*if* I could afford it."

I didn't know what to make of this, so I said, "They *did* already give you some money, didn't they? Like half now, half when it's all over—something like that?"

"I got ten thousand—outta thirty. Fifty if I got semen, but that…" She looked at me, eyes glossy, and gripped her knees. "It wasn't for the money, though, just for your information." Then she shouted: "Money's piss-shit anyway! It's what husbands use to get rid of you when they want to fuck some wetback fifteen years younger 'n you. Even the judge backs 'em up: 'Here, Sugar-babe, take fifty grand and the kid and let him get it on with Fernanda in peace. This way they can fuck in the kitchen and don't have to worry about—'" She broke off and turned her head sharply away. After a moment, she poked a nagging tear out of one eye.

So if not for the money, why? I asked, but she waved me away and muttered, "No comment."

I left, careful to shout a cheery "Bye, Betty, and thanks again" for one and all to hear. I even called to the girl across the street and inquired about the names of her dolls, but, social nimrod that I am, received an indignant *SHHHHH!* The little darlings were asleep. I performed a stage-whisper "Whoops! Sorry!" and was gratified to see a maternal face grinning from between parted living-room curtains—to which I waved copiously.

Two blocks on I passed the salesman in his car. It was running just fine now, thank you, the windows up for the air-conditioning. He had a cell-phone ear jack in his ear—waiting for the call that would never come, I supposed—and a hand-held console pressed against the steering wheel. He was concentrating so hard on his video game that he didn't even look up as I passed.

Still: Why? I discovered Betty's motive much later, while preparing this addendum to *The Saddest Election*. I called her and asked for permission to use the incident in it, though I fully expected a roaring *no* for an answer. To my galactic astonishment, she agreed. She agreed, in fact, eagerly, with the only condition that I send her at least two copies of the book with the addendum.

"Hell, this is the greatest—this is, this is the best thing that's ever happened to me! Somebody'll come to interview me, won't they?" she asked. "I mean, like, interview me on TV?"

"It's possible," I said, fully doubting it. I asked her if she could tell me anything about the people who had put her up to the dirty deed, but no luck: it had all been handled by the "salesman" in the car, who had gone by the name of Shawn.

"Hey, and like I'll have to get my hair done or somethin', won't I? Hey, you think I'd look any good redheaded?"

I was sitting in my study watching Naima sitting against an embracing maple tree and bouncing our tiny son from leg to leg and singing something in Arabic.

"It's worth a try," I said cautiously. "Try an actor's wig. See how it looks first."

"Hey, that's a good idea. Point is, my asshole ex is finally gonna see for himself how much of a woman he lost. I mean, it's not like they set up my sister *Hannah* the flight attendant to trap you; they asked *me*."

So that was the answer: she had risked deep legal trouble for her fifteen minutes and one good shot at the shitty ex-husband. No doubt one of the copies I'd promised her was destined for him— probably via the hand of their child during a weekend visit.

I hung up and watched Naima bouncing David around, and not for the first time in this whole mess marveled at how fragile a personality is, how easily dented, dented, dented, dented, until it is something new altogether.

18 I still had one interview with a person who had attended Terry's funeral, his great aunt in Toledo, Ohio, who was over seventy, but I didn't dare. My brush with public-relations meltdown had me spooked. The idea possessed me that Laura or her underling in the car had a backup plan in case Betty didn't come through for them. I would just have to lump it if I didn't have a witness who saw Laura there.

Driving on to Columbus, I ran the route of Laura's latest scheme to smear me. First, she had started the sexual harassment rumor about me: it would dovetail perfectly with Betty's story of my attempted rape and lend both a vicious synergy. Against them I merely had the mere denial of a mere man, who in matters sexual inspires less confidence than a Mexican street cop. Probably the plan had been to put America's Honestest Woman herself on the stand at the trial, cameras rolling, tears streaming, and let her lay into me. After that, anything bad I had to say about her would smack of grandstanding and revenge.

This time I had dodged the bullet; Laura would not take long to shoot another from her endless supply. It could happen anywhere: a rental-car parking lot, a hotel hallway, an elevator containing a pretty woman. And happen it would: all over the country now, candidates were declaring for the primaries. Laura could not chance a run for Congress until she had me out of the way.

Editor Walt called me at this point and, with his British lightness, demanded the prologue for the sixth edition: "It's the printer, you know, dear," he sniffed. "They simply will not let a man write in peace."

I told him that I was re-checking a few facts, though I refrained from telling him just what facts, and that he would have it soon. Walt groaned and said he could hold off the "forces of evil" for one more week.

"And we *are* remembering our sales figures, aren't we, Sam? I mean, nobody buys the same book again—unless the author adds a *lengthy, weighty, tragically profound* prologue 'Looking Back on It All' that no student of modern politics could possibly be without, one that makes the edition look *considerably* fatter. It will be lengthy, won't it, Sam? You know, we *were* a bit indulgent with *The Saddest Election* on that count, remember?"

I did: Walt had kicked up a fuss because *The Saddest Election* had weighed in at just one hundred seventy-five pages, and because I had refused to bore anyone by padding it out. I told him not to worry. "Once I get it all looked back on, we're talking about a good sixty-seventy pages minimum, maybe a hundred."

"Marvelous!" he exclaimed in relief. "And after all, your prose is so....Well, you know what Janine told me once? She says there are times when Sam's prose just *dances!*"

"Oh, it'll dance, Walt. No question. Dance, sing and tell jokes."

Walt laughed. He didn't know yet that the joke was on us.

For a day, still trying to place Laura at the funeral, I looked through old Columbus newspapers and checked possible leads on Laura's whereabouts on the day of Terry's funeral; I called her PR agency's clients and tried to run down old agendas. Not a single soul gave me the time of day. I mentioned that I was the bestselling author of *The Saddest Election* and that I was working on a short highlight of Laura and Terry. Zilch—only Betty had been thirsty for fame. I also considered making a simple, square assertion: I had seen Laura at the church—period. I had people saying they'd seen some-one at the back of the pews, so why not? Such are the black holes of a desperate writer's universe.

The next day I spent entirely in my hotel room—no more fleabags, incidentally, though I knew well that I had produced nothing that deserved an upgrade. I actually started on the balmy preface Walt had suggested. My dancing prose would see me through, right? But by dinnertime I saw the shaky, teetering crap I'd written and deleted every bit from my computer while the spurt of sanity lasted.

Well. Enough about that.

Finally, as I watched the local evening news and chewed a raw "Texas burger" in my room, an idea winged me. The TV film crew. They had been at Terry's funeral—outside. Had they seen Laura go in? Had any of them later recognized the face—"Hey, that's the one at the funeral!"—and made the connection to Laura?

It would be a miracle if anyone had; I jumped into my car, anyway, the first thing the next morning. Miraculous confirmations were as welcome as sweated-for ones.

The immediate answer was no, none of the three-person film crew, two of whom still worked for WCMS-TV, remembered Laura. But one of these people—Hank Keister, a cameraman—got the news item out of the video library and tried to jog his memory with it. Faye Richmond, the reporter, also took a look.

Here was Terry's mother, supported by Terry's two embarrassed brothers, relatives behind them—including "max-sexy" Hannah, pale and long-faced as if she'd just worked a round-trip to Honolulu. The camera panned to the hearse, where the coffin was being smoothly off-loaded to a sort of rolling catafalque, and the funeral-home people wheeled it past everyone into the church, though at this point there was a one-second gap of black video that made Hank start. The mourners followed.

There was no audio on the report. I asked why. "After a newscast is six months old, it's taken apart and filed," Faye said from the couch of the station viewing room. "This was a walk-through, so there's—"

"A walk-through?" I asked.

"Just the anchor talking over the vid," Hank said. "Yeah, so when they file it, they don't re-record over the vid file," Faye said. "They just keep the anchor's script." She offered to get it, but I said not to bother.

"You didn't stick around after filming, did you?" I asked.

"No. We already had a copy of Gotchell's statement. We just filmed that part"—Hank motioned to the screen, which now froze on the clean, shiny church steeple—"and a bit of the church. That was all we needed for a thirty-second walk-through. We had to move on to other assignments."

I thanked them and, alone, watched the report a few more times, swore in a whisper at the black gap, checked and re-checked the faces, the background, the name of the funeral home—which I called. I wanted to ask if they had stayed outside and seen anyone come in late, but the Henry Halbee of Halbee Funeral Home told me that company policy was not to speak to reporters under any circumstances. I explained my mission in brief terms and asked if these circumstances included the robbery of an American presidential election; Mr. Halbee assured me that they did.

So: nothing. I ate something in some fast-food place in some shopping mall. And a curiosity grew on me. No doubt you spotted it fast, simply because I had to mention it: the gap in the video, 1.2 seconds according to the digital timer at the bottom of the screen. But at the time—back there in real life—it was just a mistake, a bad piece of tape, a blip in the broadcasting machinery, a spatter from the magnetic spigot that applies the electronic crud to the slipping surface of the videotape. It wasn't worth raising a fuss.

I called Hank at the station. Was there another copy of the report?

No, was the answer. Once the newscast is broken up into its aliquot stories and filed, those are the only copies that exist. Neither did outtakes exist.

Thanks.

I shot dinosaurs in the mall's video arcade. They were astonishingly real, their ribs cages expanding with each breath, the blood from the wounds flowing correctly down their contours. I wondered if Laura Prestini's machinations wouldn't make a good video game. Why not? Let realism pass for reality. By the end of the game, I had the rules and weapons figured out, but a hairy teenager insinuated himself before the rifle when I bent down to put in more money.

"Sorry," he said, not sorry at all. "Here." And he placed the equivalent amount I'd already put in the machine on top of the next game down the line. So much for those old traditions of waiting your turn, respecting your elders, and not being a prick. I left his coins where they were, hoping to insult him, though I probably just gave him a free game.

I bought some athletic socks, looked over flights to Minneapolis, dithered about reserving, called my wife to ask about her sore throat, reconsidered a new prologue, and finally remembered Terry's mother, so proud to read the message from Senator Gotchell at the funeral. I called. Did *she* have a copy of the TV report?

She had three.

Thirty-five minutes later, over her desiccated beef curry that had spent easily a week in the fridge, I confirmed that the original broadcast had had no gap in it. At first glance, it contained nothing interesting. Which was why I gave it a second glance.

The camera pans from Terry's mother back to the hearse—it had arrived late, remember?—where the casket is being off-loaded. Just past her shoulder, up the street, at the very top of the screen, a lone car sits parked, and it appears to have a single occupant, in the driver's seat. Mrs. Letizzle's shoulder, however, blocks the lower part of the car and the license plate. The camera, trained on the coffin being wheeled towards the church doors, again passes over the car; this is the one-second gap in the station's video. Now the car is fully visible—except its occupant, who has disappeared. And nobody is anywhere near the car. Obviously, whoever was inside was ducking down.

An hour later, I was at WCMS-TV with Mrs. Letizzle's tape, where Hank kindly interrupted the frenzied work on the five-thirty report to snag a film technician for me. For an hour, LaVonne Dohle worked on the key frames while I vomited Mrs. Letizzle's beef curry into the men's toilet.

She also explained to me about the gap in the station film. If not a mechanical error, it was due to someone erasing it. The public can ask to see and record the station's six-month archives—for example, when some charity needs footage of its work in order to raise funds. The only condition is that the tapes stay in the station's viewing room. But the VCR in the viewing room has a recording function, and it would have been easy as pie to erase 1.2 seconds of tape without anyone noticing. Unfortunately, the station kept no records of people asking to see broadcasts. No one remembered Laura.

The results of LaVonne's work were not terrific, but sufficient: one person of white skin and neck-length dark hair was in the car, though nothing more was certain. The license plate, however, was clearer.

Among the four possibilities that she would swear to was HKR 173. This, according to the state licensing authorities, was the plate number of Laura's car at the time. The car model, a full-bodied Volkswagen Passat, was reasonably similar to the silhouette of the car in the image.

At last.

Now that I had a solid dent in Laura's story, I rented a deposit box in the nearest bank and locked up the video, LaVonne's photo enlargements and a brief, written explanation in case I never lived to see them. Paranoid? You bet. I was on the lookout for Laura's agents. I even made a blazing fool of myself in front of a restaurant lavatory with a well-dressed executive who asked me to hold her purse while she put on her suit jacket; and who has since raised her estimate of the number of nut-cases running around this crazy old world. Laugh if you want; any danger can look peachy-keen in hindsight.

At any rate, the good break on the video brought back my confidence; that night I ordered a steak the size of a life raft and moistened it with a bottle of red wine that cost me the royalties of ten books. I had proof in hand of two basic points: Laura's acute sense of guilt over Terry, and her willingness to lie. The latter meant I could stretch for another, riskier theory—about the Gotchell dressing-room videotape. It would wrinkle Phyllis Kirk's credibility, but tear Laura's straight down the middle.

The problem was that Phyllis liked her credibility smooth. So I used two precious days to prepare the ground for my final interview with her. I flew to Minneapolis—again daring the terrorists, but that day it was the turn of the poor folks in the Detroit traffic jam, wasn't it?—and picked up my old campaign notebooks.

By phone I tracked down and questioned a few staffers who had worked under Phyllis, flew to Washington and had a cup of coffee in the Watergate Hotel just to soak up the atmosphere, flew to Columbus, and in an exorbitant hotel suite pored over my copy of each campaign's log—that is, Gotchell's and Frakes'. I had one shot at Phyllis, and I had to get it right.

After some thought, I chose Phyllis' house for the encounter. In the first place, because I needed to charge her all at once. I didn't want the interruption of the office phone to pull her out of the emergency I was about to drown her in. Second, if my suggestion of a casual interview at home warmed the chance of the Ultimate Sexual Experience With a Bestselling Author, so much the better: my first task was to get her off balance. It would only help matters if I doused her desire with a bucket of water first.

Her Columbus mansion was as big as Mount Everest, of course, if not bigger. I arrived at eight-thirty on a Tuesday, and in the dark it looked like a hulk of ivy with circumspect yellow windows peeping on the driveway. Its surface was gravel, which made a rich, starchy crunch under the wheels of my rented Porsche. I wanted to give Phyllis the illusion that this was Sam The Nouveau Riche, who now had Nouveau morals, too.

Phyllis had come out in a grand, frilly bathrobe and leaned herself against the pillar of the porch and was flapping her curly perm around with a hand. "Well, Sam, my goodness! What a few million in sales will do for a man!"

I shut the Porsche's thick, confident door. "If you can't guzzle a little gas in your life, Phyllis, what's it all about?" I said, locking the car out of habit, though in the security man's booth at the gate, two automatic rifles stood at attention like Dobermans.

"Absolutely, Sam. Ditto, ditto."

Phyllis bounced off the pillar and threw her arms round my neck and kissed me. I kissed back—it seemed proper that she got one decent gesture out of the evening. "Great to see you again, Phyllis. You're looking fantastic."

"Fantastic and *alone*, Sam. The help is off tonight, so you have me at your mercy."

"You'll pay for *that* mistake," I purred because I meant it.

She winked. "I did it on purpose."

"Naughty you."

I had been in her house once before, at a political cocktail just after her candidate—Governor Frakes, remember him?—had breezed to victory in the Ohio primaries.

It was what you would expect of a divorced airline exec too busy to decorate for herself: lots of stripes and overstuffed sofas and chairs upholstered in fabric made in Italy. Tables as heavy as train cars lined the walls, covered with pictures here and antique musical instruments there. The table by the front window supported a bath-sized tropical aquarium with oodles of clown fish in it. Soft music wafted from speakers as big as washing machines, tastefully hidden in the corners; atop one lay a hand-sized teddy bear, and I remembered that Phyllis must be a grandmother. The liquor cabinet stood to one side full of all manner of sinister bottles; in front of the fireplace, unlit and dark, the coffee table displayed carefully laid magazines. *Playboy* was one, for why shouldn't a modern, progressive woman read *Playboy?*

And in a gesture to homey hospitality, the busy airline exec herself had assembled a tray with a decanter and tumblers and ice and chip and dip; also a fist-sized jar of Vaseline, lest vigorous conversation should turn into Matters of Force Majeure.

I took all of this in as I slipped out my new toy: a tiny and very expensive tape recorder guaranteed to pick up a hiccup across a Saturday-morning bowling alley. Passing the table with the musical instruments, I hit the Record button and slipped the thing between a french horn and a redwood clarinet with gold-leaf keys. Then I wove through the overstuffedness to the coffee table, where I noisily dropped ice into tumblers.

Meanwhile Phyllis was turning off computers and lifting phones off hooks and making a last fluff at her fluffy perm and finally swishing into the room, lace flying. There's nothing like an entrance.

"So, Sam, how is our rising star of investigative journalism? I trust that you are *disrobing* with cruel defiance the high and mighty of the land?"

"Yeah, and getting disrobed at the same time," I answered, dangling one last hope before her.

She looked at me, pleased. "How lovely," she said in a low voice. "Doesn't practice make it ever so perfect?"

"You can say that again. Is that one finger or two, Phyllis?"

"Give it two for starters, and we'll see how the night progresses."

I poured two for her and two for me, handed her one and took the other.

She raised her glass. "Cheers—may our ships pass and re-pass in the night."

I smiled, nodded, sipped and dumped the cold water over her. "They won't. Unless you plan on coming clean with me about the 'Gotcha' Gotchell videotape."

Phyllis, to give her credit, did not even break her rhythm; she took an extra sip of whisky and swirled it around her mouth. "Coming clean? Sam, whatever have I got to—"

To my tone, I now added a deceived man's bitterness. "Tell you a story, Phyllis. This rumor about Laura and me that's going round? You've heard it, no doubt?"

"What? That you wished to be the first to try the fruits of Laura's new face? Sam, my god, we're *friends.* Don't think *I*—"

"That's the one," I interrupted her. "I went to Washington a few days ago and had a little chat with Laura about it. She wouldn't receive me in her White House office, of course; I'm just a hack. But she condescended to a cup of coffee at the Watergate. Which turned out to be appropriate." Another gulp of whisky to open the floodgates of glibness. "I ask Laura what it's all about, she says she's sorry, it was a comment she made that was blown all out of proportion."

"What comment might that be?"

"In some cocktail party. She told some people that after I grilled her in her apartment, quote: 'Sam was really sweet to me afterwards.' Which is true—I made her some soup. Seemed the least I could do for someone bawling her head off. I didn't mention it in *The Saddest Election,* though—didn't seem important."

"So what does—"

"Hang on, hang on. Anyway, the usual cocktail party dumbass asked if the sweetness involved carnal delights, and Laura just laughed it off—when she should have stomped on it with both feet. And that got the ball rolling."

"So what did—"

"Let me finish!" I snapped. "All right, we're in the Watergate, and Laura tells me she's sorry about the rumor, right? Apologizes, says she'll put out a statement if I want. Miss Congeniality."

"Well, you did rather launch her White House career—why not?" Phyllis muttered.

"And then Laura, all contrite—you know how she gets—figures she's going to give me a little consolation prize." I wetted my tongue. "Which, before I go on, brings me to a question. Very straight, very clear here, Phyllis. Yes or no: That video of Gotchell in the dressing room with a woman? The one you showed your staffers at the party and then destroyed? *Did* you make a copy of it, after all?"

A few seconds earlier, Phyllis had concluded that the night was not going to be as sensual as planned. She had lowered her tumbler till she held it by the rim, her arm straight down. She might have been explaining poor quarterly results to angry shareholders.

"Of course I didn't, Sam. I told you everything I could. I saw it and I got rid of it."

"Well, that's too bad for you, Phyllis. Because now you're in big trouble. Because Laura told me the truth about the video. Something you should have told me a long time ago and that really puts a new turn on my story."

"Why? It's her word against mine: I say it existed, she says it didn't. So fucking what? I'm not going to put up with—"

"What?" I dropped my glass from my lips. "No. No—that's not it at all. Laura says that the woman Gotchell pulled into his dressing room was *you.*"

Shock and dismay brighten the face of our airline executive. Her tight mouth has wrinkles orbiting around it, and the spidery tendons of her neck jump to attention.

After sundry sputterings: "That's the most ridiculous thing I ever heard! You couldn't sell a bullshit story like that to—"

I didn't let her get in another word; I had to drive the story through her like a sword. "Phyllis, *Phyllis:* Is it really bullshit? Is it really? It certainly makes everything fit together: why you didn't make a copy—which seems to me and everyone else incredible; why you didn't slip the media a copy when OutFrakes destroyed your candidate."

Then Phyllis laughed, tilting her bony face up to the ceiling and making her broad curls flop backwards. "Of me with Alan Gotchell? Marvelous! And let everyone in on the secret? Sam, this is really—"

"Oh, come *on*, Phyllis. For morbid motive we're not exactly hurting, are we?" I clinked my ice at her lacy bathrobe. "Phyllis Kirk certainly likes a good roll in the hay. Not too particular about the whos and whys and wheres. And what better high than with Alan Gotchell, the opposition candidate? Oh, that must give some orgasm, Phyllis: the ultimate treason. And from there, we get into all kinds of ramifications."

I would have articulated these—I had lots thought up—but Phyllis threw her drink in my face and screamed at me to shut up. The ice cubes stung like hell; one hit me just over my left eye and would leave a bruise. I just managed not to do the same, figuring this would give me an advantage.

Phyllis strode around, then whirled. "That is the most, most *stinking, disgusting, conniving* bullshit that I have ever heard! How can a responsible person like you believe bullshit like that? And from *her?*"

"*How?* Well, since you asked..." I was trying to wipe off my face on my short sleeves and gripping my left temple. The whisky burned in my eyes. But I didn't want to let up. "You're right, Phyllis. I *am* a responsible person and I *don't* believe everything people tell me, especially when they come from Laura. And especially when she's talking about someone she has no great love for. So I checked the facts. That's what I've been doing for five days and nights: checking facts."

"Which are?" Phyllis said.

"One: the campaign logs." I fished in the crystal bowl for an ice cube and pressed it to my eye. "It turns out that the only time you and Gotchell were in the same city at the same time before the general campaign was on March twenty-fourth during the primaries. In North Carolina. So I went to Charlotte to see the basketball arena where Gotchell spoke. Building manager remembered his coming and showed me around. We found his dressing room. And it turns out Laura was right, Phyllis—the camera angle was looking straight *into* the dressing room because it's at the end of a hallway and there's no hallway on either side."

"Oh, is that so?" Phyllis said with a laugh. "Well, what excellent detective work, Sam. I *am* impressed. That's worth—"

"Two: Greg Wright—ring a bell? Assistant press agent?"

"Of course I remember Greg. We enjoyed several vivid fucks in several dull hotel rooms."

Which was why I had selected Greg, as well as for his presence at the nomination-night video fest.

"Well, your lover didn't want to say anything at the time, but he thought he recognized you in the video. He was sitting there stoned beside Laura Prestini—at that post-nomination party where you gave the one showing? He told me the memory was hazy, he wasn't even sure it was Gotchell; but he did remember a grainy vid and a certain well-kept ass he knew."

"Sam, that's hardly—"

"Right. So Greg wisely stayed mum. But I tracked him down yesterday. He lives in Kansas City now, writes birthday card jingles for Hallmark. I told him what Laura told me and, to make a lot of prodding short, he *now* says that if Laura is willing to go on the record first, he'll confirm. It was you."

Phyllis stared at me. "This is getting into complete idiocy! This is—" She stopped. She seized the belt of her bathrobe and gave it a harrowing tug. "These people...These people are so completely full of *bullshit.*"

"Maybe they are, Phyllis, maybe they are. But I am right now re-writing a big section of the sixth edition of *The Saddest Election*, and believe you me, it will read differently than the fifth."

"You mean you're just going to take what these, these shit-for-brains say at face value? Sam, what the hell's gotten into you?"

I was holding an ice cube against the upper socket of my left eye, and I think now it was the only thing that kept it from swelling shut the next day. "All right, Phyllis, all right: *your* side of it, then. Pay no attention to the whisky you see dripping down my shirt here; I'm all ears. And don't even *bother* going back to your original story, got it? I'm not interested."

"Well, no..." She was walking in circles between the fireplace and the coffee table. She made a last stab: "But why would I show them a video if I knew I was in it?"

"That one's given *me* a lot to think about, too. Vanity? Pure foolishness? Showing off your trophy? Figuring nobody would believe the story anyway? And certainly Gotchell was the star of the film, not the girl. Who knows? That question doesn't interest me at the moment."

Phyllis licked her lips. Her neck tendons stood up like a mesh.

"C'mon, Phyllis, give it up. This is your one chance, though I don't know how—"

"All right! Shut up! All right!" She untied and tied the belt still tighter till it bit into her ribs. All the while, she searched the carpet for a trap door that she could escape through. "Oh for Chrissakes…" She breathed heavily, like a sprinter at the end of the race.

"Tick-tock-tick-tock," I sang.

In a tiny, disembodied voice, as from an evil spirit: "Shut the fuck up. This isn't a courtroom; it's not like I'm up for a libel charge or anything. I don't have to say anything."

"Fine. I'll send you a new copy of my book." I headed for the door. "You can just throw the old one out. It's not worth a—"

"No, no, no, Sam. That's not what I meant. *No,*" she moaned. I turned, and from across the room she looked very much her age, elongated, bending slowly like an inverted U over the coffee table and pouring herself a new drink into my former glass. Then she grasped it by the rim and labored to a more-or-less upright posture.

I shrugged: Well?

"There was no video. Okay? There never was. Laura is a liar. *I'm* a liar."

I waited.

"I wasn't given any tape, and I never saw any. You told me in my office that day that Laura had seen it at the post-convention bash." A gulp. "So I ran with it. I ran with it. Why not? I'd already run a losing campaign we should have won easily, and I thought I'd make a little mileage: 'Yes, I'd seen it; I showed it to the kids, and I threw the tape away because I believe in democracy and fair play.' It sounded great, and why not? I would've, anyway."

Which was just what I'd suspected. Laura trafficked in rumors— about Gotchell in the dressing room, about me, about whatever served her purpose.

"I see," I said slowly. "Well, that certainly explains why you never turned it over to the media."

"Doesn't it, though," Phyllis muttered into her glass. She poured the rest of the whisky down her throat and pointed a shaky finger at me. "You put what I've told you in your book, Sam—it's the truth. I want to see how that bitch weasels out of this one. Or better yet—go back and ask her point-blank, cameras rolling."

I nodded. "That would sure be the best thing," I said, walking to the table with the musical instruments. I picked the recorder from between the clarinet and the french horn. "But I can't. Laura's always refused to talk to me again since the book came out. No follow-ups, no nothing. Complete stonewall. Bye, Phyllis."

And before her shining stupefaction, I hit the Stop button and walked out.

Still, there was no joy in Mudville. I now had to face the country and admit that my account of The Miracle Election of President Mitchell Taylor had steered them all wrong. I wondered if America would be as forgiving with me as with Laura.

And as you can see by this website with the revised story, I'm still wondering. Fate had one last elbow to throw at me.

19 The prologue I wrote for the sixth edition is a short version of what you are reading on this website. The present text intends to revive memories and put events into context with the ending of the Taylor Administration; and of course, my key interview with Rolf Obermeyer and the spying incident involving Mrs. Evans and the tetchy Brad Bailey have not appeared before.

Three days after my showdown with Phyllis, I called Walt Greene-Halver at the publishing house and told him I would be in his office the next morning at nine with the prologue.

"Bring Janine and be prepared for a headache," I added.

At eleven-thirty, I was still sipping tea and awaiting their verdict. I spent most of the time scanning the isle of the Manhattoes from the thirty-ninth floor of one of those monstrous, mute shafts that Naima's brothers love postcards of; they must have a dozen by now, all tacked up on the walls of their bedrooms. The coffee-break room was silent. Now and then a line editor dashed in, filled her cup, and dashed back to whatever profit her labors were eroding. A scattering of plastic cups lay across the tables and chairs like the dead after battle. They gave off a cloying fug—not unlike the publishing industry itself.

My cell phone hummed, and I pulled it out of my pocket: Naima.

"How are things, Sam? Did you had your meeting with Walt and Janine?" said Naima in English, which she was still trying to perfect.

"They're still reading it," I said, glancing at my watch. "We started a little late." Only five minutes late; I hadn't expected them to take two-and-a-half hours over ninety-four double-spaced pages. Naima turned to French, which we habitually used for important matters. "I just wanted to tell you that I'm sorry about yesterday, Sam. This is very important to you, and it's okay if we have to go back to the way we were living. We've had a good time being rich. I just don't want to see you doing silly translation jobs again. But for me, it's okay."

"Yesterday" meant our argument about the revelations in the prologue and the likelihood that Laura would sue me and the whole country pelt me with eggs; even my writing career could be in jeopardy.

But why bother with the truth, Sam? she'd said. *Public life is the same everywhere; it is tradition more than anything else. It's like King Mohammed the Sixth of Morocco. Nobody elected him; people only care that he was the son of Hassan the Second. That's enough for them; and if tradition said that the person with the longest legs in Marrakech would always be the next king, it would be the same. It is the tradition. Here in America, the tradition is a legal tradition. Legally, Taylor won, right? People accept this, even if one person changed the entire election. And people like him and they love his daughter with her big ass. Well, that is enough. And Laura Prestini? She is untouchable. She is still America's Honestest Woman, an 'example to youth everywhere.' This has turned into public truth. The political class will not be happy if you question it.*

"In the worst case," she went on now, "we can always sell the house. It is noisy to cut the grass every week, anyway. I think I prefer apartments. You only need to clean the windows on the weekend. Then you can take a walk and have a drink in a café." The careless Moroccan tone in her words brought tears to my eyes.

"Well, we'll see how it goes," I said.

"Okay, *bonne chance, cherie!*"

I hung up and looked at my watch. Walt was supposed to call me in, but enough was enough. *He* had been the one whining for "mustard" on the sixth-edition sales; if it turned out to be Dijon mustard and burned his tongue, too bad. I walked to his office, for my mother's sake knocked politely, and went in.

It was proudly spacious, done over in what Walt called an "honest-wood" motif: the cherry desk, oak floor, and pine lamp stands all done in natural woods. It would have looked great in Arlen Barrington's chalet, but in a steel-and-glass building, it struck me as faintly crazy, almost a joke. Awards lined a wall like hunting trophies, along with a picture of an electrically happy Walt shaking hands with Saul Bellow. The carved mahogany pencil can on the desk displayed an arsenal of yellow pencils topped by fleshy erasers, with a few light-blue galley-editing pencils mixed in, just to show you that Walt could actually use them like old-time editors.

Walt and Janine sat on one of the rustic sofas conferring, Walt as far from the smoke of Janine's stinking hand-rolled cigarettes as he could get.

"Well?" I said. "Pretty strange turnaround, huh?"

"*Strange* is a many-splendored word, Sam," said Janine with a tremor of aggressiveness, and blew a huge cloud of smoke as if daring me to object to either her observation or her smoking; that Walt permitted it was, I think, the symbol of her editorial prestige in the company. Her long hair was stiff; the gray had collected on it in clumps, like the yellow on her fingers. She wore a dull-pink dress, voluminous like a hospital gown, and expensive low-heeled shoes. Her glasses that day were a frameless single pane that covered the middle third of her face. Their pink tint matched the dress.

Walt had recently grown a mustache, which he now stroked with Grave Reflection. "Indeed," he said—a very pointed, British "indeed." He got up and offered me a drink, and with shock I recognized the mossy rites of rejection.

"But *strange* is what life's all about," Janine said. "That's part of why I do books: to record the strangeness."

"I'm in it to record the truth," I said, firing my first shot, and not across the bow. "And the fact that the truth is not A but B is something that needs to be recorded. And published."

"Yes, but what is truth?" cried Janine. "In part it's what everybody agrees on, right? I mean, just because you say the sky is blue doesn't mean it is. It's an observation that needs corroboration before it becomes a truth." To Walt, giggling (and did I hear a British accent?): "Oh, gosh, that sentence re-e-ely does need a spot of work, doesn't it?"

I went on: "That's why I put in months digging up—"

"Shall we cut to the proverbial chase, Sam?" said Walt. He tested his martini cautiously as if it were thin ice he was about to step on. "We can't use it, old man. Totally out of the question."

"Not a question of can or can't, Walt. As I said right in the first line, 'In the light of new evidence, another interpretation of the available facts is—'"

"'Necessary and appropriate,'" Janine finished with a placating nod I resented. "Your problem is that the case you make is utterly circumstantial. The first part is based totally on two questionable observations: that Laura Prestini attended Terry's funeral and that she tried to bury some hatchet with him a few weeks after the election. Then there's something about a video box with a suitcase alarm in it that *nobody* understands."

I stared. By now I was sitting on the sofa facing her, the heavy chestnut coffee table between us. The pages of my prologue lay on top, face-down in a sloppy pile amidst the ghosts of glass rings on the wood. "'Some hatchet'? What do you mean, 'some hatchet'?"

"Sam, we're *reasonable* here," Walt reminded me in a schoolteacher's sing-song.

"Janine, it's not like she had a little fender-bender with him; she was trying to apologize for ruining his life, and Terry wasn't buying it. He knew the story would almost surely come out and that he was as exposed as a duck in a barrel. And he knew that Laura, who can play the media like a violin, had written herself in for the heroine-defender of democracy and Terry the turncoat."

"'Surely,'" Janine mused and lit another cigarette. "*Almost* surely."

"*Almost* is the word for the whole essay, Sam," Walt said, bending to the coffee table and picking through the stack of paper as if it were dirty laundry. "Then there's the other part: that the Gotchell-in-the-dressing-room tape probably never even existed?"

"'Probably'—there's that word again," said Janine, though I hadn't heard it before. "Phyllis was *probably* telling the truth about the tape? Frankly, between her and Laura, I know where my vote goes."

"Then how do you—" I began.

Janine: "Has it occurred to you, Sam, that we might be dealing with *two* tapes?"

"*Two?* How do you figure two?"

"Easy. One that Phyllis made up that never existed, and one that did, that Laura Prestini actually saw and knew about?" Janine gave me a triumphant smile, which I gladly would have slapped off.

"That's completely....I won't, I won't even argue about that. If Laura saw it, so did other people."

"But possibly," Janine said, blowing a new cloud that her possibility inhabited, "only Laura saw it and put it away in the video files where she could get it. I mean, maybe there's something even the great Sam didn't—"

"Janine, that's utterly ridiculous."

Walt: "Sam, we're—"

"All right, all right! I'll humor you, Janine." Though I knew I was taking a dangerous step downwards. "With her own dressing-room video she could have sunk Gotchell and promoted herself in the Frakes campaign—with no risk, and she wouldn't have needed Terry at all. And self-promotion was the idea, right from the start."

"But what *was* the start, actually, re-e-e-elly, Sam?" Janine pleaded, definitely using Walt's British accent. "I mean, that's the whole thing. There's not even a start to your—"

"Yes, there is. There very much is," I snapped, tapping the pages. "Page three, if I'm not mistaken: the reporters' crisis in Indianapolis, when Laura blew up at her campaign's top execs. That was the start. Phyllis said she would never hire Laura on at the White House, and Laura took her literally. That's why Laura was so amazed when I told her that Phyllis had spoken highly of her work."

Janine started to speak, but Walt held up the hand that signed her salary increases. "So we're saying, in short—just to put this in context for all of us, Sam—that from that point on, Laura was out for revenge."

"Right. Laura figured that if *she* wasn't going to the White House, then neither was anybody else. Problem was, she couldn't stand the idea of Gotchell getting the White House, either. Remember how she talked about him in *The Saddest Election*? I *think* I'm quoting here: 'Gotchell is a vicious bastard—a congenital liar all throughout his career, and not only about sex.' She knocked him off *first*—to be sure he was out of the way. Her modus operandi? The well-placed rumor."

"Explain yourself, old boy," Walt interrupted.

I'd already explained it in the prologue, but I did it again:

"In the ten days or so following the reporters crisis, Laura stopped by campaign HQ in Columbus twice. On one of those occasions—probably the first, but the security video on those dates doesn't show anything—she put the Squeel-EE alarm she'd already been using into a video box. This was just in case the false security i.d. she gave Terry didn't do the trick to alert the guards. Around the same time, she started a rumor about the existence of a Gotchell-in-the-dressing-room videotape and just let it cook. The rest was easy. She called Terry and told him where to find the 'Gotcha' video; she figured Terry would go for it himself. Get it? Gotchell's *bodyman* makes the snatch. How could the orders come from anyone *except* Gotchell? Turns out Jover did the deed, but it didn't matter much. Once Terry took the bait, everything played itself out, and Gotchell had a major scandal on his hands."

Walt smoothed his mustache again. "Which made Terry doubly eager to even the score once he found the OutFrakes video in his hot little hands."

Janine frowned.

Why so much resistance? I was wondering. The prologue would surely send my book back to the bestseller lists. That was Walt's only real concern—that and taking the credit. The one catching hell before the public would be me.

"Right," I said. "And good-bye to Frakes' candidacy. Laura left it all arranged for some post-election writer to investigate and make her out the heroine who was just trying to keep the elections fair." For Janine's benefit, I added, "And that part of it is as clear as water."

"Clear? I'd call it more like absolutely preposterous!" Janine said, and Walt sighed, hearing his stomach grumble.

"Really?" I counted it out for her. "One: I've uncovered Laura's little pantomime sticking the putative Gotchell video in her suitcase in front of the security guard. Two: I've got—"

"Wasn't that just marvelous when she nipped that guard on the cheek?" Walt interrupted with an alcoholic chuckle, and I reached for another jar of patience.

"Two: I've got the key copies—all of the same key and otherwise useless—that she used as props, which prove that her whole security-tape comedy was really just a grab for the Squeel-EE. Three—"

"Keys that you say she needed in order to put something metal on the counter," said Janine. "You see, Sam, that's another one. It's not only circumstantial, it's sheer speculation: it doesn't make a flying bit of sense."

I stared at her helplessly. "Why the hell not?"

"Don't you think a ring with the exact same keys would have looked pretty funny to the guard standing right across the counter?"

I was starting to wonder if I was dealing with an adult. "Janine, the guard was busy looking down her shirt. The indentations of her keys were not a high priority."

"Not the indentations, the type of key!" Janine said triumphantly. "None of those keys were round, none were car keys. That could well catch his attention."

"Catch his attention? What kind of..." I looked to Walt for help, but he merely watched me flatly as he would a movie screen. I struggled for calm. "So, so what other reason would she have for carrying so many copies in her jacket pocket?"

Janine shrugged happily. "Hairy great masses of reasons!" she cried, using another Britishism. "Maybe she found them around the airport."

"She *bought* them, Janine," I said heavily. "I have the receipt, remember?"

But Janine was campaigning for her heroine. "Fine. Maybe she intended to distribute the copies later on. Sam, do you seriously call this hard evidence?"

"Yes, I do. Actually I would say the key business nails her to the wall pretty goddamn firmly."

Janine sniffed and adjusted her colossal pink glasses.

I moved on, fast, though I felt like a straggler in the desert being steadily ground down by the sun. "Three, I've got Phyllis Kirk saying that there was no dressing-room footage at all of Gotchell with a woman. Four, I've got Arlen Barrington saying he covered for Laura. Five, I've got Laura for sure at Terry's funeral when she denied it. What else—"

"Which is again circumstantial," Janine said. "How many times do I—"

"Circumstantial but very strong, Janine."

"Oh, this is all…" snapped Janine, shaking her head and long hair. "Bottom line is, Laura Prestini just isn't that kind of person."

I gave a hard, tiny laugh; it just burbled out of me. "Oh, and I suppose you know her personally? You've seen her on TV, Janine, that's all, just like the rest of us. You probably cried with her, too."

"I don't find her suffering a bit funny."

"Her suffering—Jesus!" I didn't know what to do. I appealed to their vanity. "C'mon! This is Manhattan. You're smart, articulate, well-read, thinking people. You're a cut above the rest. Don't tell me you're buying the same cream puff as the guys at the truck stop."

"Oh, what difference does it make?" Janine growled. "Look, we have a great, new president. He's fun, he's smart, and after all, he did win the vote."

Then I blew up. "This woman rigged an American presidential election!" I shouted. "And you're going to let her get away with that?"

Janine screamed back. "I'm not going to rock boats just because a woman—it's always a woman, isn't it?—this wonderful woman was nice enough to forgive and forget and go to an old friend's funeral! To offer to buy him a drink and bury the hatchet! Doesn't that itself prove that she's the most decent woman in this whole fucked-up country?"

"All right, now let's calm the fuck down!" said Walt. "Bloody hell, Sam, you need a drink." And over my objections, he made one for me and yet another for himself, which was the whole point.

During this time I said nothing. I went to the window and let my eyes wander: a garbage truck charged like a madman into an intersection far below, making me catch my breath till it cleared the other side. On a freeway, the stream of cars raced like blood through the veins. The puttering report of a jackhammer heckled somewhere out of sight. A pallet loaded with sacks of cement soared up fifty stories on the strands of a crane and settled atop yet another Manhattan skyscraper. On the horizon, an airliner arrowed upwards. It was a busy country.

"So in short," Walt said, noisily mixing the drinks, "your theory is that she planned this whole thing—don't interrupt me—planned for you to catch her up, planned to confess to you her 'innocent mistake,' planned to be made to look ridiculous once your book came out, planned her mea culpa campaign, planned her attempted suicide, planned to gain public sympathy and rise to the heights she's reached?"

I smiled grimly. "Don't forget the topless segment in the pool."

"Oh, that is such chauvinist…" Janine snarled, but her snarl lacked force because she was unable to summon a noun.

"And end up America's Honestest Woman," Walt finished.

"Right. Exactly right; probably things have worked out better than she'd imagined." I reined in my voice because anger would sink me. "Don't you see? It's love on the rebound, the prodigal daughter returned to the family and given a feast. She made a mistake, we forgave her, and now we feel great about it. That's why she blew a bundle of money on her nose before taking the plunge: because it's easy to be sympathetic, not to mention noble, to a pretty woman. Simple as that. The country's taking terrorist attacks, the economy is soft, people are under a lot of pressure, so Laura has moved up next to George Washington."

Walt delivered my drink to me and sat down again, inviting me to sit as well. I stayed where I was. I wanted their surrender first, or at least a willingness to listen.

Janine picked up one of the last pages of the prologue and scanned it. "'Laura Prestini's downfall was not her nerve or vision, but her guilty conscience,'" she quoted. "What is this, Sam? Trailer-park psychology?"

"She has a crucifix in her apartment that would scare away crows."

"So does the bloody Pope!" Walt cracked. "So much for that theory!"

I looked at them, laughing like squirrels on the fence. Why, why, why were they defending her?

"There's nothing funny about it," I said, drawing cries of "spoilsport" and "party-pooper." "Her acts are perfectly consistent with a guilty conscience."

"Why?" Janine demanded.

Anger seized me again. "Goddammit, didn't you even finish that?" I growled, pointing at the pile of paper. "Laura's from an old-fashioned Catholic family. Her father is a lifer bureaucrat, her mother's never worked outside the home, her brother is studying to enter the Church. What do you think that means? That she's never been inside a confession box? That she's a little fuzzy on what's right and wrong?

Like hell. Laura lost her head when Phyllis Kirk said she wasn't going to the White House. Laura's big dream up in smoke. Her—"

"Conjecture," said Janine like a bored attorney.

"Her ambition got away with her, and before she knew it, she'd mucked up a whole presidential election. Then she had some kind of spasm of bad conscience and tried to rationalize it all to Terry Letizzle and wanted his forgiveness, and he wouldn't give it."

"To the chase, Sam, to the chase," said Walt tiredly. "I'm really getting—"

"Here's your chase, Walt," I snapped. "Here's the last five pages, which you'd do well to look over before you shove me out the door. Laura tried to make up with Terry; I'd bet anything she tried to convince him that she would bring him into the story as a hero of democracy just like herself. But he wasn't about to play ball. Later, seeing the writing on the wall when I showed up at his door, he committed suicide. So she went to his funeral. And all for what? Don't you see it? Doesn't it slap you in the face?"

"Gosh, I guess not," Janine said innocently.

"Shut up!" I shouted, and this made both of them jump. "Because she owed God penance! *Huge* penance! Probably she'd promised Him one right from the start. She was doing penance for contributing to Terry's suicide: she was risking being recognized at the funeral, which would've trashed her whole plan. Get it? Just the phrase I quoted from her book: *Creative Penance.*"

Janine grinned. "People only do penance for the IRS anymore, Sam."

She stopped because I'd whipped my still-full martini glass at them, and only barely managed to aim it over their heads so that it shattered against a window and smeared Walt's view of upper Broadway.

"For the love of Christ!" I shouted. "Didn't you read what Hopkins said about Terry in the bar? He turned his back on her! And Laura Prestini—*the* Laura Prestini—who has her own government agency, who kisses movie stars and adorns the covers of a half-dozen magazines every month—*that* Laura Prestini ran around the other side still trying to convince him. Get it? She groveled! Laura Prestini groveled! And when Terry wouldn't forgive her, she ran out of the place in tears! Doesn't that say anything at all to you? This is goddamn Lady MacBeth here! How else could she make such a convincing show of regret on those interviews? Christ alive—it was self-flagellation! She practically had *me* in tears! Now would somebody please tell me *what the fuck is going on around here?*"

An elegant, bored silence. Neither one looked at the broken glass; they were probably thinking it was the latest Cool thing and they ought to try it sometime in a meeting.

Finally, with an I've-heard-enough-of-this sigh, Walt re-smoothed his mustache, stood, picked up the pages of the prologue and slipped them into the file jacket. "All right, Sam, all right. Bottom-line time. This is what I will do. I myself will take this down to Legal. The lawyers will read it with a magnifying glass, and if we can put it in the sixth edition under the heading of, 'Another Interpretation' or something equally neutral, fine: in it goes. If not, I'm sorry."

"So you're telling me that none of this—"

Janine interrupted stridently from the sofa. "Sam! That's fair. It's their call, and especially in this time of total, utter terrorism in the nation it is all anyone is willing to do against America's newest and brightest star. And I do not mean you."

Walt sloshed a fresh wad of martini into his mouth and gulped it down, sadly watching my wasted drink running down his window. Then he put down his drink, came over to me and dipped his head by mine.

"But I do think, Sam," he said softly, "that under the circumstances, we would do best to simply enjoy that three-point-something million in royalties we've made, and not advertise too loudly that we might well have obtained it by playing mouthpiece to a fraud." A hard smile that I did not return. "I mean, let's be just a wee bit realistic, shall we?"

"So you think—" I began.

Walt tapped my ribs with the folder. "I will wait for the lawyers' decision, Sam—Uncle Walt's word on that now—but I think the bottom line here reads: 'This is inappropriate.'"

Waiting for the elevator under the indignant gaze of the receptionist whose copy of *The Saddest Election* I had refused to autograph, I looked over the publishing group's huge, pompous logo. It was a single theater mask—the grinning one—white edged in gold. Beneath, in gold letters on purple like the roll of members in a club, were the many imprints of the group, and I wondered if any of them had standards higher than that of a comic book, or editors that—

My eye stopped at the penultimate on the list: Saint Linus Children's Books. It was Laura's publisher for *Standing Tall*, which every shiny-faced schoolkid would read that autumn.

"You bitch," I whispered. "You ungodly, clever bitch."

20 The lawyers, of course, screamed bloody murder. I asked Walt and Janine to cancel new editions of *The Saddest Election*, but Walt said the sixth was already steaming ahead, and coldly hinted that big money and big lawyers could get involved if I raised hell. In compensation, he promised to head off any call for a seventh edition. He did this, although months later he and Janine tried to wine and dine me, to get me to agree to the seventh. I took a page from Terry's book and turned my back on them.

For a frantic June, I contacted publishing houses, starting with the majors and working down. Nobody would touch it. Several people went as far as to read the manuscript—a one-third-shorter version of what you have here—and request copies of photos and footage to examine, but all of them rejected. Walt's "inappropriate" was "delicate" in one house, "definitely non-PC" in another, "not our kind of thing" in another, "unappropriate" in another, and "just totally beyond us" in another that had published *Trash Talk with Al Smokel* and that I was foolish to try at all.

The editor added this gem: "At this so-not-pleasant juncture in our national security situation, to knock a major national figure off her stature would not be in the best interests of the American people."

Another editor, in rejecting by phone, took the opportunity to bawl me out for spoiling Laura's reputation: "How dare you tear down this country's national heroes!" she cried, and hung up.

But my favorite was this one, from a major Los Angeles firm: "While we are in sympathy with your passion to publish a spellbinding new take on your book and all the monetary rewards accruing thereto, we are not comfortable dealing in frameworks that cast doubt on our nation's electoral processees, and all that concerns our sacred national duty."

And at least half of them at one point or another used the phrase "conspiracy theory."

I wondered about calling a press conference. I called a veteran, street-wise TV reporter in Minneapolis who had interviewed me and e-mailed him the prologue with Naavy Thao's photos of the keys, which nearly everyone requested. He read it and called me the next day.

"You've got it uphill, man," he said. "Yeah, you're right, the keys really lay this bitch bare. You know and I know it. But what are you going to do once the cameras start rolling? Hold up a glossy B-and-W of door keys?"

"I was thinking of displaying a blow-up on an easel, actually."

He laughed at that; I didn't know why. "Yeah, yeah, yeah, they're important, I grant you. But that's not the issue. To understand *why* they're important, you've got to build the whole story around them: that they prove she planned all that sequence in front of the security counter, that she bought them *just for that,* which means she was trying for a certain effect during it, to communicate certain self-evident truths, blah-blah-blah. And *that's why,* good citizens, her claim about the vid mix-up is false. And then someone will pipe up about motives—story's no good without that—and then you're into the Indianapolis thing and Laura getting pissed off with her boss, and more blah-blah-blah. All pertinent, yeah, fine, great, *but...*see what I mean?"

"I guess."

"Now, guy sits down and reads your prologue, fine: he gets it. Lotsa heat behind it, good reference stuff. But for a press conf? No way, man. Not press-conf material. Besides, next day Laura refutes coast-to-coast, crying and wearing her best push-up bra, and you're gonna need more than door keys to beat her. Our anchor-chick, for example? Thinks she's Joan of Arc, I kid you not. Anyway, bottom line is, people won't believe it—rips up too much of the bedrock."

Which must be the way that Laura saw it—her spies had surely informed her of my progress by now—for the next day, and to national applause, she declared her candidacy for U.S. Congress. Her campaign slogan: *Put America's Honestest Legend in Congress!*

Honestest—that was "the frame." And just as Laura had told me, anyone who tried to go outside it would look like a fool. I still wonder if that word, "honestest," wasn't Laura's quiet suggestion to some impressionable interviewer from a women's magazine, for that was where it had first appeared.

In July, two candidates who were also in the race for the party nomination against Laura called me—or rather, their campaign people did. Rolf Obermeyer, with my permission, had contacted them and summarized my findings. I talked with each briefly. One said that he would talk to the candidate about the matter, "but I don't know if this is going to seriously fly." He never called back. The other cleared his throat nervously and said he thought this route might be "taking the campaign into uncharted waters." He did call back a few days later, however, and urged me to "hang it on the Net and see if you get any nibbles," as if it were trout bait.

Which is why I remained reluctant to open up a website, e-cheek by e-jowl with on-line poker and *Mayberry R.F.D.* hobbyists. Internet turns everything into nothing. Also, it was—and is—a matter of pride, for long and dismal is the drop from bestselling author, baptized by a national tour, to Internet hack.

Maybe it was pride that prodded me to fly to Ohio and confront Laura myself.

I felt strangely sheepish on the flight there, though it wasn't until I had arrived at the Columbus shopping center and stood in the clinging heat waiting for her that I understood why I felt that way: I was just trying to convince myself that I still had someplace to go with my story. I didn't. I was through. It was all over, and Laura had won. For the whole truth and nothing but, the public needed look no further than *Standing Tall*: Laura Prestini's silly mistake had resulted in the election of Mitch Taylor; but the country had forgiven her; and Laura had gone on to work in the White House and run for the U.S. Congress. Thus would generations of schoolkids be taught.

After I'd waited for some time at the shopping center, Laura had not appeared, and I saw no crowd awaiting her. I began to wonder: had I read the wrong time or date on her campaign website? And then I saw an ad hung up at the entrance: "Laura Prestini for U.S. Congress."

It was a four-color poster taped to a wall: the clean hair, the smile, the straight nose, the crucifix high up near the throat now. She wore a stretchy top, and the one-quarter profile of womanly convexity made its case to the red-blooded-male vote. At the bottom, a hurried calligraphy read: "Laura will appear, TODAY JULY 21! 1:00 P.M. in the South Parking Lot, Roxbury Mall II."

It was already one-twenty. I checked my bearings again and decided that I was as south as south could be from the mall. I went inside and stopped a strolling security guard. He told me that I was at Roxabury Mall I; the second in the series lay yonder across the highway. "Hey, may-an, I'll give you fifty bucks if you can git me Laura's phone number," he joked as we walked outside, where he gave me directions. "When she's in Congress, I am gonna be on my phone to her bitchin' and whinin' every day o' the goddamn week, I'll tell you that right now."

"So you're going to vote for her?" I asked.

"You kiddin'? Against fat ol' Will Halflin? Hell, yes. 'Bout time we got some new blood in Washington."

"Halflin's in his first term," I said. "And he can't be forty yet."

The security guard's face turned cold. "Mister, it just goes to show ya: there's two things you shouldn't never talk about with nobody: politics 'n' religion."

Chastised, I arrived as Laura was finishing her speech. She stepped down and began shaking hands and signing autographs. She had a well-run operation: a traveling trailer-van pulled by a semi-truck with Laura's face on the sides and flat front. The driver was scrubbing it with a sudsy sponge-mop; it wouldn't do for Our Lady of the Honestest Visage to be seen full of smashed bugs. Speakers opened from special panels at the front and rear of the trailer; the speaking platform slid forward from the trailer's underbelly. The fresh campaign colors were—what else?—red and blue, with white trim.

Her fans, a.k.a. political base, were women between college and second-divorce ages; and retired men in their sixties who, like Saint Thomas, preferred to touch in order to believe.

I had a plan worked out for getting to see Laura alone, but it turned out that I didn't need it. I was fanning my face with a campaign flyer when I saw a pasty-faced, thirtyish guy sweating in a suit near the semi. His security pass read Duane R. Hale. I stepped up and bopped him lightly on the shoulder and said hello. He looked at me with annoyance, then recognition, then alarm.

"You're—"

"Tell your candidate that I want five minutes alone with her."

"Oh? To proposition her again? Think this time she'll take off her clothes for you? Fuck she will. She's scared stiff of you." And he really believed it; Laura must have cried for her staff, too.

"Then tell her this: I'd like to apologize—just as she apologized to the nation. All I want is five minutes."

Now he didn't know what to do. He stood swaying from side to side like a tall tree in a wind.

"I also have some news to give her that will affect the campaign," I added.

"Like what?" he sneered as if I'd said my hot rod could beat his.

"Information I have that she needs. Get me Laura for five minutes."

More swaying.

I leaned closer and said, "If you don't, I'll tell everyone that I made a good-faith effort to see her and was turned away by"—I read his card—"one Duane R. Hale. Now: do you want to get your butt kicked back to wherever it came from?"

He didn't. A moment later, a security man led me around to the other side of the trailer, well away from Laura, who was still signing autographs and nodding wisely over the hard lot of the paunchy and limp-of-breast.

I was body-searched and metal-detected, for the contents of the conversation were not to be recorded by any means, including my Bic pen. Hale also informed me, with an evil grin, that the van was "completely sound-proofed. So you can forget about the directional mikes."

I assured him of my disappointment.

I was discreetly whisked inside. Silent as a bookend, the security guard kept me company; I was not to read any papers on any desks "in any way, shape, or form," according to Hale.

The trailer was a carpeted box. Campaign posters and some fifteen-inch-square windows broke up its walls; the carpet was dark and synthetic, made for the tread of many feet. Desks and seats were arranged on the sides like booths in a restaurant.

I looked for Laura's presence—the Barbie doll, the stuffed dog— and finally found it: a small mountain of beanbag animals before the tabletop mirror with adjustable lights where Laura did her makeup before appearances. When she entered, ten minutes later, the first thing I noticed was the layer of base on her face, thick like a flight-attendant's. (Yet on the five-o'clock local report that evening, I would notice she looked terrific.)

I said hello; she said nothing. She would not say a word until the guard closed the door after himself.

"I hear you've been working night and day to spread bullshit about me. What? You helping out the other party now? I don't know why Duane didn't call security on you."

"But you couldn't say no to my five minutes, could you?" I said. "That wouldn't look right to the troops."

This annoyed her. "Five minutes, dearie." She looked at her watch. She slipped off her suit jacket—sweat streaked the back of her blouse—and turned her attention to a table full of papers. She leaned over it with a pen, honoring me with my own personal view of the famous cleavage.

"Actually, that's what I came to tell you. I've called it off. Nobody will publish me, and your opponents won't touch it, either."

Laura's head lifted from the papers. "Which is as it should be." But I could see she was relieved.

"Looks like you made the frame pretty strong."

Laura nodded. "And the press only paints inside of it—what did I tell you." I put no question mark in that sentence because there was none in her voice.

Still, she decided she did have something to tell me, and put down the pen and crossed her arms. "You know, Sam, you are the ingrate of the century. I could have given that story to any of a dozen writers. But I chose you. You were smart, my generation, your editors had tricked you into covering a dull election. And you were poor as dirt—you write *history* books, I mean." This as if history books were a form of weeds.

"And it late January when we really talked for the first time," I said. "You wanted to let the first books about the election come out, right? See if anything had come up about you or Terry?"

"Yeah, that too. Point is, I chose *you*, and you went to the top. I made your career. And here you are, trying as hard as you can to throw it all away." She shook her head. "I never took you for that kind of fool—my mistake, I guess."

"Maybe it's because I don't like playing the role of dupe," I said.

A pitying look. "And you can't get over that? Well, poor you. Make up for it on your next bestseller."

"No, Laura. Don't pity me. Pity the country whose election you rigged."

"Rigged?"

"Yeah, and don't play innocent. You know, I've always wondered: What penance did you do for that? No vinegar potato chips for a month?"

She scowled, swung away, snatched a bottle of water out of a low refrigerator, took a long drink.

"Handy book, that *Creative Penance*."

"Fuck you. And I didn't rig anything. This country voted in a free and fair election. They elected Mitch Taylor."

I stared at her. "A free and fair election? After you trashed the two main-party candidates?"

"Free and fair as the birds, Sam. And I did not trash the two main opponents."

"Really?" I said with a chuckle. "Well! This is enlightening. So what do you call it?"

Laura sighed as if she were talking to an idiot. She glanced in the mirror, brushed her hair back, smoothed it over her the collar of her business-white blouse, tapped it in a few places, and said, "Who did you vote for?"

"No, no. You're not going to squirm out of my question. I asked you—"

"Oh, I'm going to answer you. But before I do, tell me—who did you vote for?"

I shrugged. "All right. Gotchell. Happy?"

"Despite the scandal? Why?"

"I thought his environmental policy was strong. And he's been on the Foreign Affairs Committee in the Senate for five years, and he would enter office knowing what the score is globally, which is more than you can say for most presidents. As for his sex problems, I don't give a damn. He has a good head, has an obvious passion for the welfare of normal people, and that's more important."

She nodded, standing now with her arms crossed like a stern schoolteacher. "And the scandal with Jover? That meant nothing to you? His own chief of security trying to enter the opposition's campaign headquarters?" I noticed that the collegiate "like" had disappeared from her syntax. "Don't answer knowing what you know now—just what you knew back then."

"What the hell are you—"

"Just tell me, Sam. All that meant nothing to you?"

I shrugged. "People do stupid things in the heat of a campaign," I said. "I'm much more concerned about a decent environmental policy before we cook the planet to toast. Compared to that, what's one rogue security guy?"

Laura clapped her hands, slowly, sarcastically. "Well, let's hear it for Sam."

"So who did the great Laura vote for? Can I know?" I countered, mainly to stop her clapping.

"For my candidate, of course—Governor Frakes!" she said with a grin.

"After you sank him?"

With mocking sincerity: "Hey, Sam, I'm just like you: I liked his stands on the issues: tax policy, nuclear energy, an integration of the four branches of the military that will save trillions. I figured, hell, what's one rogue video? A candidate at the end of a long day of filming spots; has to get it done because tomorrow, well, it's a tough seven-stop through Pennsylvania. He's pissed about having to kowtow to the geriatrics, but he has to, since they actually have the gall to go and vote. I'll give him a pass on the outburst."

Then she shrugged, as if that answered it all, and picked up her pen and began to look at her papers. From outside came a rising chant: *Lau-ra, Lau-ra, Lau-ra, Lau-ra.*

"Okay, so where are we going with this?" I asked finally.

"Nowhere. Or at least nowhere else." She signed something with a brief zigzag of her pen. "We're there."

"We're where?"

She looked up, rolling her eyes as if forced to explain multiplication to an idiot. "Here, Sam. Don't you get it? If you don't, too bad—you're five minutes are up."

"So what are you saying? That a presidential campaign is—"

"Uh-uh. Five minutes is five minutes. In fact, I gave you more than that, and I haven't heard you say thank-you." A seventh-grader's smartypants grin, cold as salami.

"That's an answer?"

"Yeah—why don't you just sleep on it?"

Bristling, I figured I'd better leave before I did something stupid. When I reached the door, however, a laugh bubbled from her. I turned and saw that she was shaking her head.

"You know, Sam, that's another reason I chose you: you're a total believer, you're a democrat. You want to see cynics? By the hundred? Take a step out that door. Go ahead: ask 'em why they back me. Oh, they'll give you all kinds of answers, I guarantee you that. But boil 'em down—I mean boil 'em right down to the base. What do eighty-ninety percent of 'em come to? This: no fucking idea."

She lowered her head to her papers, dismissing me, but raised it fast when she heard my three long strides—providing me the perfect target of her left cheek, which I slapped as hard as I could.

"What?" she screeched. Jerking backwards, she threw a knee at my groin and connected harmlessly with my right thigh. Then I slapped her other cheek, and the fight ended.

She stumbled back into a chair, tears welling up. The crucifix on her chain hung crooked over one side of her collar, swinging in vivid little circles.

"One of those was for Terry," I growled over her. "The other was for the rest of us."

"You...hurted me!" she squealed in a little-girl's voice. A tear ploughed a muddy furrow in the makeup of her cheek.

"Chalk it up to 'creative penance,'" I said. "Like going to Terry's funeral."

Her head snapped up. "Bastard!" She kicked me in the shin—hard. Which is what happens when a light shines on a dirty truth; so now we were even.

Not allowing myself to limp so that she wouldn't know how much pain I was in, I walked out. The chant—*Lau-ra, Lau-ra, Lau-ra*—washed over me as I opened the door.

"You're lucky—you got ten minutes," shouted Duane Hale as I stepped down and closed the door behind me. The crowd of some two hundred people, many with "I Love Laura" placards, stood at a police barricade, their lonely, envious eyes upon me: *That guy talked alone with her.*

Laura's voice buzzed over an intercom beside the door, quite composed if you weren't listening for hints of stronger emotion: "Duane, you want to wake me in about a half hour? I'm going to take a little nap."

"You bet," Duane replied, grinning at me: whatever we'd talked about certainly wasn't making Laura miss her sleep.

It turned out, though, that he was wrong: a few days later, Laura withdrew from the congressional race.

Three days after my dust-up with Laura, another bomb went off in an airport parking lot—in Orlando, Florida—and killed four people. Laura visited the bomb site and declared that she was rescinding her candidacy. With her unmatchably modest boilerplate, she said that she could not leave her YouthGo post during a national emergency.

The cascade of praise from the Highest in the Land, especially from Taylor and her own party, made the very airwaves weep. Laura, sweet and shrugging like a movie star, orchestrated her appearances like a maestro. The outpouring would see her nicely into her own afternoon talk show a year down the road, when she would be introduced every day, "And here she is, ladies and gentlemen: America's Honestest Woman—Laura Prestini!"

As Goebbels said, there's nothing like repetition for creating a truth.

And nothing like a talk show for national exposure and healthy campaign coffers for a new congressional run in the future.

But YouthGo and national crisis, I think, had little to do with her withdrawal from the race that year. Rather, her motives were, first, defensive. If Sam had guessed right about creative penance, what else?

Second, and more important, is that my two slaps really shook her. This is only my gut feeling, but it is reinforced by the fact that Laura never told a soul about the incident, though it certainly would have served her purposes to do so. For months, Rolf Obermeyer kept his ear to the political earth for me, and even managed to clink fundraising martinis again with Duane Hale:

"Duane—just between you and me and the whiskey here—I heard that Laura and Sam Walker had a last chit-chat in Columbus last summer, and for some unknown reason it wasn't too bowls-of-cherry-like. True?" Hale replied with his dirty grin that indeed it wasn't; Sam had left, "face beet-red and hands stuffed in his pockets."

Rolf swears it sounded as if he never suspected a thing.

Back in Minneapolis, I continued to cast lines to publishers. In the last year of the Taylor Administration, I finally nailed down an offer from a very nervous small publisher who was willing to commit suicide in the name of truth, and a publisher in Paris who was willing to put out my French translation. Neither was really what I wanted, but I was ready to sign. Then the big bombing in Miami happened—one hundred and fifty-four dead—and the wretched cycle of terror-war-terror-war flared up again—in Chad now, of all places—like a fire that just won't die.

Many young people had heeded Laura's call to join the armed forces. She was perfect—"the high priestess of Cool Patriotism," as the newsmagazines called her, as if patriotism were another fad, like tattoos and yo-yos. At any rate, the small publisher was scared off; the Parisians said the book had to come out in America first, which I suppose is true.

For the last year of the Taylor Administration, my new account of the Miracle Election sat in a drawer.

But about twenty people—some I'd talked to, some who'd heard from others—urged me not to give up the fight. Even Janet Evans, when I recounted the matter to her over a Washington lunch, was indignant:

"Sam, put that story in front of the people! I always thought her video-mix-up story was a little thin, but she cried so hard over it, I figured it had to be true. Send me a copy. I'm going to call a special session of the League of Women Voters just to discuss this!"

I told her to be careful; Laura was a member of the Ohio chapter.

Rolf Obermeyer, who had got involved in another presidential campaign, also called me—from the desk of his Czech grandmother in his West Wing office. Because of the campaign (his previous one, for Sally Visterman, had lost), I had hardly seen him since the midterms, and he gave me hell for letting the Laura matter languish:

"Whaddaya mean, 'given up on it'?" he boomed. "That bitch committed mockery, Sam—pure mockery of our democratic system. Now you go stick your two cents in front of John Q. Taxpayer and don't be afraid to bust a few bulls in the china shop. 'Bout time someone gave this country a hard shake by the scruff of the ying-yang and read it the riot act. First sentence: 'Full vetting of all shit-heads on election campaigns.' Some things in this old world are true-blue solid gold, Sam. And I'm not talking flags and cherry trees and

'In God We Trust.' You like that stuff, go pray to your baseball bat. I mean columnists and whiskey and back-scratching and everybody sweating and shoving down the back stretch to the pork pile, which is where the wash comes out anyway.

"Democracy is a horse race, isn't it? Writing bills and twisting arms and spending your political capital down at the congressional convenience store. Damn right. People's lives at stake, guns, butter, Mom's apple pie—not some sweet-tits hogswallowing a whole presidential election just to get a White House mess pass."

Spoken like "a total believer," as Laura would say.

So for Mrs. Evans and Rolf and my many hoodwinked readers who plunked down good cash for *The Saddest Election*—here's the whole story, free for all on the Internet. True, it's but a drop in the cyberocean; look up Laura Prestini on an Internet search engine, and you'll get twenty-three sex pages, her ongoing Laura-for-Congress Web page, seventeen "unofficial" fans-of-Laura pages, and four government ones before you reach my website. But it's better than nothing.

I immediately received a letter from her lawyers and another, two days later, from her. The lawyers' you can well imagine: twenty-seven pages of apocrypha and excessive punctuation, all on good-quality bond paper. Laura's single page—folded in perfect thirds so that you confuse the top and bottom of the page; ring a bell?—is calculated to be brought up as evidence of Laura's goodwill once we get to court:

"...Like the country, I am putting the whole matter behind me and moving on, especially important in these days of crisis in our nation's existence. I am extremely hurt that you have, like so many ugly, disreputable reporters, gone in for this level of hate-mongering. This when the president himself has absolved me of any guilt."

Which must have referred to the guilt she had felt over Terry. What she had done to the election was perfectly consistent with her view of democracy—the view of a jaded advance woman who knows that a picture is worth a thousand speeches.

No, she was free of sin, free as her rise into the highest levels of American government, free as the millions of dollars that flow through her bank accounts, for *Standing Tall* has been on the bestseller lists ever since it came out.

The lawsuit, said my lawyer, will bankrupt me either with legal bills or an unfavorable decision if Laura gets lucky with the jury. He tried to cheer me by adding that at least the publicity should make publishers eager for my new work. Nice of him, of course. The prospect of a hot market for history books, though, strikes me as faint.

But so be it. Apartments are cheap, and you don't need to cut the grass.

THE END

encompass
E D I T I O N S

ENCOMPASS EDITIONS is a young publishing house, founded in 2009 and based in Kingston, Ontario, Canada but dedicated to providing access to traditional publishing to a wider spectrum of writers than is often the case—writers in the United States, Canada, the United Kingdom and the European Union.

Although Encompass does not accept unsolicited manuscripts, the company relies upon several agents who work closely with writers at every level of experience. This policy permits Encompass to focus on what it does best: publish books good to read.

You can visit the Encompass website at www.EncompassEditions. com or contact editor Robert Buckland at words@encompasseditions. com

www.ingramcontent.com/pod-product-compliance
Lightning Source LLC
Chambersburg PA
CBHW031349170626
46807CB00002B/880